LOST LETTER LOVE

JERRY_V

Contents

Acknowledgements

I must begin by thanking the one companion who has been with me through every word, every twist, and every emotion of this journey—my own free time. In the stillness and quiet moments, it was in the spaces between my days that the story began to take shape. Time, unhurried and unbothered, allowed my thoughts to wander, explore, and create.

I owe a deep gratitude to my thoughts, which were constantly at work, weaving together emotions and experiences to bring this story to life. It was in the quiet corners of my mind where the most profound emotions stirred, urging me to write, to capture every feeling, every nuance of the narrative. They pushed me forward when doubt crept in and helped me stay true to the essence of what I wanted to share.

To the quiet moments, to the flow of inspiration, and to the emotions that guided me—thank you. Without them, this story would not have been possible.

1

Pages of Now

As Sameer stepped into his new room, he was struck by a sense of calm he hadn't felt in years. The room was bathed in soft, golden light from the afternoon sun, filtering gently through cozy curtains that swayed faintly in the breeze. Outside the window, thick branches of trees framed the view, their leaves rustling softly, as if sharing secrets with the wind. He could just make out patches of blue sky peeking through the canopy, while birds called out lazily from somewhere within the trees.

The walls, painted a soft, faded cream, were covered in old pictures and paintings, each with a touch of warmth and mystery. There was a small wooden desk by the window, perfectly placed for someone to sit and write letters or lose themselves in a book. The bed, with its quilted cover and neatly fluffed pillows, looked as though it had been waiting for him.

The air in the room carried a faint scent of lavender and something earthy, like freshly fallen leaves after rain. As Sameer placed his camera bag beside the desk, he felt that even his belongings softened in the room's gentle atmosphere. The quiet, paired with the distant murmur of trees swaying, made the world outside feel far away.

Outside, the weather was just as peaceful. A light breeze played through the trees, and soft rays of sunlight streamed in from gaps in the leaves, casting dappled shadows that danced across the floor.

It felt like a small haven, wrapped in the embrace of nature, and as Sameer took it all in, he felt an unexpected peace settle in his heart.

As if summoned by his thoughts, Mrs. D'Souza's warm, sing-song voice floated up the stairs, breaking the stillness. "Sameer, beta, you must be tired! Do you want some chai? You look like you need a break, my dear!"

Sameer couldn't help but smile to himself, even though she couldn't see him. Ever since he'd moved in two days ago, Mrs. D'Souza had been showering him with motherly warmth, offering advice and endless cups of tea. She hovered around with a kindness that felt comforting, if a little overwhelming, like a distant aunt who cared more than necessary.

Before he could respond, he heard her footsteps on the stairs. Moments later, she appeared, holding a steaming cup of chai in her hands, her eyes crinkling with a warm smile. "Here, here, beta. Fresh chai for you," she said, extending the cup toward him. "You'll feel better in no time."

"Thank you so much, Mrs. D'Souza," Sameer replied, taking the cup gratefully. "I don't know what I'd do without your tea breaks!"

"Oh, nonsense!" she laughed, brushing off his gratitude. "I'm just happy to have someone like you here. It's been so quiet since the house's owners moved abroad last year." Her expression softened, a trace of wistfulness in her eyes. "I really miss them, you know. They were like family to me. When they finally decided to rent the place, I prayed someone nice would come along—and here you are!"

Sameer chuckled, sipping the chai, savoring its warmth. "Well, I hope I can live up to your prayers," he said, smiling.

"You already have, beta," she said with a grin. "And if you ever need anything—or just want a chat—you know where to find me. Call me Masi, if you like! You know, like a mother."

He laughed and nodded. "Okay, aunty. Sorry, I mean...Masi," he corrected, and her face lit up even more.

"Ah, now that's better!" she said, clearly delighted. "Enjoy your tea, Sameer," she added, giving him a warm pat on the shoulder before retreating down the stairs.

As her footsteps faded, Sameer took another deep breath, soaking in the quiet again. He turned his gaze toward the end of the hallway, where the attic door stood. It was a small door, almost hidden behind a dusty old coat rack, and he'd noticed it on his first day. For some reason, he'd avoided it—something about the weathered edges and old brass knob seemed to hold secrets.

Setting down his cup, he moved toward it, feeling a growing sense of curiosity. Gripping the doorknob, he noticed its worn, cool surface, with grooves from countless hands before his. With a gentle twist, the door creaked open, and a gust of stale air greeted him, carrying with it the faint smell of age and dust. It felt like stepping back in time.

Inside, the attic was dim and cramped, packed with forgotten relics of the past—old trunks with faded leather, cobweb-covered chairs, and boxes stacked haphazardly. The only light came from a single bulb overhead, its glow casting long shadows across the space. Dust swirled in the air as he pulled the string to turn on the bulb, illuminating the attic in a soft, yellow light.

He coughed lightly, the dust settling around him like whispers, as if each particle carried a story, a memory.

He took a deep breath, the air thick with dust and the faint scent of old paper. Carefully, he lifted the bundle of letters from the chest, feeling the delicate weight of time in his hands. The name "Aditya" stared back at him, written in ink that had faded but still held a quiet strength. Sameer's curiosity was tinged with hesitation, as though he were holding someone's secrets, moments frozen in words that had never reached their destination.

Slowly, he untied the frayed twine and unfolded the first letter, his fingers gentle, careful not to tear the fragile paper. The handwriting was a beautiful, flowing script, though certain letters wavered, as if the writer's hand had trembled under the weight of emotion. He scanned the first few lines, feeling a strange sense of familiarity as if the words themselves carried a heartbeat.

"Dearest Aditya," it began. The words were simple, yet they seemed to carry the weight of longing, a voice reaching out from the past.

Sameer's pulse quickened. Who was this person pouring their heart out? And what had kept these letters hidden away, unread, for so many years? He couldn't shake the feeling that he was meant to find them—that somehow, these letters held a story that was waiting to be told.

"Dear Aditya,"

It's strange to write this, knowing you'll never read it. But I need to put these words somewhere, even if they stay hidden forever. I'm not brave enough to say them to your face. The truth is, I've carried these feelings for so long, tucked away like a secret treasure I never dared to share.

Do you remember the first time we really spoke? Not just in passing, but truly connected. You were standing by the riverbank with your camera, waiting for the perfect light as the sun dipped below the horizon. The golden hues lit up everything around us, and you were so focused, so completely lost in your work. I remember watching you in that moment, wondering how a person could be so consumed by something so beautiful.

I stood there for what felt like hours, just watching you. And then, you looked up. You caught me staring, but instead of looking away, you smiled. It wasn't just any smile, Aditya—it was soft, like you were inviting me into your world. And for that one brief moment, everything around us seemed to fade, as if the universe had paused, holding its breath just for us.

I wanted to tell you so many things then. I wanted to tell you that your smile felt like warmth I hadn't known I was missing. I wanted to tell you that your presence had become a gentle comfort in my life, like a song that lingers long after the music stops. But the words stayed caught in my throat, trapped by my own fear and hesitation. So I just smiled back, pretending like it was nothing.

But it wasn't nothing, Aditya.

That moment left a mark on me. I think about it more often than I'd like to admit. Sometimes, when I'm alone, I close my eyes and picture it all over again, as if reliving it could somehow bring me closer to you.

I imagine what it might have been like if I had just spoken up, if I had found the courage to tell you the truth—that you were becoming something I couldn't ignore, something I didn't want to lose.

And now, here I am, pouring my heart out on paper, knowing these words will never reach you. Because I'm still not brave enough, Aditya. I'm still hiding behind these letters, hoping that one day I'll find the strength to speak my heart. Until then, this is all I have—a secret confession written in ink, a love that stays hidden in silence.

With all the pieces of my heart,

Tara

Sameer felt his own heart tighten as he read the letter, sensing the depth of Tara's unspoken feelings, her longing and regret. It was as if her words echoed something he understood deeply, something he might have felt himself at some point, for someone or something that slipped through his fingers.

As Sameer carefully unfolded the letter, a photograph slipped out, landing gently on his lap. He picked it up and examined it with a photographer's eye, his gaze drawn into the depth of the image, as though it held a heartbeat of its own.

The photograph was a black-and-white portrait of a woman, captured in a side profile against a blurred backdrop. Her expression was soft and distant, as if she were lost in a world only she could see. Her hair was styled in loose waves, held back with a delicate pin, and she wore a simple, elegant saree that seemed to belong to a different era. Her features were timeless—graceful and poised, with a serene beauty that seemed to linger between the past and present.

The light in the photograph was soft, the shadows carefully framing her face, highlighting the curve of her cheek and the slight upward tilt of her lips. It was a subtle smile, but one that held a quiet mystery, as if she were holding back a thousand unsaid words. Sameer could see that this was more than just a photograph; it was a glimpse into a moment heavy with emotion—a secret the camera had captured, one that words might never express.

In the corner of the photograph, written in delicate script, was a single name: Aditya.

Sameer's pulse quickened as he traced the signature with his thumb. He felt a sudden connection to the man behind the camera, as though he could understand the tenderness with which Aditya must have captured this image. It wasn't simply a photograph. It was a love letter in light and shadow, an unspoken confession immortalized in a single frame. As a photographer, Sameer understood the feeling of wanting to capture someone's essence, to hold onto a fleeting moment that felt significant beyond explanation.

He felt a pang of empathy for Aditya—a man who had seen this woman, not just as she appeared, but as she felt, and had tried to capture that feeling in his lens. The photograph seemed to whisper of love, longing, and perhaps even regret, as though Aditya's emotions had seeped into the film, leaving behind an imprint of his soul. And in that moment, Sameer knew that these letters and photographs held a story—a story he was now a part of, a story that perhaps needed to be told.

As Sameer continued reading, he felt a strange connection, one he couldn't fully explain. Tara's words seemed to echo his own unspoken thoughts, capturing feelings he hadn't even realized he shared. Her descriptions of longing, fear, and the hesitation to embrace love struck a chord deep within him, as though she had given voice to emotions, he'd never been able to put into words.

A sudden buzz in his pocket broke the spell, pulling him back to the present. He glanced down to see Rohan's name lighting up on his screen. Smiling slightly, he answered.

"Settling into the haunted mansion yet?" Rohan's voice crackled with humor. "Found any old family skeletons or maybe a creepy doll?"

Sameer chuckled, glad for the lightheartedness. "Close, but not quite. Just found a box of old letters."

"Letters? Like, handwritten ones?" Rohan sounded genuinely surprised. "Are you sure they're not cursed?"

Sameer laughed. "Pretty sure. They're all addressed to someone named Aditya. I haven't gone through them all, but... there's something personal about them. Almost like they weren't meant to be found."

A pause on the other end was followed by a more serious tone from Rohan. "You're goanna dive into this, aren't you? I can tell. You've got that curious face on already, don't you?"

Sameer leaned back against the attic wall, staring at the letters in his hand. "Maybe. It feels like these letters hold a story. I don't know why, but I can't shake this feeling that I need to know it."

"Just don't get too carried away with someone else's drama," Rohan warned, his voice softening. "Remember, you've got that exhibition coming up. It's big for you."

Sameer nodded, though he knew Rohan couldn't see him. "Yeah, I know. I'll keep my head in the game." But even as he said it, he could feel his thoughts drifting back to Tara's words. The exhibition that once filled him with excitement now seemed distant, replaced by a newfound pull toward these letters and the people in them.

As he ended the call, he looked at the letters again, his thumb running over the worn edges. Whoever Tara was, whatever had happened between her and Aditya, it felt unfinished. And for reasons he couldn't fully understand, he knew he wasn't ready to walk away from it just yet.

With a renewed sense of purpose, Sameer took out another letter, feeling the anticipation build within him. He unfolded it gently, eager to dive deeper into Tara's world and uncover the mystery of her unspoken love. This felt like a puzzle waiting to be solved, and for the first time in a long time, he sensed a flicker of direction and meaning. Perhaps by unraveling their story, he might discover the connection he had been searching for—a reason to finally call this place home.

Dear Aditya,

I imagine a world where I can tell you everything. A world where I can confess that I've fallen in love with you. But then, the fear comes creeping in. What if you don't feel the same? What if I'm just another person you've smiled at by the river?

I can't seem to push my fears away, Aditya. I'm not strong enough for that. So, instead of speaking to you, I write these letters. Letters that will never reach you. At least this way, I can keep the hope alive that maybe, somewhere deep down, you loved me too.

I wish I were braver. I wish I could be the kind of woman who could stand up for her feelings, who could look you in the eye and say, "I love you," without feeling scared. But I can't do that.

I'm scared, Aditya. That fear is stronger than my love.

Tara

As Sameer read Tara's heartfelt words, he felt the weight of her emotions. He could sense her struggle, the longing for connection mixed with the fear of vulnerability. Each line spoke to him, echoing his own doubts and hesitations about love. Tara's courage in writing these letters, even if they would never reach Aditya, made him admire her strength.

He could feel her heart on the page, the tenderness behind her words, and the sadness of a love that remained unspoken. In that moment, he realized that this story was more than just a collection of letters; it was a reflection of the human experience—love, fear, and the longing for connection. Sameer closed his eyes for a moment, letting the emotions wash over him, feeling an inexplicable bond with Tara and Aditya, and he knew he needed to discover what had happened between them.

The attic felt still and quiet, almost like it was waiting for Sameer to explore more of its secrets. Just as he prepared to dive deeper into the letters, his phone buzzed again, breaking the silence.

"Meet us at Chai Adda in twenty minutes," Rohan's voice came through the line, filled with energy. "Rhea was already there. I told her you're finally getting out of your cave."

Sameer couldn't help but smile at Rohan's playful tone. It was just the encouragement he needed to step away from the attic and the mysteries it held.

"I don't know if I'm ready for your usual antics," Sameer replied, slipping on his jacket. "But fine, I'll come. I could use some fresh air anyway."

"Good! If you keep hiding in that dusty house, I'll have to drag you out myself," Rohan joked. "Rhea's already complaining about missing your brooding face. See you soon, man!"

Sameer ended the call and tucked his phone into his pocket. Although he felt drawn to the letters and the story behind them, he knew Rohan was right. He needed a break and a chance to reconnect with the outside world. Besides, Chai Adda was one of the few places in town where he felt relaxed.

Stepping outside, the cool autumn air wrapped around him like a comforting blanket. The town had a unique charm that had captured Sameer's heart from the very beginning. As he walked down the narrow streets, he admired the old buildings that lined the roads. Their pastel colors were faded from years of sunshine and heavy rains, giving the town a nostalgic feel.

He noticed women walking along the sidewalks, carrying baskets filled with bright marigolds, their colors adding vibrancy to the scene. Vendors shouted out about the day's fresh produce, their carts overflowing with colorful vegetables. Somewhere in the distance, the gentle sound of temple bells rang softly, creating a peaceful atmosphere that blended perfectly with the lively hustle and bustle of the market.

Sameer took a deep breath, feeling the life of the town around him. It was a beautiful day, and he was ready to enjoy it with his friends.

Sameer loved this city because of its unique mix of fast and slow life. It felt like everything rushed by, but at the same time, some things stayed the same. There was a beautiful chaos in the city, balanced by moments of quiet stillness. Swarna Nagar was surrounded by hills, their sharp edges standing out against the sky. From almost any corner, you could see the river flowing gently through the valley. Sameer had spent many evenings by that river, watching the sunlight dance on the water, just like Tara had written about in her letter to Aditya.

As he walked along the cobblestone streets, Sameer thought about his time in the city. He was always on the move, constantly searching for something—whether in his photography or his life. This busy lifestyle kept him from ever really settling down. But something about Swarna Nagar made him feel that maybe, just maybe, he could find a place to belong.

At the end of a narrow lane was Chai Adda, Rhea's café. Its faded yellow walls blended in beautifully with the other shops nearby. As Sameer stepped inside, he was welcomed by the delicious smell of freshly brewed tea and baked goods. The café felt cozy, with mismatched furniture and walls covered in photographs and local art. Rhea had a special talent for making the space feel like home—warm, welcoming, and full of life.

Rhea stood behind the counter with her shoulder-length hair framing her face, styled in soft waves that added a playful touch to her look. Her eyes sparkled with mischief, and her smile had a way of lighting up the café.

"There he is!" Rhea called out, her wide smile teasing Sameer as he walked in. "The prodigal photographer returns! I was starting to think you'd been buried alive in that creepy old house."

Sameer laughed, shaking his head. "Don't give Rohan any ideas."

Rhea had a unique talent for reading people, always knowing when someone was feeling down or when they needed a good laugh. She had a sharp wit but a heart that remained soft, no matter how challenging life became.

"So, how's it going? Found anything interesting in that antique museum you're living in?" she asked, pouring tea into three mugs.

"Depends on what you define as interesting," Sameer replied, sliding into the chair beside Rohan, who was busy scrolling through his phone. "I found a box of old letters. From someone named Tara to a guy called Aditya."

Rhea raised an eyebrow as she set the mugs down. "Letters? That sounds like a story waiting to be uncovered. You planning to dive into that mystery, or are you still pretending you don't have time?"

Sameer took a sip of the steaming chai and leaned back, letting the warm, spiced liquid calm his restless thoughts. "Honestly, I don't know. It feels... personal. Like I'm reading something I shouldn't."

Rohan looked up from his phone, a mischievous glint in his eyes. "But you're definitely going to read them, right? You've always been the guy who loves a good mystery. Plus, come on, what's more interesting than other people's drama?"

Sameer rolled his eyes. "Not everything is drama, Rohan. But yeah... I don't know. There's something about them that's pulling me in."

Rhea sat down across from them, her expression thoughtful. "I think you should do it. Maybe there's a reason you found those letters. Sometimes the universe works in weird ways, you know? You might find something that resonates with your own life."

Rohan snorted. "Or you could find out that Aditya was a psycho killer. Ever think of that?"

Sameer chuckled, shaking his head. "Always the optimist, Rohan."

Rhea smirked. "Ignore him. He's just bitter because the last time he tried to read someone's diary, it turned out to be a grocery list."

"Speaking of pulling in," Rohan teased, eyeing Rhea's hair. "What happened to your hair? I barely recognized you!"

Rhea smirked, flicking her hair over her shoulder. "Oh, you mean this? I decided to make a change. Why, do you not like it?"

Rohan grinned, leaning back in his chair. "I actually dared you to change your style. But I didn't think you'd actually do it!"

"Is that so?" Rhea shot back, her eyes narrowing playfully. "What's next? A dare to dye it pink?"

"Only if you promise to keep it for at least a month," Rohan replied, his laughter infectious.

Sameer chimed in, "I think you should do it! It would match your colorful personality!"

Rhea rolled her eyes but couldn't suppress a smile. "Alright, alright. No pink hair, I promise. But you guys owe me for making me question my style now!"

Sameer laughed, grateful for the light-hearted banter. It had been a long time since he'd felt this relaxed. Despite the weight of Tara's letters lingering in his mind, being here with Rohan and Rhea made the world feel a little less heavy.

"So," Rhea said, leaning forward, "are you still working on your exhibition piece?"

Sameer hesitated. The exhibition, the one that was supposed to be the crowning achievement of his career, had been looming over him for months. But lately, it felt distant, like something that belonged to a version of himself he wasn't sure he recognized anymore.

"Yeah," he said, his voice lacking the conviction he wished he had. "I'm still working on it. But, honestly... I'm not sure if I'm going to make it."

Rohan frowned, his usual playful expression slipping away. "You're kidding, right? This is your dream, man. You've worked your ass off to get here."

"I know, I know," Sameer sighed. "But lately... I don't know. Something's missing. It's like I've lost my spark or whatever it is that made me love photography in the first place. And now, with these letters..." He trailed off, unsure how to explain the pull he felt.

Rhea gave him a sympathetic look. "Maybe that's why you need to read them. Maybe they'll help you figure out what you're looking for."

Sameer nodded, appreciating her insight. As much as he loved photography, he couldn't deny that something about Tara's story had awakened a part of him he hadn't felt in years. Maybe Rhea was right. Maybe these letters would help him see things differently.

The conversation shifted, with Rohan cracking jokes and Rhea talking about a new blend of tea she was working on, but Sameer's thoughts kept drifting back to the attic. The letters. Tara. Aditya. There was something there, something unfinished, and as much as he tried to push it aside, he knew he couldn't ignore it forever. Their banter continued, the warmth of friendship wrapping around them like a cozy blanket as they settled into the comforting atmosphere of Chai Adda.

....

Later that evening, Sameer walked back to Mrs. D'Souza's house, the sky turning dark with deep blues and purples of twilight. The streets were quieter now; the busy sounds of the day were replaced by the calm of night. He walked slowly, his footsteps echoing against the cobblestones, feeling the cool air brush against his skin.

When he reached the attic again, it felt different—less scary and more familiar. He opened the chest he had found earlier and pulled out another letter. The paper felt fragile and trembled slightly in his hands.

"Dear Aditya,"

I don't know how to explain what I'm feeling. I want so badly to be with you and to tell you everything that's in my heart. But every time I get close, something pulls me back. Fear, I suppose. Fear that you won't feel the same, fear that I'll lose you altogether if I speak the truth.

Sometimes, I think I could be braver. I imagine a world where I tell you everything, where I confess that I've fallen in love with you. But then, the fear sets in. What if you don't feel the same? What if I'm just one of many people you've smiled at by the river?

I can't fight my own fears, Aditya. I'm not strong enough. So, I write these letters instead, letters that will never reach you. At least this way, I can hold on to the hope that maybe, somewhere, you loved me too.

I wish I were stronger. I wish I could be the kind of woman who could fight for you, who could stand in front of you and say, "I love you" without trembling. But I can't.

I'm scared, Aditya. And that fear is stronger than my love.

Tara

As Sameer read Tara's words, he felt a deep sadness. Her pain, her self-doubt, her fear—it all felt very real. Folding the letter, he realized it wasn't just Tara's story that captivated him. It was how she expressed her feelings so openly. This reminded him of why he had fallen in love with photography in the first place: to capture the unspoken moments, the feelings that words often couldn't express.

But there was something special about these letters. They felt personal, like a connection he had been searching for without even knowing it. With his exhibition approaching, Sameer knew he needed something unique to showcase—something more than just beautiful pictures of landscapes or portraits. He needed a story, a story that could touch people's hearts. And perhaps this was the story he had been looking for.

The letters, Tara's love for Aditya, and the mystery of why they had never been sent—it all felt like a puzzle waiting to be solved. For the first time in a long time, Sameer felt a sense of purpose, a desire to uncover the truth behind this unfinished love story.

As the night grew darker, he made a decision. He would find out what happened to Tara and Aditya. And maybe, just maybe, this journey would help him discover what he had been searching for in his own life.

2

Pages of Now

The attic felt colder than before, or maybe it was the weight of Tara's final letter that sent a shiver through Sameer's body. Each word from her letter echoed in his mind, filling him with a sense of loss for a love that had ended before it even had a chance to begin. He stretched, his legs stiff from crouching over the letters for so long, and looked out the small window. The morning light had changed, pouring into the room in soft, golden beams that danced through the dust in the air.

As he carefully made his way down the creaky wooden stairs, the scent of something warm and comforting drifted up to meet him. The sweet smell of freshly baked bread, blended with a hint of cardamom, reached him just before Mrs. D'Souza's familiar, cheerful voice.

"There you are, beta!" she called from the kitchen, her tone bright and welcoming. "I thought you were going to stay in that attic forever! Come, I've made some sheera for you. It'll clear your head."

Sameer gave a small, grateful smile as he entered the kitchen, where Mrs. D'Souza was moving around with a lively energy that seemed to fill the entire room. She wore a floral apron over her dress, her arms decorated with colorful bangles that jingled as she moved. Her face was warm, her eyes bright—a woman in her sixties but with a spark of life that seemed as fresh as a young girl's. She reminded Sameer of someone who truly knew how to cherish life.

He took a seat at the small, round table, and she set a steaming bowl of sheera in front of him. The sweet semolina pudding glistened, warm and comforting.

"This will fix that brooding face of yours," she teased, giving him a playful look. "You've been so quiet lately. I know that look—you've got something on your mind, don't you?"

Sameer stirred his spoon through the sheera, watching the steam rise and feeling its warmth in his hands. "I found something in the attic," he said, looking up at her. "A box of old letters."

Mrs. D'Souza's face softened with curiosity and interest as she sat down across from him. "Letters? Whose letters?"

"They're from someone named Tara. She wrote them to a man named Aditya," Sameer explained. "But... they were never sent."

A gentle smile touched her lips, a kind of sadness mixed with understanding. "Ah," she said, her voice quiet and reflective. "Love letters. So many of us leave things unsaid, don't we? We think we have all the time in the world, and then one day, the chance is gone." She paused, her gaze thoughtful. "I hope you learn from their story, Sameer. Life is too short for unspoken words."

Sameer took a bite of the sheera, the sweetness warming him, but he felt a weight in his chest from her words. There was something in her tone—a wisdom that came from life experience.

"Did you ever feel like that?" Sameer asked gently, unsure if he was crossing a line but curious to know.

She gave a wistful smile and nodded slowly. "Oh, yes. My husband and I, we were young once, full of dreams and arguments," she laughed softly. "We fought over silly things—what color to paint the kitchen, where to go on holiday. But we loved each other deeply, with all our flaws and fights." She paused, lost in a memory. "He used to say that our love was like the sheera I make—sometimes sweet, sometimes spicy with a hint of bitterness, but always something we'd come back to."

Sameer watched her, intrigued by her story. He could almost picture her, years ago, with her husband, sharing these moments together.

"When he passed," she continued, her voice softening, "my children wanted me to come live with them. They didn't understand why I wanted to stay here, in this city, in this house. They thought I was clinging to old memories, to ghosts." She looked around the room, her eyes thoughtful. "But this isn't about being bound to the past, you see. It's about freedom."

"Freedom?" Sameer echoed, curious.

"Yes," she nodded, smiling at his surprise. "Freedom is different for everyone. For some, it's traveling, exploring, leaving places behind. For me, it's staying. I feel free here, close to his memories, close to the life we built together. There's a kind of peace in that, a feeling of belonging."

She reached for his hand, her touch warm and comforting. "You see, Sameer, love isn't always about grand gestures or moving on. Sometimes, it's about choosing to stay—staying with the memories, with the laughter and tears, even if it means being in one place. That's freedom for me. It's not being stuck; it's being rooted. It's having a place to come back to, a place where love still lives, even if the person is gone."

Sameer looked down at his bowl, feeling a strange emotion welling up inside him. Mrs. D'Souza's words struck a chord, resonating deeply. He had spent his life moving from city to city, avoiding attachments, thinking that he was free. But here was this woman, who had found freedom in a place, in the memories of a life she had shared with someone she loved.

"It sounds like you really loved him," he murmured, his voice soft.

"Oh, I did," she said, her eyes twinkling with a mixture of joy and sorrow. "He was my biggest love and my greatest annoyance," she laughed. "But that's the beauty of it, you know? Love isn't perfect. It's messy and flawed. But it's real."

Sameer felt a pang in his chest, thinking about Tara's letters. They were full of love, yet they were also filled with doubt, fear, and hesitation—emotions that had held her back from expressing how she truly felt. Maybe, he thought, there was a lesson in that, too.

"I guess you're right," he said, his voice thoughtful. "Life is too short for unspoken words."

Mrs. D'Souza gave him a gentle smile, patting his hand. "Remember that, beta. Don't let fear keep you from saying what's in your heart. One day, you'll look back and wonder why you held back. And by then, it might be too late."

As he finished the Sheera, Sameer felt something shifting within him, a newfound determination taking root. Mrs. D'Souza had shared her story, and through it, he felt he had glimpsed a different way to live—a way that embraced love and memory, not as a chain but as a home.

He looked up at her, gratitude in his eyes. "Thank you, Mrs. D'Souza. I think I needed to hear that."

She smiled, her eyes warm and understanding. "Anytime, beta. Now go, live your life. And don't be afraid to love. It's the one thing worth taking a risk for."

Sameer was about to say more, but his phone started buzzing again. It vibrated insistently on the table, and he saw his father's name lighting up the screen. He sighed, feeling a mix of hesitation and relief, and answered the call.

"Sameer," his father's voice came through steady and calm, the way it always did. "How are you, beta? You sound tired."

Sameer leaned back in his chair, glancing up at the ceiling. "I'm alright, Dad. Just... have a lot on my mind."

There was a pause on the other end. His father was a man of few words, the kind who listened deeply before he spoke. It was something Sameer admired but didn't always understand until he grew older. Now, he realized that he, too, had inherited this habit—keeping emotions hidden, processing things in silence.

"You know, Sameer," his father said gently, his tone a little softer, "life doesn't always go the way we plan. It twists and turns, sometimes in ways we don't expect. But there's a rhythm to it, a kind of purpose that we might not always see. Even when we feel lost, we're still moving forward."

Sameer closed his eyes for a moment, letting his father's words sink in. It was comforting, hearing these thoughts from someone who had lived through so much and come out stronger.

"I know, Dad. It's just... there's this photography exhibition coming up," Sameer admitted, his voice quiet. "And I'm not sure if I'm ready. Or if what I have to show is even worth sharing."

His father gave a soft chuckle, almost as if he expected Sameer to say this. "You've always been too hard on yourself. Do you remember when you were young and picked up a camera for the first time? You didn't know what you were doing, but you loved it. You loved how everything looked different through that lens. You believed in it. Why don't you believe in yourself now?"

Sameer felt a wave of emotion rise in his chest. It was rare for his father to speak so openly, to express himself in a way that touched on the vulnerabilities they both often hid. But here he was, offering Sameer the kind of support only a parent could give.

"I don't know, Dad. It's hard to see things clearly sometimes," Sameer replied, his voice barely above a whisper.

"Maybe you're looking in the wrong places," his father said, his tone warm but firm. "You mentioned that you found something, something that stirred something inside you, right? Don't ignore that feeling. Let it guide you. Believe in the journey, beta. It will lead you to where you need to go."

His father's words seemed to settle into a deep part of Sameer, reaching places that felt tangled and confused. There was wisdom there, a kind of steady reassurance that Sameer needed but hadn't realized. Maybe his father was right; maybe the answer wasn't about forcing himself to complete the exhibition, but rather in uncovering the story he needed to share.

After a long moment of silence, Sameer managed to say, "Thanks, Dad. I really needed to hear that."

"Take care of yourself, Sameer," his father said gently. "I believe in you, and you should too."

As the call ended, Sameer sat in the quiet kitchen, feeling the weight of his father's words settling over him. They lingered in his mind, intertwining with the memory of Tara's letters, as if both were trying to nudge him in the same direction. There was something here, something he needed to uncover, not just for the sake of the letters, but for his own journey.

Sameer felt the weight of his father's words lingering even after the call ended. The kitchen was quiet, the silence thick but somehow comforting. He glanced around at the familiar surroundings, letting the memories of family dinners, late-night conversations, and laughter fill the room.

Just as he stood to clear the table, Mrs. D'Souza shuffled in, her soft slippers pattering against the floor. She glanced at him with a knowing smile. "Phone call from the family?" she asked, setting a fresh cup of tea down for him.

Sameer nodded, a faint smile on his lips. "Yeah, my dad. He... he always knows how to say the right thing."

Mrs. D'Souza sat down across from him, settling into her chair with the ease of someone who'd spent years finding peace within these walls. "A good father is like that. My late husband was the same, you know—always had just the right words, especially when I doubted myself. We used to bicker over the silliest things," she chuckled, her eyes sparkling with a far-off memory. "But, even through the fights, he'd find a way to remind me I was loved."

Sameer's curiosity was piqued. "Sounds like you two were really close."

She nodded, her gaze softening as she looked out the kitchen window. "Close? Oh, yes, like two halves of a whole. It's funny; we were opposites in almost every way, but that didn't matter. He was practical, and I was always the dreamer. We balanced each other out. Even when he passed on, that love didn't go anywhere. It just... transformed, I guess."

Sameer watched her, sensing the quiet wisdom in her words. "Didn't your kids ever ask you to move in with them after he passed away?" he asked gently.

She smiled, a hint of mischief in her expression. "Oh, they did, alright! Both of my sons were ready to pack up my things and take me with them. They live in big, bustling cities, so they figured I'd have more company there. But I refused. I wanted to stay here in this city, in this house. People think it's sad to live alone, but for me, this place holds his memory."

She took a sip of her tea and looked at Sameer thoughtfully. "It's not like I'm clinging to the past or that I'm bound by memories. No, it's... freedom. For me, freedom isn't moving to new places or running from the past. It's staying in the space that holds my heart and reminds me of what we shared."

Sameer was quiet for a moment, absorbing her words. "I guess everyone's idea of freedom is different."

"Exactly," she agreed, a glint of understanding in her eyes. "Some people find freedom by moving on, by changing their surroundings, by letting go. Others, like me, find it by staying. By honoring what was. For some, freedom is the ability to fly wherever they want. For others, it's the choice to stay grounded in a place that gives them peace."

Sameer felt a deep sense of respect for the woman sitting across from him. "You make it sound so simple," he murmured. "Like you've figured it all out."

She laughed softly, her voice warm. "Oh, beta, nobody ever figures it all out. I'm still learning, every day. But I do know that love has a way of sticking around, even when it's not visible. Whether it's love for a person, a place, or a memory, it never really leaves us. It changes us. And I think... I think that's what your dad was trying to say too."

Sameer nodded, remembering his father's advice from earlier. "He said that life doesn't always go the way we plan, but there's a rhythm, a purpose to it. And that even if we feel lost, we're still moving forward."

Mrs. D'Souza's face softened. "He's a wise man, your father. Sometimes we need that little nudge to keep going, to keep believing in our own journey."

A gentle silence settled between them, warm and reassuring. Sameer felt his doubts begin to loosen their hold on him, as if the simple conversation had unlocked something within him. "Maybe I need to stop looking so hard for answers and just... follow where the path leads," he said, half to himself.

"That sounds about right," Mrs. D'Souza replied, a twinkle in her eye. "Trust your heart, Sameer. Sometimes, when we stop searching, we find exactly what we need."

They shared a comfortable smile, the connection between them deepened by this moment of shared understanding. And as Sameer sipped his tea, he realized that he felt lighter, the weight of his worries softened by the quiet wisdom of the woman across the table.

The journey ahead was still unclear, but maybe, just maybe, he was ready to take the next step.

After hours of trying to find inspiration for his exhibition, Sameer still felt lost, unable to connect with his work in a way that felt real. Frustrated and weary, he made his way back to the attic, hoping that something—anything—might spark an idea. This time, he wasn't just searching through Tara's letters; he was searching for something deeper, some lost connection that had eluded him.

As he sifted through an old wooden chest, pushing aside faded fabrics and worn books, his fingers brushed against something small and delicate. Pulling it out, he found a bracelet covered in a layer of dust, its once-vibrant crystals dulled by age. As he wiped it clean, the crystals caught the faint light filtering through the attic window, revealing a soft, shimmering glow.

A strange wave of familiarity washed over him. He stared at the bracelet, realizing with a pang that it looked remarkably similar to the one his late mother used to wear. She had always been fond of crystals, believing they held energy and healing properties. She used to say that each stone had a purpose—a way of keeping people grounded, helping them find peace, or even love. She'd often run her fingers over her own bracelet, telling him how she felt a special connection to the stones, how they reminded her to stay true to herself.

The memory of her voice, the calm warmth it always carried, filled his mind. He remembered how she'd encourage him to live with an open heart, to see the beauty in small things, just as she did with her crystals. This bracelet, once cherished and full of purpose, now seemed to pulse softly in his hand, almost as if it were alive, whispering reminders of his mother's wisdom and love.

Sameer held the bracelet carefully, feeling a deep connection to both his mother and Tara. It struck him that his mother and Tara, though they'd never met, shared a similar kind of quiet strength, a sensitivity that saw the world beyond the surface. Tara had poured her love and unspoken fears into her letters, just as his mother had poured her own dreams and love for life into every crystal she wore.

In that quiet attic, with the weight of the bracelet in his hand, Sameer understood something he hadn't before. This piece of jewelry wasn't just a relic of the past; it was a reminder of what mattered—of love, connection, and the courage to embrace the journey, no matter where it led. He realized that his exhibition didn't need to be about perfection. It needed to tell a story, one that was raw and deeply human.

This bracelet would be his anchor, a symbol he would carry forward. It was the link between his past and his present, connecting him not only to his mother's memory but to his own path. He could almost hear her gentle voice telling him to trust himself, to follow his heart, and to remember that sometimes, the smallest things—like a crystal bracelet—held the greatest power to heal and inspire.

That evening, Sameer met Rohan and Rhea at Chai Adda again, clutching the photograph tightly in his hand. The café was peaceful in the dim glow of evening lights, with only a few patrons chatting softly over their chai. Sameer spotted Rohan and Rhea at their usual corner table, and as he slid into the seat across from them, Rohan looked up, raising an eyebrow.

"You've got that look again," Rohan teased, eyeing Sameer's determined expression as he took a sip of his chai. "What did you dig up this time?"

Without a word, Sameer placed the photograph on the table, sliding it towards them. Both Rohan and Rhea leaned in, their faces softening as they took in the faded black-and-white image. Tara stood by a riverbank in the photo, her eyes distant, her expression filled with something fragile yet powerful, as if she were waiting for something—or someone.

"It's her," Sameer said softly, his voice filled with awe and a touch of reverence. "Tara. The woman from the letters."

Rhea's eyes widened as she carefully traced the edges of the photograph with her fingers, almost afraid to disturb the delicate beauty of the moment captured there. "It's beautiful," she whispered. "There's so much emotion in her eyes. Like she's waiting... holding onto something."

Sameer nodded, lost in thought. "That's just it. This picture, these letters—they've shown me the story I've been looking for. I think I know what I want to do for the exhibition now."

Rohan's eyebrows shot up in surprise. "Really? And here I thought you were going to ditch it and become a full-time attic explorer."

Sameer chuckled, rolling his eyes. "Yeah, I thought about it. But my dad reminded me why I started taking photos in the first place. And these letters... they gave me more than just a story. They gave me something real, something I want to share. I'm going to use this photograph, maybe even some of Tara's letters, to create a piece that doesn't just show a love story, but captures the fragile beauty of human connection."

Rhea's face lit up, her smile warm and proud. "Sameer, that sounds incredible. You're not just taking a photograph—you're creating something with meaning, something that tells a story people can feel."

Rohan smirked, patting Sameer's shoulder playfully. "I knew you'd come around, man. But don't go getting all poetic on us, or next thing we know, you'll be quoting love sonnets at the exhibition."

Sameer laughed, shoving Rohan's hand off his shoulder. "Hey, I make no promises."

As they laughed, Rhea's gaze drifted around her cozy café, and she suddenly turned to Sameer with a spark in her eyes. "Sameer, would you mind taking a few photos of Chai Adda? I could use them for some publicity, you know, make the place look as special as it feels."

Sameer's face softened, and he nodded. "I'd love to. Let's make Chai Adda shine."

He stood up, adjusting the settings on his camera, his posture shifting to that of a focused artist as he scanned the café with a thoughtful look. His expression was calm yet intense, his eyes taking in every detail, from the warm lights casting soft shadows on the walls to the worn, comfortable chairs that had seen countless stories unfold. He moved with quiet concentration, tilting his head, squinting slightly, completely absorbed in the moment.

As he framed each shot, he seemed to transform, his usual easygoing nature replaced by a seriousness that surprised even Rhea and Rohan. Sameer angled the camera towards a corner filled with books and cushions, capturing the quiet, cozy feel of the space. He moved to the counter, focusing on the glass jars of colorful spices and tea leaves, their warm tones creating a sense of comfort and nostalgia. The faint reflection of fairy lights danced in his camera's lens, making the café glow softly.

When he finally showed Rhea the images, she couldn't believe her eyes. The photographs seemed to capture the heart of Chai Adda in a way she had never seen before.

"Sameer... this is amazing," Rhea murmured, her voice filled with wonder. "It's like the café is telling all its stories. I never realized how much life was here until now."

Sameer smiled, his usual playful grin returning. "Your café does tell a lot of stories, Rhea. You just don't know how to read them."

Rohan chuckled, nudging Rhea. "Well, looks like Sameer's not just a photographer. He's a storyteller for cafés now too."

Sameer laughed, shaking his head. "Hey, don't start giving me new titles. Next thing you know, you'll be calling me a poet like you feared."

As they all laughed, Sameer's heart felt light, the weight of doubt easing as he looked around the café, now feeling more certain than ever about his path forward.

3

Pages of Before

The year was 1994, and the city had a special kind of magic in the air. Life wasn't rushed like it is today. People took their time, and the world seemed calmer, as if even time itself had slowed down.

The streets were lined with tall, old trees. Their branches stretched wide, creating cool, shady paths. When the wind blew, the leaves danced, and the sunlight peeked through, making patterns on the stone roads. The city felt alive, as if every corner had its own story to tell.

In the middle of the city was a lively marketplace, full of colors and sounds. Sellers called out, showing off fresh fruits, vegetables, and shiny trinkets. The smell of spices, fried snacks, and sweet treats filled the air, making your mouth water. People chatted, laughed, and bargained with the shopkeepers. Kids ran around, giggling as they played, adding to the cheerful chaos.

Away from the busy market, narrow lanes led to quiet neighborhoods. The buildings stood close together, their walls painted in faded pinks, yellows, and blues. Small balconies were filled with flowerpots, and neighbors leaned out, chatting with each other. In these lanes, life felt slow and simple, like everyone had time to stop and smile.

There were cozy little cafes hidden in these streets, perfect for taking a break. The wooden doors creaked when you opened them, and inside, the smell of coffee and old books welcomed you. Artists and writers often sat at the small tables, sketching or writing while sipping on steaming cups of tea or coffee. These cafes were peaceful places, full of quiet dreams and ideas.

The city also had beautiful parks, full of green grass and colorful flowers. Couples strolled hand in hand, while children played and chased butterflies. In the evenings, the streetlamps glowed softly, and sometimes you could hear someone playing a flute in the distance. It felt magical, like a scene from a storybook.

But the rooftops were the most special part of the city. They weren't just for drying clothes or storing old things. People went up there to enjoy the breeze and look at the stars. On clear nights, the sky was full of shining stars, so close it felt like you could touch them. Friends laughed, lovers whispered promises, and dreamers wrote their thoughts under the open sky.

This was a city untouched by the fast-paced life of today. There were no tall buildings blocking the view, no phones buzzing constantly. It was a place where people enjoyed the moment—whether it was sipping a cup of chai or watching the sunset.

In this peaceful, beautiful city, a story was waiting to unfold—a story of love, life, and the connections that make life truly special.

The café by the river had a charm of its own, a quiet warmth that made it a haven for dreamers and thinkers. The golden light from vintage lamps cast a soft glow over the wooden furniture and faded walls adorned with paintings by local artists. The scent of fresh chai mingled with the faint sweetness of baked goods, creating an atmosphere that felt like a warm embrace. On most evenings, the hum of gentle conversations and the occasional clinking of cups created a soothing background melody. But for Tara, tonight was different.

Tara sat by the large window, her favorite spot. The view outside showed the fading evening light reflecting on the calm river, while inside, the world around her melted away. She was lost in her notebook, the pages filled with small, neat handwriting that carried her thoughts and emotions. Tara was not the kind of person to stand out in a crowd. Her nature was quiet, her presence soft, yet there was something about her that was unforgettable.

She wore a simple lavender kurta paired with a scarf that seemed to blend into the calmness of the café's ambiance. Her hair, dark and slightly wavy, was tied loosely, with a few strands falling around her face. Her almond-shaped eyes held a world of depth, as though they carried stories she wasn't ready to share. Every so often, she'd pause her writing, tapping the pen against her lip, her brows knitting together in thought. Tara's movements were gentle, her expressions unhurried, as though she lived in her own rhythm, away from the rush of the world outside.

Aditya entered the café with a familiar air of curiosity. His day had been spent wandering the streets of the city, his camera slung over his shoulder, capturing the little moments most people missed. He wore a crisp white shirt, the sleeves rolled up just above his elbows, paired with dark jeans. His black hair was slightly messy from the breeze outside, and his sharp features carried a quiet intensity. There was a calmness about him, but his eyes—oh, his eyes—were always searching, always observing. Aditya was a man of few words, but his camera was his voice, capturing the stories he struggled to express out loud.

As he stepped inside, the warm light of the café enveloped him, and for a moment, he stood still, taking it all in. The familiar faces of artists and writers filled the space, their laughter and chatter blending seamlessly with the soft music playing in the background. But then, his gaze fell on Tara.

She was sitting by the window, bathed in the last rays of the setting sun filtering through the glass. The light framed her like a painting, highlighting the soft curves of her face and the thoughtful furrow of her brow. Her pen moved across the page with a grace that seemed almost deliberate, as though every word she wrote carried a piece of her heart.

Aditya felt something stir within him. He wasn't sure what it was—curiosity, admiration, or maybe a bit of both. He couldn't look away. There was a stillness about her that contrasted with the hum of the café, a quiet intensity that made her seem like she belonged to another world.

Almost without realizing it, Aditya reached for his camera. His movements were instinctive, careful, as if he were afraid to break the spell of the moment. He adjusted the lens, framing her in the viewfinder. The soft glow of the golden light, the focused expression on her face, and the serene backdrop of the window made for the perfect composition. He clicked.

The sound of the shutter broke through the silence around her. Tara's hand froze mid-sentence, and her eyes lifted from the notebook to meet his. Aditya felt a jolt of panic. She had caught him. He was about to stammer out an apology, but then something unexpected happened—Tara smiled.

It wasn't a big smile, just a small curve of her lips, but it lit up her entire face. Her eyes softened, the faint traces of curiosity and amusement dancing within them. She didn't seem offended, only surprised, as if she couldn't quite believe someone had chosen to notice her in that way.

Aditya lowered his camera, his own lips quirking into an awkward, sheepish grin. He raised a hand in apology, but Tara tilted her head slightly, her smile growing warmer. In that brief moment, it was as if the bustling world around them faded, leaving just the two of them locked in a silent exchange.

The connection between them wasn't loud or dramatic—it was quiet and unspoken, like the first note of a melody yet to be written. Tara, with her guarded heart and stories tucked away in her notebook, and Aditya, the observer who saw beauty in the ordinary, had unknowingly taken the first step into each other's lives.

Aditya finally looked away, his heart beating faster than he cared to admit. Tara, too, returned her gaze to her notebook, though her pen didn't move this time. She glanced up once more, just for a second, to see Aditya still standing there, his camera hanging at his side.

For Aditya, it was a moment he wanted to freeze in time—not just with his camera but in his memory. And for Tara, it was a moment that left her wondering if, maybe, someone had finally seen her—not just her face but the person she was inside.

With a shy smile, Aditya walked across the room, holding his camera carefully as if it were an extension of himself. "I'm sorry," he said, his voice warm and sincere. "I didn't mean to disturb you. You just looked like... a moment worth capturing."

Tara looked up at him, surprised but not annoyed. His honesty caught her off guard. She wasn't used to being noticed like this, let alone described as something worth capturing. There was something about him—his genuine tone, his slightly nervous expression—that made her feel at ease. Closing her notebook, she gestured to the empty chair in front of her. "It's okay," she said softly, her voice calm but friendly. "I didn't even notice you were there."

Aditya chuckled, the sound light and easy. "I guess that's part of the job," he said with a wider smile. "Sneaking around, trying to catch people in their natural moments. I'm a photographer—it's kind of my thing."

Tara's lips curved into a faint smile. "A photographer," she repeated, nodding. "That makes sense. I'm a writer—always chasing the perfect word."

His eyes lit up, a spark of curiosity shining through. He pulled the chair out and sat down, placing his camera gently on the table between them. "A writer? That's interesting," he said. "What kind of things do you write?"

Tara hesitated, unsure how to explain the world she carried inside her. Writing was such a personal thing for her, something she rarely shared with anyone. "I write about... everything, I guess," she said, her fingers brushing the edges of her notebook. "But mostly about people. Their lives, their thoughts. I believe everyone has a story worth telling."

Aditya leaned back slightly, his expression thoughtful as he took in her words. "I think you're right," he said after a moment. "That's why I take photos. Sometimes, words can't capture what a moment feels like. A picture can tell a story that words never could."

They both fell silent for a moment, but it wasn't awkward. Instead, it was comfortable, like they had slipped into the same rhythm without even realizing it. The noise of the café seemed to fade away, leaving just the two of them in their little bubble by the window.

Tara glanced at Aditya, studying him for a moment. There was something disarming about him, something honest and grounded. His messy hair, his easy smile, and the way he held his camera like it was a part of him—it all felt genuine. She realized she didn't feel the usual nervousness she often felt with strangers.

Aditya, too, felt something stir within him. There was a calmness to Tara that drew him in, like she carried her own quiet world around her. Her soft voice, the way she held her notebook like it was her lifeline, and the depth in her eyes—it all felt special, like he was sitting across from someone extraordinary.

"You know," Aditya said, breaking the silence, "I think writing and photography are pretty similar. Both are about capturing something real, something that matters, whether it's in words or in a frame."

Tara tilted her head, a soft smile touching her lips. "I've never thought of it like that," she admitted. "But you're right. Maybe we're both just trying to make sure the world doesn't forget the little things."

Aditya nodded, smiling back at her. "Exactly."

The conversation wasn't long or overly complicated, but it was enough. Enough to create a memory, to leave an impression. As Tara and Aditya sat there, their words weaving a connection, they both felt it—something unspoken but real.

It was the kind of moment that lingers, the kind you carry with you long after it's gone.

Two Days Later

Tara paced back and forth in the living room, her heart racing with a mix of nerves and excitement. She wasn't sure why she was so anxious. It was just a casual visit, but the thought of seeing Aditya again made her stomach flutter.

Her mother was busy adjusting a basket of flowers they were taking as a gesture of goodwill, ensuring every petal looked perfect. "Tara, can you stop pacing? You're making me nervous," her mother said without looking up.

"I'm fine, Maa," Tara replied, smoothing her saree for the tenth time.

Her father, on the other hand, grumbled from near the door. "If we don't leave soon, we'll be stuck in traffic. Then we'll end up spending more time on the road than our friends."

Manav, Tara's younger brother, sat slouched on the couch, already bored with the whole plan. the excitement that seemed to buzz in the air. "Why do I have to go? It's not like I even remember those people," he complained, barely looking up.

Tara ignored him, her mind elsewhere. The name Aditya repeated in her head like a faint melody she couldn't shake.

Aditya.

She remembered him, though not vividly. Back when they were kids and neighbors, he had been the quiet boy . He was always wandering around, playing with trees, birds, and occasionally people, though they'd never interacted much. Her family had moved away before they'd had the chance to truly know each other but they used to very close. It is like one family.

"Tara are you ready?" her mother called, snapping her out of her thoughts.

"Yes, Mama. I'm ready," she said, taking a deep breath.

The car ride to Aditya's house felt surreal. Familiar streets passed by, bringing back flashes of her childhood. She could see her younger self playing outside with Manav, running up and down the lanes. But today, the past felt closer, as if she was stepping into it again.

When they arrived, Tara's breath hitched. The house looked the same as she remembered—whitewashed walls, a small garden with neat flowerbeds, and wind chimes swaying gently in the breeze, their soft tinkling creating a sense of calm.

Aditya's parents greeted them at the door, their smiles warm and welcoming. His mother, a kind woman with a soft voice, embraced Tara's mother. "It's been so long!" she exclaimed. "And look at Tara! Such a beautiful young woman now."

Tara smiled politely, feeling a bit self-conscious under the praise.

As everyone exchanged pleasantries, Aditya appeared at the door. Tara's heart skipped a beat.

"You remember Tara, don't you?" his mother asked, gesturing toward her.

Aditya nodded, a small smile tugging at his lips. "Of course," he said, his voice soft but steady. "How could I forget?"

The families settled into the living room, reminiscing about the old days. Tara's parents were busy catching up with Aditya's, laughing about shared memories and exchanging updates about their lives. But Tara barely heard a word.

Her attention was on Aditya.

And his was on her.

They exchanged small smiles and polite greetings, their unspoken connection growing with each glance. It wasn't awkward, but there was an energy between them that Tara couldn't quite put into words.

It was Manav who finally broke the silence. "So, you're the famous photographer, huh?" he teased, his tone playful. "Tara told me you sneak up on people with your camera."

Aditya laughed, a genuine sound that made everyone in the room glance over. "Guilty as charged," he said, reaching out to ruffle Manav's hair in a brotherly gesture. "But only when I see something—or someone—interesting."

Tara's cheeks flushed a deep pink. She tried to focus on smoothing a crease on her dress, but she couldn't ignore the way Aditya's words seemed to linger in the air.

"What do you mean by someone interesting?" Manav teased, his grin widening as he looked between Tara and Aditya.

"Manav, stop bothering him," Tara said quickly, shooting her brother a warning glance.

Aditya chuckled, leaning back in his chair, clearly amused. "It's okay," he said, his gaze shifting back to Tara. "Photography is about capturing the things that make life beautiful. Sometimes, that's a sunrise or a street corner. And sometimes..." He let the sentence trail off, his meaning clears without needing to say more.

Tara looked away, her heart racing. How could such a simple exchange feel so significant?

The rest of the visit passed in a blur of conversations and laughter, but for Tara, the moments that stood out were the quiet ones—the way Aditya listened intently whenever she spoke, the shared smiles, and the unspoken understanding that seemed to grow with every passing second.

As they prepared to leave, Aditya walked them to the door. "It was nice seeing you again, Tara," he said, his voice low enough that only she could hear.

"You too," she replied, her voice barely above a whisper.

As they drove home, Tara stared out the window, a soft smile on her lips. The visit had felt like the beginning of something—something she couldn't quite name yet, but she knew it was important.

Aditya wasn't just a boy from her past anymore. He was someone who had found his way back into her present.

Aditya caught up with Tara as she stood in the garden, admiring the blooming flowers while her family chatted inside. The late afternoon sunlight bathed the space in a golden glow, making everything feel warm and surreal.

"Tara," Aditya called softly, and she turned to find him standing a few steps away.

"Yes?" she asked, her voice light but curious.

He rubbed the back of his neck awkwardly, his usual confidence faltering. "I wanted to say... I'm sorry I didn't recognize you right away the other day. It's been years, and you've changed so much. But I should have known."

Tara smiled gently, tilting her head. "It's alright. A lot of time has passed. People change." She hesitated for a moment, then added,

"But I recognized you."

Aditya's eyebrows lifted in surprise. "You did?"

She nodded, her smile widening. "Of course. Some things don't change—like the way you always look at the world as if you're seeing something no one else can. You still have that same spark in your eyes."

Aditya chuckled, a little embarrassed. "Well, I guess that's one way to put it. But honestly, I don't know how you remembered me. I was just a shy kid with a camera back then."

Tara shrugged playfully. "Maybe I have a good memory. Or maybe you left an impression."

"An impression?" he asked, intrigued.

She laughed softly. "Don't let it go to your head. I just remembered you as the boy who was always chasing sunsets and trying to capture magic in ordinary things."

Aditya's gaze softened as he took a small step closer. "And now? What do you think of me now?"

Tara paused, meeting his eyes. "I think... you're still chasing magic. Only now, you've grown into someone who knows how to find it."

His smile deepened, and for a moment, they stood in a comfortable silence, the unspoken connection between them growing.

"You know," Aditya said after a beat, "I think I owe you more than an apology. Maybe I could make it up to you?"

"How do you plan to do that?" Tara asked, raising an eyebrow.

He grinned, the playful spark returning. "I'll let you choose. Coffee, a walk, or maybe... you could teach me how to put magic into words. I've always admired writers."

Tara laughed, shaking her head. "You don't have to make it up to me, Aditya."

"Maybe not," he replied, "but I'd like to."

She hesitated for a moment, then nodded. "Alright, coffee sounds nice."

"Then it's a plan," he said, his eyes twinkling with excitement. "Tomorrow?"

"Tomorrow," Tara agreed, her heart fluttering as they shared another smile.

4

Pages of Before

The sun was just starting to rise when Tara's family got an unexpected call from Aditya's parents, inviting them over for breakfast. It was a pleasant surprise, and soon, Tara was walking with her mom, dad, and younger brother, Manav, towards Aditya's home again.

Manav, as usual, couldn't resist teasing her. He nudged her playfully and grinned. "You seem pretty excited to see him again."

Tara rolled her eyes, trying to act indifferent. "He's just a friend, Manav. Don't make it a big deal."

"Just a friend?" Manav smirked, his tone dripping with mischief. "Then why do you smile every time someone says his name?"

Tara didn't reply, but her cheeks turned pink. It wasn't just that she liked talking to Aditya—there was something about him that felt special. He made her feel like she belonged, like they understood each other in a way she couldn't explain.

When they reached Aditya's house, his mother opened the door with a big, welcoming smile. "I'm so happy you could come," she said warmly. "Aditya hasn't stopped talking about you, Tara."

Tara's heart skipped a beat, but she managed a polite smile as she stepped inside. The smell of fresh parathas and chai filled the house, making it feel cozy and inviting. Laughter and cheerful chatter echoed from the kitchen, and Tara instantly felt at ease.

As everyone settled in the living room, Aditya walked in, his usual calm smile lighting up his face. His eyes met Tara's almost immediately.

"Hey," he said softly, his voice warm. "I'm glad you're here."

Tara smiled back, feeling her shyness creep in. "I wouldn't miss it."

While their parents started chatting about old memories and laughing about their childhood, Manav wandered off to explore the garden. Tara and Aditya soon found themselves alone on the back porch.

The morning sun was soft and golden, casting a warm glow over everything. The gentle sound of birds chirping made the moment feel peaceful.

Aditya leaned against the railing, looking relaxed. "You know," he began, "I was looking through some old photos last night, and I found one of us from when we were kids."

Tara looked at him, surprised. "Really? I don't remember that."

Aditya chuckled. "You wouldn't. You were maybe ten. You were sitting under a tree, completely lost in your own thoughts. You looked like you were imagining something amazing."

Tara smiled, a little embarrassed. "That sounds like me. I guess I've always been a daydreamer."

Aditya's gaze softened, and he shook his head slightly. "Even back then, you were different. You didn't just sit there like other kids. You seemed... curious. Like you saw things no one else did."

Tara's cheeks grew warm, and she looked away, unsure how to respond.

Before she could say anything, Manav burst onto the porch, dragging Aditya's parents with him. "You have to see the garden! It's so cool!"

The moment between Tara and Aditya faded into the bustle of their families, but the connection they shared lingered in the air, unspoken yet undeniable.

Over the next few weeks, Tara and Aditya's friendship blossomed in the most natural way. They spent countless afternoons walking through the city's parks, the paths lined with trees that swayed gently in the wind. The air always felt fresh, the scent of blooming flowers filling the space around them. They didn't have a set destination in mind, often wandering without purpose, allowing the peaceful surroundings to guide their steps.

With each walk, they grew more comfortable in each other's company. The moments felt timeless, like they had all the time in the world. The sunlight filtered through the leaves, casting playful shadows on the ground, and the world around them seemed to slow down, just for them. They didn't need to fill the silence with words—sometimes, just walking side by side was enough. Tara would notice the way Aditya paused to take in the smallest details: the light falling just right on a leaf, the way the wind moved the branches, as though he could see beauty in every little thing. And in those moments, Tara felt something shift inside her, a quiet realization that she too, was seeing things differently now.

It wasn't always the grand moments that left an impression; sometimes, it was the simple things—the sound of their footsteps on the path, the way they both reached for the same bench to sit on, their hands brushing lightly before they pulled away, shy but comfortable. They would sit in companionable silence, watching the world go by, occasionally exchanging a few words, but mostly just enjoying the presence of each other.

Even though their conversations were often light—talking about everything and nothing—the bond between them was growing stronger. It was in the way Tara found herself thinking about Aditya when they were apart, or how Aditya's smile lingered in her mind long after they'd said goodbye. They both knew something was shifting, but neither spoke of it. It was a quiet understanding, like the soft rustling of leaves in the breeze, ever-present and gently comforting.

The connection between them was undeniable, a subtle thread weaving them closer with each passing day.

One afternoon, while they were sitting under the shade of a large tree in the park, Tara nudged Aditya playfully. "I still don't get it," she said with a teasing smile. "Why do you take so many pictures of the same thing? How many shots of a sunset does one person really need?"

Aditya chuckled, taking his camera out of his bag with a grin. "It's not just about the sunset. It's about the moment," he explained, his eyes glinting with passion. "Each one is different, even if it looks the same. It's about the feeling it gives you—the colors, the way the light shifts, the quiet of the evening. Every sunset tells a story."

Tara laughed, shaking her head. "You're such a romantic," she teased, her voice light and airy.

Aditya shrugged, not at all embarrassed. "Maybe I am," he said, lifting his camera and snapping a picture of her as she laughed. Tara froze for a moment, her laughter caught mid-sound, and when she noticed him, her cheeks turned pink. She could feel the warmth of the sun on her skin, but also the heat of his gaze, making her suddenly aware of the closeness between them.

"You're not supposed to take pictures of me when I'm not looking," she said, trying to act casual, but her voice wavered slightly, giving away her shyness.

Aditya smiled, lowering his camera. "You look better this way," he replied, his tone soft and sincere, making her blush even more.

The moment stretched, comfortable and easy, before Aditya spoke again, his voice breaking the silence. "By the way, you and Manav are going to stay at my place tonight."

Tara blinked in surprise, her eyebrows knitting together as she looked at him. "Wait, what? I wasn't planning on staying overnight," she said, feeling a little caught off guard.

Aditya waved off her concern with a dismissive gesture. "Don't worry," he said with a reassuring smile. "My mom already asked aunty, and she's fine with it. It'll be fun. ."

Tara's initial surprise faded, replaced by a sense of warmth. "Well, if she is okay with it..." she hesitated before continuing. "I guess it'll be nice. Besides, I don't know why, but Manav really loves spending time with your mom."

Aditya's smile widened. "Oh, he's not the only one," he teased lightly. "My mom loves him too. It's like they've been best friends forever."

Tara grinned at the thought. "I can definitely see that. Manav's got this charm that people just can't resist."

Aditya chuckled, his eyes twinkling. "I think he's already got my mom wrapped around his finger," he said, shaking his head in playful disbelief. "But seriously, it'll be nice having you both over. We can hang out, relax. Maybe we can even go over some old photos from when we were kids."

Tara's heart fluttered at the thought of spending more time with Aditya. She wasn't sure when it had started, but there was something special about these moments—simple, unspoken, yet filled with meaning. "Sounds like a plan," she said, smiling softly.

As the afternoon sun began to dip lower in the sky, casting long shadows over the park, Tara and Aditya stayed there, chatting and laughing, the world around them fading into the background. In that moment, it felt like time had slowed just for them, allowing their friendship—and something more—to grow in the most natural way possible.

....

Manav was happily immersed in helping Aditya's parents. Tara watched from the doorway as her little brother handed Aditya's father tools and chatted animatedly with his mother about recipes. It was heartwarming to see how naturally he fit in here, as if their lives had always been intertwined. Tara smiled to herself, but her thoughts were interrupted when Aditya appeared beside her.

"Manav's a hit," Aditya said with a soft chuckle. "I think my parents might adopt him if you're not careful."

Tara laughed, shaking her head. "He's never like this at home. Your family must have some kind of magic."

"Maybe," Aditya said with a teasing grin. "Speaking of magic, I want to show you something. Come on."

He led her through the house, up a set of creaky wooden stairs she hadn't noticed before, their quiet steps echoing in the stillness of the night. As they emerged onto the rooftop, Tara felt her breath catch in her chest. It was as if they had stepped into a hidden world, untouched by time.

The stars stretched endlessly across the sky, brighter than she had ever seen, glowing like tiny lanterns hung in the heavens. They seemed to shimmer with life, pulsing gently as though sharing secrets with one another. The sky wasn't just dark; it was a deep, velvety canvas, painted with streaks of silvery light and faint hints of blue that seemed to ripple like waves.

The air was cool and carried a faint, soothing scent—perhaps the nearby flowers or the freshness of the earth after a long day. A soft breeze wove its way around them, playful yet calming, as though it too were enchanted by the night. Tara closed her eyes for a moment, letting the coolness brush against her skin, almost like a whisper.

Looking out, she could see the city sprawled far below, but it felt distant, almost unreal. The faint glimmers of streetlights and the soft hum of life below seemed like mere shadows compared to the brilliance of the stars above. Up here, the world was quiet, peaceful, like a sanctuary suspended between earth and sky.

The trees surrounding the house swayed gently in the breeze, their leaves rustling in harmony with the stillness. It wasn't just a rooftop; it felt like a magical balcony overlooking a world made of dreams. The boundary between reality and fantasy blurred, and Tara felt as if she could reach out and touch the stars, pluck one from the sky, and hold its light in her hands.

The night wrapped around them like a protective cloak, its beauty so vast and untamed that it made her feel small in the most wonderful way—as though she were part of something far greater than herself. The rooftop wasn't just a place; it was a moment suspended in time, a quiet pocket of magic they had stumbled upon together.

Aditya walked over to the edge and leaned against the railing, motioning for her to join him. Tara hesitated for a moment, overwhelmed by the beauty of the moment, before stepping forward.

"This is... incredible," she said, her voice hushed.

Aditya glanced at her, a gentle smile on his face. "I come up here when I need to think or just escape. It's like the world slows down up here."

Tara leaned against the railing, her gaze fixed on the endless expanse of stars. "It's like they're alive," she murmured. "Each one feels like it has its own story."

"They do," Aditya said quietly. "And maybe tonight, they're telling ours."

Tara looked at him, surprised by the depth of his words. There was a calm sincerity in his eyes, something that made her feel seen in a way she wasn't used to. She turned back to the sky, feeling the connection between them grow stronger in the quiet.

"Do you believe in moments?" Aditya asked softly after a pause. "The kind of moments that change you forever?"

Tara tilted her head, thinking about his question. The night seemed to make everything feel deeper, like even simple words had extra meaning. "I think so," she said after a moment. "But I don't think we realize how special those moments are until they're gone."

Aditya nodded, his eyes moving between her and the stars. "Maybe. But sometimes, I think you just know. Like this—this might be one of those moments."

His words hung in the air between them, but they didn't feel heavy. Instead, they felt warm and meaningful. Tara didn't say anything right away. She let the silence speak for her, the soft breeze and distant sounds of the night filling the quiet space.

Aditya reached into his bag and pulled out his camera. Tara immediately narrowed her eyes, already suspicious.

"You can't help yourself, can you?" she teased, pretending to be annoyed.

He laughed softly, adjusting the settings. "Nope. Some things are worth capturing. Like this."

Before she could react, he raised the camera and took a photo. The sound of the click made Tara gasp. She turned toward him, half laughing and half scolding.

"Aditya!" she exclaimed, quickly trying to hide her face. "You could've at least warned me! I probably look so weird."

Lowering the camera, he grinned at her. "Weird? You're sitting under the stars, glowing in the starlight, and you think you look weird? Not a chance."

Tara felt her face warm as she blushed. "You're impossible," she muttered, turning away to hide her flustered smile.

"And you're photogenic," he shot back, his grin widening. "It's not my fault I know how to spot great art."

"Oh, so now I'm art?" she asked, rolling her eyes but unable to hide her smile.

"Exactly," he said without hesitation, leaning against the railing casually. "This moment wouldn't feel complete without you in it."

His voice was light and playful, but the words felt honest. Tara glanced at him, unsure whether to laugh at his boldness or feel shy at how sincere he sounded.

"Well," she said, crossing her arms, "if I'm art, then I want payment for every photo you take."

Aditya laughed, his voice ringing out into the quiet night. "Done. Your payment will be... a free print of every photo I take of you. How's that?"

Tara laughed too, shaking her head. "You're ridiculous."

"And you're a tough critic," he replied, raising the camera again. "Hold still. The light right now is perfect."

"No way," she said, scooting away from him. "I'm not letting you turn me into your next masterpiece."

Aditya smirked. "Too late. You're already my favorite subject."

Tara groaned, laughing as she threw up her hands. "Why do I even try to argue with you?"

"Because I make it fun," he said, snapping another picture before she could stop him.

Despite all her playful complaints, Tara felt a warmth growing in her chest. The way Aditya looked at her through his camera didn't just capture her face—it felt like he was capturing the magic of the moment they were sharing.

"Fine," she said, settling back into her spot on the rooftop. "But if I see these photos anywhere public, you'll regret it."

Aditya held up his hands like he was surrendering. "I promise. They're just for me. Well, and for you, if you want to see them."

Tara gave him a playful look but couldn't stop herself from smiling. As the night wrapped around them, she couldn't help but think that Aditya was right. This really was one of those special moments—the kind you never forget.

His words struck something deep within her. She glanced at him, seeing the way his eyes lingered on her—not just seeing her, but truly noticing her. It was a look she hadn't seen before, and it made her heart feel both full and light at the same time.

"You're such a romantic," she teased, trying to deflect the emotions stirring within her.

"Maybe," he said softly, his gaze steady. "But only for things that matter."

The simplicity of his statement left her quiet. She turned her attention back to the sky, feeling the bond between them deepen in the stillness of the moment. They didn't need to say much. The stars above seemed to whisper for them, wrapping the rooftop in a sense of magic that felt almost unreal.

For the first time in a long time, Tara felt like she was exactly where she was meant to be. As they stood there, side by side, sharing the silence and the stars, she realized something: the world might be vast and unpredictable, but in this moment, with Aditya, it felt like home.

After returning home that night, the silence of her own room was almost unbearable. The quiet only seemed to amplify the things she couldn't say aloud. Tara sat at her small desk, the dim light from the bedside lamp casting long shadows across her notebook. She reached for her pen, her fingers trembling slightly as she opened the notebook to a fresh page.

For a long moment, Tara simply stared at the blank page, her heart heavy with emotions she had been suppressing for weeks. Every time she was with Aditya, she felt her heart swell, but fear always crept in, stopping her from speaking her truth. And so, as she had done so many times before, she decided to write him a letter—one she would never send.

Letter, June 1994
"Dear Aditya,"
I don't know why I'm writing this. Maybe it's because there are things I need to say but can't bring myself to say them to your face. Maybe this is just for me—a way to deal with everything I've been feeling since we met again.

You asked me what it's like to be a writer. I should have told you then, but I didn't. Writing is the only way I know how to tell the truth, even if it's only to myself.

Telling you the truth scares me. Maybe because once you know how I feel, things will change. I'm not brave like you, Aditya. You stand behind your camera and see the world so clearly, while I... I've spent so much of my life hiding. I'm good at hiding. Behind words, behind smiles, behind this fear that if I tell you what's in my heart, I'll ruin everything.

But I can't keep pretending that I don't feel anything when I'm with you. I don't want to just be your friend. I want to be the person you think about when you look up at the stars, the one you're reaching for when you're not even sure who you need.

But I'm afraid, Aditya. I'm afraid you don't feel the same way. That you'll see this confession for what it is—fear wrapped in pretty words. And once you know, everything will change. You'll look at me differently. Maybe you'll pity me. And I don't think I could bear that.

So, I stay silent. I watch the sun set beside you, I laugh at your jokes, and I tell myself that being close to you is enough. But it isn't. I know that now. And it's tearing me apart inside, this silence.

Maybe one day I'll find the courage to tell you the truth. But until then, all I can do is write it down here, knowing you'll never read these words. Maybe that's for the best.

Tara

Tara's hands shook as she finished writing the letter, her heart racing with the weight of the unspoken confession. She carefully tore the page from her notebook, folding it neatly and tucking it into an envelope. She scrawled his name across the front—Aditya—then placed it gently into the drawer of her desk, knowing it would never reach him.

For a long moment, she stared at the closed drawer, the ache of unsaid words heavy in her chest. Tara sighed deeply and stood, walking to the window. Outside, the world was quiet. The stars twinkled softly against the inky black sky, and she wondered if Aditya was looking at the same stars, thinking of her the way she thought of him.

,,

One Afternoon, at the Café

Tara and Aditya were sitting at their favorite café by the river, the warm sunlight streaming through the tall windows. Golden streaks danced on the wooden floor as the gentle hum of chatter filled the air. Tara sipped her tea, the cup warm between her fingers, while she flipped absentmindedly through her notebook. Across from her, Aditya was fiddling with his camera, as he always did when there was a pause in their conversation, his fingers adjusting the dials with care.

"So, what's next for you?" Aditya asked suddenly, his voice breaking the comfortable quiet.

Tara glanced up, her lips curving into a soft smile. "I don't know. I've been thinking of starting a new story, but I'm not sure where to begin."

Aditya tilted his head, his grin playful. "Maybe you just need a little inspiration. You should come on one of my photo walks. There's a whole world of stories out there just waiting for you to write them."

Tara laughed softly, her eyes lighting up, but before she could respond, the café door swung open. The familiar chime of the bell made her glance toward it, but what she saw made her pause.

A woman had stepped in, and her presence seemed to shift the energy in the room. Tara had never seen her before, yet she was impossible to ignore. Her confident stride made her seem like she belonged everywhere and nowhere all at once. Her dark hair flowed down her back, catching the sunlight in a way that made it shimmer, as though it held secrets of its own.

She wore a deep emerald-green dress that hugged her figure lightly, the fabric flowing like liquid with every graceful step she took. Her eyes—large, deep, and full of warmth—swept across the room as if she were taking in every detail, yet remained entirely unbothered by the attention she drew. The air seemed to carry her in, as though the world bent just slightly to make room for her.

But it wasn't just her beauty; it was the way she carried herself. There was a quiet elegance in her movements, a calm confidence that made it seem as though she belonged not just in the café but in every moment, every space she entered. Her smile was soft yet radiant, like it held a story of its own, one that you'd want to sit and listen to for hours.

"Meera!" Aditya's voice rang out, breaking the spell. He stood up so quickly his chair scraped against the floor. His face lit up with an excitement Tara had never seen before, his grin stretching from ear to ear.

The woman—Meera—turned toward Aditya with a smile that was just as bright. Her eyes sparkled as she crossed the room in a few quick, effortless steps. In an instant, Aditya had pulled her into a warm embrace, holding her as though she was someone he'd waited a lifetime to see again.

"It's been so long!" Aditya said, his voice filled with a joy that made Tara's chest tighten ever so slightly.

Meera's laugh was light and musical, like the sound of a wind chime in a gentle breeze. "It feels like forever! I've missed this city—and you." Her gaze softened as she looked up at Aditya, her expression filled with a fondness that seemed to make time slow down.

Tara sat frozen, watching the scene unfold. Meera's presence was magnetic, her beauty undeniable, but it was the way she and Aditya interacted that caught Tara's attention. There was an ease between them, a familiarity that spoke of shared moments and memories, the kind of connection that didn't need words to be understood.

As Aditya and Meera laughed together, catching up in a way that made the rest of the café fade into the background, Tara felt an unfamiliar twist in her chest. It wasn't jealousy—not exactly. It was more a quiet awareness that, in this moment, she was on the outside looking in, watching a part of Aditya's life that she hadn't been part of.

She picked up her cup of tea, sipping it slowly, her gaze drifting to the sunlight on the floor. The golden streaks didn't feel as warm as they had a moment ago.

Aditya finally turned toward Tara, his excitement still evident in his voice. "Tara, meet Meera, my best friend. Meera, this is Tara."

Meera extended her hand with a warm smile. "Hi, Tara. It's so nice to meet you. I've heard a lot about you."

Tara shook her hand, her smile polite but small. "Nice to meet you too."

Aditya grinned, glancing between them. "Meera's been out of town for six months. She just disappeared without telling anyone! This is the best surprise ever."

"Six months?" Tara echoed, tilting her head slightly. "That's a long time. Where were you?"

"Oh, I was at my uncles for work," Meera replied casually. "It was a whirlwind—beautiful, but exhausting. I missed being here, though." She turned to Aditya with a playful glint in her eye. "And I missed this idiot."

Aditya laughed. "You mean the idiot missed you too. Speaking of, where's that other idiot? Why didn't he come with you?"

Meera rolled her eyes dramatically. "Oh, him? He's being his usual self—too busy or too clueless, I don't know which."

Aditya shook his head, smirking. "Classic. He's always like that. You need to drag him here next time."

Tara sat quietly, watching the easy banter between them. There was a slight pang in her chest, something she couldn't quite name. Jealousy? Maybe. But she quickly brushed it aside.

Meera glanced at her watch and sighed softly. "I should get going," she said, her tone warm but regretful. "I knew I'd find you here, so I came to say hi before I got caught up with everything else."

Aditya's face lit up with an even brighter smile. "Oho, you found me! I'm so happy to see you, Meera. It's been way too long."

She smiled back, her eyes shining. "It really has. But let's not make it another six months, okay? We should all get together soon. Bring Tara along too. It'd be nice to introduce her to everyone."

Aditya nodded enthusiastically. "Absolutely. Let's make it happen. don't disappear on me again!"

Meera chuckled and turned to Tara. "It was lovely meeting you, Tara. I'm sure we'll see each other again soon."

Tara managed a genuine smile this time. "You too, Meera. Safe travels."

With a quick wave, Meera headed out, the café door chiming softly behind her.

Aditya watched her leave, a nostalgic smile lingering on his face. Then, he turned back to Tara, his expression warm. "That was Meera for you. Always popping in and out like she's part of some movie."

Tara nodded, her heart a mix of emotions she couldn't quite define. "She seems really nice."

"She is," Aditya said, leaning back in his chair. "And trust me, once you meet the rest of the group, it's going to be chaos. But the good kind."

Tara laughed lightly, though a part of her couldn't help but wonder about the bond Aditya and Meera shared.

The moment settled between them, quiet yet charged, as the sunlight continued to stream through the café windows, marking the end of another chapter in their unfolding story.

5

Pages of Now

The pale morning light streams through the thin curtains of Sameer's room, creating soft patterns on the floor. The house is quiet, almost eerily so, and the silence wraps around him like a heavy blanket. At his small wooden desk, Tara's letters lie scattered, their edges slightly worn from his constant handling. They feel like fragments of a story that he is desperate to piece together but cannot fully grasp.

Sameer had spent the entire night reading them again and again, as if the words could somehow reveal a secret he had missed. Each letter drew him deeper into Tara's world, filled with emotions so raw and real that they left an ache in his chest. There was a pull in her words—something about the way she wrote, about the way she held back certain truths, that made him restless. He doesn't know why, but these letters feel personal, as though they were meant for him alone.

Leaning back in his chair, Sameer rubs his tired eyes and exhales deeply. The letters aren't just Tara's story anymore—they feel like a mirror, reflecting pieces of himself he's been too afraid to confront. In her hesitant confessions, her moments of regret, and her unspoken fears, he sees his own struggles. The way he's always avoided vulnerability, how he hides behind his camera, pretending that capturing other people's lives is enough to fill the gaps in his own.

The letters have stirred something inside him that he can't quite name—a yearning, maybe, or a need to understand. He feels an urgency to know how Tara's story ends, almost as if finding her answers will help him find his own.

His gaze shifts to his camera, resting on the edge of the desk. It feels foreign to him now, almost like a stranger. Sameer used to lose himself in photography—it was his escape, his way of seeing the world in fragments of beauty. But lately, every time he lifts the camera to his eye, the lens feels heavy. Forced. Empty.

The timing couldn't be worse. His photography exhibition is only weeks away, an event he's dreamed of for years. This should be the pinnacle of his career, the moment everything he's worked for comes together in one perfect display. But instead of excitement, he feels a gnawing emptiness. For weeks now, he hasn't captured a single image that feels alive.

He stares out of the window, the morning light softening the edges of the world outside. Somewhere deep inside, he knows the problem isn't with the camera or the photos. It's with him. He's spent so much time running—running from emotions he didn't want to face, running from the pain of his past. But Tara's letters are pulling him back, forcing him to look at things he's buried for too long.

For the first time in a long while, Sameer doesn't feel like picking up his camera. Instead, he picks up another letter. Maybe, just maybe, the answers he's looking for are hidden somewhere in Tara's words.

Sameer's eyes drift back to the letters spread across his desk, Tara's handwriting pulling him in once more. Each stroke of the pen felt like a piece of her, vivid and alive, yet maddeningly out of reach. Her story with Aditya had become more than just words on paper—it had become his anchor, a connection to something tangible in a world that often felt hollow.

But it wasn't enough. The letters were a riddle without an answer, leaving gaps that gnawed at him. Questions swirled in his mind, refusing to settle. Did Tara ever confess her love to Aditya?

Did they find their way back to each other, or did their feelings stay trapped in the silence of unspoken words? He needed to know, as if their resolution might somehow offer clarity to the confusion in his own life.

Finding those answers, however, was proving to be an uphill battle. For days, Sameer had thrown himself into the search, combing through the dusty shelves of the local library, poring over old records, yellowed newspapers, and exhibition catalogs from decades past. He followed every clue the letters hinted at, but each path seemed to dissolve into nothing. It was as though Tara and Aditya had vanished, leaving behind only these letters as echoes of their existence.

Frustration had begun to sink its claws into him. Each dead end felt like a personal failure, and the weight of his obsession was becoming suffocating.

With a heavy sigh, Sameer leaned back in his chair, rubbing the back of his neck. The air in the room felt stifling, thick with the scent of paper and ink. He needed a break—a chance to breathe, to step back before the unanswered questions consumed him entirely.

He stood abruptly, grabbing his jacket from the back of the chair. The cool air outside might help clear his head, give him a fresh perspective. Maybe he'd wander the streets, let his feet guide him somewhere unexpected. Or maybe, just maybe, he'd stumble upon the missing pieces of Tara and Aditya's story—the pieces that felt so intertwined with his own.

As he closed the door behind him, Sameer couldn't shake the feeling that the answers he sought weren't as far away as they seemed. He just had to keep searching.

Sameer strolls through the empty streets, the cool evening breeze brushing against his face. His mind is a tangled mess, filled with questions about Tara and Aditya. The letters he's read have left him restless, their unresolved emotions pulling at him like an unfinished melody. He doesn't know where to look next or how to find the answers he desperately seeks.

Just as he's about to give up and turn back home, he notices an elderly man sitting on a park bench. The man is quietly flipping through a stack of old photographs, his weathered hands handling each one with care. Something about the scene draws Sameer in, and before he knows it, he's walking toward the bench.

"Excuse me," Sameer says hesitantly, "are those old photographs? They look fascinating."

The man looks up, his kind eyes meeting Sameer's. "They are," he says with a faint smile. "I used to be a journalist. These are memories from a different time."

Sameer sits down beside him, curiosity bubbling up. "A journalist? That's amazing. Actually, I'm trying to piece together a story myself. It's about two people, Tara and Aditya. I've been reading letters they wrote, but there are so many gaps in their story. I don't know where to find more about them."

The man listens attentively, stroking his gray beard as he nods. "Hmm. Sounds like a fascinating tale. But these things aren't always easy to uncover."

Sameer sighs. "I've been searching everywhere—online, asking people—but I keep hitting dead ends. It's frustrating."

The man pauses, then says thoughtfully, "Have you tried the library? Not just for books, mind you, but for the archives. They often keep old records, newspapers, and even exhibition catalogs. You might find something there."

Sameer blinks, surprised. The idea seems so obvious now that he wonders how he hadn't thought of it before. "The library... That's actually a great idea. Thank you so much!"

The old man smiles warmly. "Sometimes, the answers we're looking for are hidden in the most overlooked places. Good luck, son."

Feeling a surge of hope, Sameer stands up. "Thank you. Really. This might be exactly what I needed."

He hurries off, his heart lighter, his steps quicker. For the first time in days, he feels like he's moving toward something real, a clue that might finally lead him to the truth about Tara and Aditya.

The local library feels like a sanctuary for Sameer, a quiet escape from the chaos in his mind. As he steps inside, the familiar scent of old paper and polished wood greets him, wrapping him in a sense of calm. Rows of towering bookshelves stretch out before him, their contents brimming with stories from the past, waiting to be uncovered. The faint hum of a fan and the soft rustle of pages being turned create a soothing backdrop, making this place feel almost sacred.

Mrs. Bhargava, the elderly librarian with a warm smile and a keen eye, glances up from her desk as Sameer approaches. She adjusts her glasses, her expression a mix of amusement and concern.

"Back again, Sameer?" she asks, her voice gentle and familiar.

Sameer nods, offering her a faint smile. "Yeah, still searching. I've got to find something—anything—about Aditya or Tara. I can't shake the feeling that their story is buried somewhere here."

Her gaze softens, and she leans slightly over the counter, resting her hands on it. "Old records can be tricky," she says thoughtfully. "Sometimes, people's stories slip through the cracks. But you never know—maybe today will be your lucky day."

Her words give him a glimmer of hope. "Thanks, Mrs. Bhargava. I'll keep trying," he replies, his voice filled with determination.

He heads toward the back corner of the library, where the old archives are stored. This section is quieter than the rest, filled with rows of metal cabinets and dusty drawers. It's almost like stepping into a forgotten corner of time. The microfilm machines sit silently against the wall, their glass screens covered in a thin layer of dust. Sameer pulls open a drawer labeled 1994-1996, his fingers brushing against brittle pages and yellowed newspapers.

He sits at a wooden table, spreading the documents out before him. Carefully, he flips through them, scanning each page for any sign of Aditya or Tara. The faint crackle of the fragile paper echoes in the stillness. An old art exhibition flyer catches his eye, and for a moment, his heart leaps. He leans closer, searching for a familiar name—but it's not there. Disappointment settles in his chest like a heavy weight, but he doesn't stop.

Hours slip by unnoticed as he loses himself in the search. Each new folder, each delicate page, feels like a step closer to unraveling the mystery. The world outside the library fades away, leaving only the quiet hum of the machines and the faint ticking of the clock on the wall.

Suddenly, a soft voice interrupts his thoughts. "Anything yet?"

Startled, Sameer looks up to see Mrs. Bhargava standing beside him, her expression kind but tinged with concern.

He shakes his head, frustration evident in his voice. "Nothing. It's like they just disappeared after 1995. There's no trace of them anywhere."

She sighs, her voice low and steady. "Sometimes, people fade away, Sameer. Not everyone leaves behind a legacy, even if they deserve to."

Her words sink into him, leaving a bittersweet ache in his chest. But instead of discouraging him, they ignite a deeper resolve. He clenches his jaw, his determination growing.

"No," he says quietly but firmly. "Their story is too powerful to just vanish. I'll find something. I have to."

With renewed focus, he turns back to the scattered papers. His fingers sift through them with a new urgency, his mind racing with the thought that somewhere in this dusty archive lies the missing piece to Tara and Aditya's story. And he's determined to find it.

Frustrated and exhausted, Sameer left the library and made his way to Chai Adda, the café owned by his best friend, Rhea. It had become his refuge during the past few weeks, a place where he could temporarily escape the weight of the letters and the growing pressure of the exhibition.

The café was bustling as usual, filled with the comforting aroma of chai and freshly baked pastries. Rhea, with her signature mischievous grin, was behind the counter, chatting with customers and pouring drinks with effortless grace.

Sameer spotted Rohan, his childhood friend, lounging at their usual table by the window, already halfway through a cup of chai.

He waved Sameer over with an exaggerated gesture, flashing him a wide grin.

"Look who finally dragged himself out of the library!" Rohan teased as Sameer slid into the chair across from him. "I was starting to think you were going to live in that place forever."

Sameer chuckled, though his weariness was clear. "Might as well. I'm getting nowhere with this search."

Rhea appeared at the table, carrying a steaming cup of chai and a plate of parathas. She placed them in front of Sameer with a knowing smile. "Still no luck with Aditya and Tara?"

Sameer shook his head. "Nope. It's like they just vanished after 1995. There's no record of them anywhere. I don't get it."

Rhea slid into the seat next to Sameer, resting her chin on her hand. "Maybe you're looking in the wrong places. Have you tried asking around? Sometimes stories live on in people, not just in records."

Sameer considered her suggestion, though he wasn't sure where to begin. "I've been so focused on the library, I didn't even think about asking around the city. But who would even remember them after all this time?"

Rohan, who had been sipping his chai with exaggerated nonchalance, chimed in. "Maybe that mysterious old lady you mentioned, Rhea. The one who comes here to write. She could be a lead."

Rhea nodded thoughtfully. "It's possible. She hasn't been in for a while, but I'll let you know if she shows up. You never know—it could be a long shot, but it's worth checking out."

Sameer leaned back in his chair, staring into his cup of chai. "I just feel like I'm running out of time. The exhibition is coming up, and I've got nothing to show for it. My head's completely wrapped up in this story, but I can't find the ending."

Rhea reached across the table, giving his hand a squeeze. "Hey, you're doing your best. It's not easy, but you'll find what you're looking for. Maybe you just need to step back for a minute and focus on the exhibition."

Rohan grinned, leaning in with mock seriousness. "Yeah, Sam. Don't let these two lovebirds ruin your big moment. This exhibition is your chance to show the world how talented you are."

Sameer couldn't help but laugh at Rohan's dramatic tone, though the weight of the exhibition still loomed large in his mind. He had spent years working toward this moment, but now, with everything that had happened, it felt like he was stuck in neutral, unable to move forward.

Rhea, always quick to change the mood, sat up with a sly smile. "Speaking of lovebirds, guess what I got today?"

Rohan's eyes widened with curiosity as he leaned closer. "What? Did you finally get that free lifetime supply of chai from your favorite vendor?"

Rhea rolled her eyes playfully. "No, you idiot."

Suddenly , Sameer's bag slipped from his chair and hit the floor with a soft thud. A folded letter slid out, landing near Rohan's foot. Rohan leaned down, picked it up with a grin, and waved it in front of Sameer's face. "Uh oh, look what fell out. Carrying Tara's letters everywhere now, huh?"

Sure! Here's the revised version of that section with a more fantastical and fairy-tale-like tone to the letters, followed by the confusion in the second letter:

Sameer didn't reply, but his expression tightened slightly. He reached for the letter, but Rohan pulled it back with a playful smirk. "Come on, let's see what Tara wrote. Don't keep all the drama to yourself."

Before Sameer could protest, Rohan unfolded the letter and began to read aloud.

"Dear Aditya,"

I've always believed that some moments belong to the stars, that they're carved in the constellations long before we ever breathe them into life. That's what you were to me—a moment that felt like it had been waiting in the universe, pulling us together like the moon pulls the tides. I remember our evenings on the rooftop, the city below us fading into whispers, and the sky above us painted in colors only we could see. You made everything feel magical, like we were writing a love story the world had forgotten.

Do you remember how we'd lie there, just talking about the universe? You'd point out the stars, tracing stories between them, and I'd laugh, telling you that you could find poetry in anything. But the truth is, you were the poetry, Aditya. Every smile, every touch, it felt like fate—like we'd been written in the same breath as the wind that rustled through the trees.

I've always wondered what I did to deserve you. You saw me when no one else did. You found beauty in my silence, in the words I was too afraid to speak. With you, I felt like I belonged in a fairy tale—a story that was too perfect to be real. But that's what scares me now. What if we were too perfect, too fragile? What if love like this can only exist in dreams?

I wanted forever with you. I still do. But forever seems like a place I can't reach, no matter how much I long for it. I can't stay, not when every moment feels like it's slipping away, like the stars that once guided us are fading into the dark. And I... I don't know how to bring them back.

I love you, Aditya. I always will. But I'm afraid this love was never meant to last beyond the fantasy we built. Maybe that's why it's so perfect—because we were never supposed to live it. We were only meant to dream it.

Yours, forever in that dream,

Tara

Rohan's voice trailed off, his expression turning serious as he absorbed the weight of the words. The whimsical, fairy-tale love described in Tara's letter made him pause. He glanced at Sameer, then back at the letter.

"Wait... does this mean... they didn't end up together? Are you sure?"

Sameer nodded slowly, pulling out another letter from his bag. "Yeah. Tara wrote this as her final goodbye to Aditya. She left the city, knowing how much he loved her. But she couldn't stay, no matter how perfect it all seemed."

He handed the letter to Rhea, and Rohan leaned over to look at it as she unfolded the pages. This time, her voice carried a somber tone as she began to read.

"Dear Aditya,"

I've been thinking about us a lot lately. The way we've built something so beautiful—something so pure that it scares me. I never told you how much I've feared this love. Not because it isn't real, but because it's too real. When I look at you, I see a part of myself that I didn't know existed, and that terrifies me.

You've always given me more than I could ever ask for. You've held me in moments when I didn't deserve to be held, loved me even when I was too afraid to love myself. But Aditya, I've been lying to you. I've been lying to both of us.

I told myself I was strong enough to stay, that I could handle the weight of this love. But every day, I feel like I'm losing a part of myself, bit by bit. I'm not scared of losing you in the way most people are scared of losing love. I'm scared of losing you by holding on too tightly, of breaking what we have by staying when I don't have the strength.

I don't want to be the one who ruins us. And I think if I stay, I will be. Because deep down, I know I'm not ready for what this means. I'm not ready to give all of myself the way you have. I don't want to hurt you, Aditya, but I think I already have.

It's not your fault. It's not mine either, maybe. But I can't keep pretending that love is enough when I'm not enough for it. I know how much you love me—I've seen it in every glance, every word you've left unsaid. But I'm afraid that if I stay, I'll break something in you that I can't fix. And I don't want to leave you broken.

This isn't a goodbye forever. Maybe we'll find each other again, in another time or place, when we're both ready. But for now, I have to go. I have to leave because I'm afraid of staying, and I know that's something you'll never understand.

Please don't hate me for this. I'm scared too, Aditya. More than you'll ever know.

Love always,

Tara

Rhea's voice faltered as she finished reading. The room fell silent as the weight of Tara's words sank in. The confusion, the fear, the self-doubt—it all swirled together into a confusing mess of emotions that left more questions than answers.

Rohan was the first to speak, his brow furrowed in thought. "What... what does that even mean? It's like she's blaming herself, but at the same time, she's not? She says she's scared of hurting him, but she's leaving because of that fear? Was it Aditya's fault? Did something happen?"

Sameer sighed, running a hand through his hair. "I don't know. That's the part that's been driving me crazy. Tara loved him, but she was afraid. It's like she was caught between wanting to stay and feeling like she didn't deserve to."

Rhea leaned back in her chair, her expression thoughtful. "It's almost like she's leaving to protect him... but from what? From herself? Or was there something more?"

Sameer shook his head. "That's the thing. I don't know if it was just her fear or if something else happened. All I know is that she left, and whatever they had—it ended because she thought she wasn't enough."

The room remained heavy with the weight of Tara's letters, the lingering questions they left behind. No one could pinpoint exactly what had gone wrong, but the love between Tara and Aditya, once so pure and fairytale-like, had unraveled into something painful, something neither of them could fully explain.

Sameer sighed, glancing at his friends. "I wish I knew what really happened. If it was just fear or if there was something else. But that's what's been haunting me, and I can't stop thinking about it."

Later That Night – Sameer's Place

After spending a few more hours at the café, Sameer invited Rohan and Rhea to his place to hang out. It was a spontaneous decision, but he needed their company more than he cared to admit. The letters had left him feeling emotionally raw, and he didn't want to be alone with his thoughts.

As they entered the old house, the familiar creaking of the wooden floors greeted them. Sameer's landlady, Mrs. D'Souza, appeared at the door with a tray of freshly made snacks, her usual wide smile lighting up her face.

"Ah, Sameer! I knew you'd bring company today. I made some of your favorite aloo Tikki. Come, come, sit!"

Rhea's eyes widened as she caught the scent of the warm food. "Mrs. D'Souza, you're an angel. I'm starving!"

Mrs. D'Souza chuckled, setting the tray on the table. "Enjoy, my dear. And don't forget, Sameer—you promised me you'd fix that leaky tap in the kitchen."

Sameer grinned sheepishly. "I'll get to it, I swear."

The three of them settled into the living room, munching on the delicious snacks as they talked about life, their careers, and the uncertainty of the future. The conversation shifted between lighthearted teasing and more serious reflections on their personal struggles.

At one point, Rhea suddenly reached into her bag and pulled out a small, rose quartz bracelet. "Oh my God, I forgot! Look what I found. I've been searching for this forever."

Sameer glanced at the bracelet, raising an eyebrow. "That's the famous bracelet? The one you were so distraught about losing?"

Rhea nodded eagerly. "Yes! This is super special to me. It's a rose quartz bracelet, and it's supposed to bring love and healing. I've had it since I was a kid."

Rohan leaned in, inspecting the bracelet. "Love and healing, huh? Maybe you should give it to Sam. He needs it more than you."

Rhea smirked, slipping the bracelet back onto her wrist. "No way. This is mine. Meera gave it to me, and I'm never letting it out of my sight again."

Sameer looked up, his expression softening. "Meera... she really did love you, didn't she?"

Rhea grinned playfully. "More than you, Sam. And definitely more than Rohan."

Rohan gasped in mock outrage. "Excuse me? You know what's funny meera always thought that I want to marry you , Rhea ,she used to tease me all the time "

Rhea wrinkled her nose. "Ew, no way. In your dreams, Rohan."

Sameer laughed, though his heart ached at the mention of Meera's name. He hadn't thought about his mother in a long time. The memories were too painful, too raw. But now, sitting here with his closest friends, the weight of her absence hit him all over again.

Rhea, noticing the shift in his mood, placed a hand on his shoulder. "You miss her, don't you?

6

Pages of Before

The year is 1994, a time when life feels simple, and each day seems full of endless possibilities. The streets of the city are bright under the warm sun, alive with energy. Students hurry to their college classes, their laughter and chatter filling the air. The distant hum of traffic adds a soothing rhythm to the lively atmosphere, blending with the occasional ringing of a bicycle bell or the honking of a scooter.

For Aditya and his group of friends, this is the golden age of their lives. College days bring a kind of freedom they've never known before, where responsibilities feel like a distant worry. Their world revolves around the college campus, the corner tea stall, and the small park where they gather every evening.

Late-night conversations are their tradition—moments where they pour their hearts out, dream big, and sometimes argue over silly things, only to laugh about it minutes later. They tease each other endlessly, their playful banter often masking the deep care they share. It's a bond so strong, so pure, that they believe nothing in the world can ever tear them apart. For them, these days are not just memories in the making—they are the best days of their lives.

Meera was the heart of their group. She had a calm and caring, welcoming nature; she was like a happy, peaceful soul, always knowing when someone needed a kind word or quiet support. When things got tough, she was the one they turned to, the one who kept them together. But Meera had a secret—she had deep feelings for Aditya. She always loved him, quietly, and without asking for anything in return. She never said a word about her feelings because she knew Aditya's heart was somewhere else.

Shaan, the group's joker, was the only one who noticed Meera's hidden feelings. He was always the first to make them laugh, the one with endless jokes and playful energy. But behind his fun personality was someone who saw everything. Shaan noticed the way Meera's eyes softened when she looked at Aditya and how her smile grew just a little brighter when Aditya spoke. He never said anything to her, but every time he caught her looking at Aditya, his own smile would turn sad for just a moment.

Aditya, completely unaware of all this, was the dreamer. He lived with his camera in hand, capturing the world in ways that no one else could see. To Aditya, photography wasn't just a hobby; it was how he understood life. While others walked past ordinary streets and moments, Aditya saw beauty and stories in them. His friends teased him, calling him "the storyteller with a camera," but they loved the way his photos made their memories feel special.

The group was more than friends—they were like family. They shared laughter, dreams, and late-night talks about the future. Together, they created a world where they could be themselves, free from worries and judgments.

Then Tara came into their lives, and everything started to change.

Tara was a writer, a free spirit who joined their college halfway through the year. From the moment she arrived, she stood out—not just because she was new, but because of the energy she carried with her. Tara seemed to bring life into every room she entered. Her laugh was open and genuine, the kind that made others smile without even knowing why. Her bright, curious eyes were always taking in the world around her, as if everything held a story she couldn't wait to uncover.

At first, the group wasn't sure how she'd fit in, but Tara had a way of making people feel at ease. She quickly found her way into their circle, blending in as though she had always been part of their world. It didn't take long before she became one of them—an inseparable part of their tight-knit group.

Aditya noticed her right away. There was something about Tara that he couldn't ignore, something that drew him to her from the moment they met. She had a way of seeing the world that reminded him of himself. While Aditya captured life through his camera, Tara captured it through her words. She was always scribbling in her notebooks, filling the pages with thoughts, ideas, and bits of poetry. She said she was searching for the perfect way to describe the things she saw and felt, and Aditya admired that about her. It was as if they spoke the same language, just in different forms.

The rest of the group welcomed Tara with open arms. Her lively nature and quick wit made her easy to like. She had a gift for making people laugh and feel included, whether it was by cracking jokes during study sessions or by insisting they all go for ice cream after class. Tara had a way of bringing everyone together. She wasn't just fun to be around; she was the kind of friend who made others feel seen and valued.

Tara's energy was infectious. She added something new to their group, something they hadn't even realized was missing. In no time, she became the glue that held them together. Her presence turned their shared moments into memories that felt more vibrant, more alive. Tara was one of them now—a true friend who made their world feel a little brighter.

But there was something more between Tara and Aditya that neither of them realized at first. It wasn't obvious, not even to them, but everyone else could sense it. It showed in the small things—the way Aditya would look at Tara a little longer than usual, his eyes following her as she moved around. And how Tara's laugh was always louder, more joyful, whenever Aditya was around, as if his presence made her happier.

There was a connection between them, something deeper than just friendship. It wasn't a simple look or a quick smile; it was something that quietly grew between them. The rest of the group could see it. They noticed how Tara and Aditya would naturally drift towards each other, as if pulled by something they couldn't explain.

It wasn't loud or obvious, but it was there. It was like a soft, unspoken bond growing between them. Neither Tara nor Aditya had said anything about it, but everyone could feel that their friendship was turning into something more. Neither of them was ready to admit it yet, but it was starting to show.

One lazy afternoon, the group sat together on the college lawn, sprawled out under the shade of a large oak tree. Shaan was busy recounting a ridiculous story from his weekend, making everyone laugh, while Meera leaned back against the tree, her gaze drifting to Aditya, as it often did.

Tara sat beside Aditya, her legs crossed beneath her, a notebook resting on her lap. She was scribbling something—perhaps a story or an idea—but every now and then, she would glance up at Aditya, watching as he fiddled with his camera, snapping random photos of the group.

"Are you ever going to let me see the photos you take?" Tara teased, nudging Aditya playfully with her elbow.

Aditya grinned, lowering the camera to look at her. "Maybe one day. But only if you let me read what you write."

Tara laughed, closing her notebook with a dramatic flourish. "Deal. Though I warn you, my writing might make you cry."

Aditya's smile softened as he looked at her, his eyes filled with warmth. "I wouldn't mind that."

The group exchanged knowing glances, sensing the quiet affection growing between the two. It was subtle, but it was there, in the way Aditya's voice softened when he spoke to Tara, and in the way Tara's playful teasing was laced with something deeper—something more than just friendship.

Shaan, always quick with a quip, leaned forward and raised an eyebrow. "Oh, so it's a deal now? Aditya gets to read Tara's emotional novels, and she gets to see his 'perfect' photos?"

Aditya chuckled. "It's a fair trade, Shaan."

Tara smirked. "Fair, maybe. But I don't know if Aditya's ready for my masterpiece yet. It's about a love story that might just make him rethink his whole romantic outlook."

Shaan leaned in, grinning widely. "Ooooh, sounds intense. Are you sure you can handle that, Aditya?"

Meera, who had been quietly watching, finally spoke up, her voice light but teasing. "Maybe we should add a warning label to Tara's writing: 'Caution—emotional overload ahead!'"

Tara rolled her eyes. "You guys are the worst."

Shaan laughed. "Hey, we're just looking out for you. We don't want to see Aditya crying his eyes out, unable to take any more of your tragic love stories."

Aditya chuckled, holding up his hands in mock surrender. "I'm ready for anything, Shaan. I've seen a lot of things through my camera lens. I think I can handle a few tears."

Tara smiled, her eyes twinkling with mischief. "Oh, it's not just the tears. It's the heartache, the twists... I might even break your heart."

Meera raised an eyebrow at her, joking. "Oof, if that's true, Aditya might need a backup tissue box."

Shaan joined in with a grin. "I'll be there for the emotional support. Don't worry, Aditya, I'll have your back through all the plot twists."

Aditya laughed, shaking his head at his friends. "I think I'm in for more than I bargained for. But it sounds like I'll need to read it just to survive the teasing."

The group laughed together, the easy rhythm of their friendship flowing naturally, as always. The teasing, the jokes, the small moments of connection—they were all part of the same bond that had always held them together. But now, there was something more between Aditya and Tara, something no one could ignore.

Tara's teasing smile lingered a little longer, and Aditya's gaze held hers with an unspoken understanding, a new layer of something between them that had begun to shift ever so quietly.

Shaan glanced at Meera, a mischievous grin tugging at his lips. "Hey, you know I'm terrible with paperwork, right? I've got to submit some forms at the office, and I swear, I'll mess it up if I go alone. You're the only one who can help me. Plus, everyone knows you're the topper here, and I'm sure it'll take no time if you're there."

Meera, rolling her eyes playfully, leaned back against the tree, arms crossed. "You know I'm not good at this either. But fine, I'll come with you, just to make sure you don't get into trouble. But you owe me, Shaan. You're treating me to pani puri after this, okay?"

Shaan's face lit up immediately, the relief in his eyes clear. "Done! I promise you'll have as many pani puris as you can eat. Deal!" He grinned like a kid who had just gotten away with something, his excitement infectious.

"Fine," Meera replied with a small smirk, already standing up. "Let's go before you waste any more time trying to convince me."

With that, Shaan grabbed his bag and they headed off, leaving the peaceful atmosphere of the lawn behind.

Now, under the large oak tree, it was just Tara and Aditya. The quiet between them wasn't uncomfortable—far from it. It was a calm, almost sacred silence that enveloped them. The gentle rustling of leaves in the breeze filled the air, but it felt as though everything else had faded into the background. The world beyond the tree didn't exist for them in this moment.

Tara, glancing out of the corner of her eye, couldn't help but notice how Aditya looked so effortlessly at peace, his camera resting on his lap as he gazed ahead. She felt a warmth rise in her chest, something she hadn't expected. It was the simple joy of being near him, of existing in this moment together without the need for words.

"I like this," Tara said quietly, her voice soft, barely louder than the whisper of the wind. She kept her gaze fixed on the ground for a moment before looking up at Aditya, a small smile playing at the corners of her lips. "Just... being here with you."

Aditya turned his head to look at her. His gaze was gentle, his smile subtle but genuine. "Me too," he replied, his voice warm and sincere. It was the kind of statement that didn't need any elaboration. It was enough.

They didn't need to say anything more. Time seemed to slow down around them as they sat together, simply being. There was no pressure, no rush. The connection between them was quiet but undeniable, a soft thread that seemed to tie them together without either of them acknowledging it explicitly.

It was as if the rest of the world had slipped away, leaving only the two of them, wrapped in the comfortable silence. The usual noise of everyday life—exams, deadlines, expectations—didn't matter in that moment. All that mattered was the peace between them, the simple presence they shared.

Tara shifted slightly, leaning back against the tree, feeling the coolness of its shade. She didn't need to say anything else. Just being there, in that shared space with Aditya, was enough to make her heart feel light. She felt like she could sit like this forever, just quietly with him, and it would be perfect.

Aditya, for his part, had never felt more at ease. There was something about Tara's presence that calmed him, something in her quiet nature that mirrored his own. In a world that often felt overwhelming, this moment—this simple, serene moment—was all he needed.

Neither of them moved, both content in the peaceful stillness, letting the world fade away as they sat side by side, feeling a connection that was growing, yet still unspoken. It wasn't a need for more—it was enough to just be in that moment, together.

Shaan and Meera walked side by side toward the office, the sun beating down on them, the bustling campus life behind them. Shaan, as usual, was in a playful mood. He kept glancing at Meera, trying to catch her attention with his light teasing.

"You know, you're seriously addicted to pani puri. Every time we go out, it's the first thing you crave! Do you have some secret obsession with it?" Shaan grinned, nudging her with his elbow.

Meera, though, wasn't as quick to respond. Her mind wasn't on the pani puri she loved so much or the playful banter that usually made her smile. Her gaze was distant, her thoughts drifting. But she quickly masked it, giving Shaan a casual look.

"I'm not addicted," she replied, her voice light but not as spirited as usual. "I just like it. That's all."

Shaan raised an eyebrow, clearly not buying it. "Uh-huh, sure. You're probably dreaming of it right now. Just admit it, you can't live without it!" He laughed, but there was a knowing glint in his eyes, like he could see through the mask she was trying to put up.

Meera rolled her eyes, trying to seem unaffected, but her heart fluttered. Shaan always knew her too well. She hated how easily he could tell when something was off. She didn't want to show it, though, so she focused on keeping her voice steady.

"I can live without it," she said, but the words felt hollow even to her own ears.

Shaan, noticing the subtle shift in her tone, softened his teasing. He didn't want to push her too far, but he could tell something was bothering her. He fell into step beside her, his expression turning serious for a moment, his usual playful energy fading.

"You okay?" he asked quietly, his voice just loud enough for her to hear. His eyes locked with hers, full of understanding, knowing that there was more to her silence than just not wanting to eat.

Meera hesitated for a brief moment, her heart heavy with unspoken feelings. She wanted to say something, but she wasn't ready. Instead, she gave him a small smile, the kind that didn't quite reach her eyes, and shrugged.

"Yeah, I'm fine, whyyy??" she replied, her tone soft but distant.

Shaan wasn't convinced, but he didn't press her. He could see the way her eyes had shifted whenever Aditya and Tara were near each other, and it hurt him to watch, even though he didn't say anything. He knew Meera's feelings for Aditya, though she'd never voiced them. And it broke his heart a little to know that she was silently carrying this love, a love that was likely never going to be returned.

"You know," Shaan said softly, his words more sincere now, "it's okay to feel what you feel. You don't always have to hide it."

Meera's smile wavered, her gaze falling to the ground as she tried to hold back the emotions that bubbled up inside her. She wasn't sure how to respond, unsure if she even could.

"I know," she murmured, her voice barely a whisper. "But it doesn't change anything, does it?"

Shaan didn't have an immediate answer for that. He didn't know if anything could change the situation. But what he did know was that Meera was his friend, and he cared for her deeply. She didn't have to face everything on her own. So, without saying another word, he placed a comforting hand on her shoulder, a silent gesture of support.

Meera glanced up at him, the smallest hint of gratitude in her eyes. They didn't need words; they never did. Over the years, their friendship had deepened in ways that needed no explanation. Shaan understood her in a way few people did. He knew when to tease her and when to step back. He knew when to make her laugh and when to be the silent listener.

Their friendship wasn't about grand gestures or constant conversation. It was in the moments of quiet understanding, in the shared silences, and in the little things that spoke louder than words.

"Thanks, Shaan," Meera said softly, the words carrying more meaning than she could express. She appreciated the way he always had her back, even when she didn't want to admit she needed it. Shaan just smiled at her, giving her shoulder a gentle squeeze.

"No need to thank me. I'm always here, remember?" His tone was light, but the sincerity in his eyes spoke volumes.

Meera nodded, a quiet smile tugging at her lips as she felt a weight lift off her chest, even if just a little. With Shaan by her side, she knew she didn't have to carry everything alone. He understood her in ways she didn't even realize sometimes, and in that understanding, she found a kind of comfort she never expected.

As they reached the office, Meera felt a little lighter, a little more at peace. Even though the feelings she had for Aditya still weighed heavily on her heart, she knew that Shaan would always be there to catch her when she fell, just like he always had. And that, in itself, was enough.

As the weeks passed, the feelings between Tara and Aditya only seemed to grow stronger, but neither of them had yet found the courage to confess what they both knew deep down inside. Their friends teased them constantly, knowing full well that there was something between them. But Tara and Aditya remained silent, caught in their own thoughts, unsure of how to say what they both felt. It wasn't until a rainy evening that everything finally changed.

The day had been long, filled with classes and endless notes, and Tara was exhausted as she packed her bag to leave the campus. Her friends were already heading out, but she stayed behind for a moment, rummaging through her things. As she pulled out a small cloth, she unwrapped it carefully to reveal a photo album. It was a small, simple album, but the pictures inside were something special—pictures that Aditya had taken over the past few months. Each page was filled with memories, moments they had shared together, caught in the frame of his camera. There were candid shots of Tara laughing, her face glowing with joy, and others where she was lost in thought, unaware that Aditya had been watching her from behind the lens. Every photo seemed to capture a piece of her, a piece of their journey together.

Tara smiled softly to herself as she turned the pages, feeling a warmth in her chest. But the weather outside seemed to mirror her mood. As she flipped through the album, she heard the first drops of rain against the windowsill. Within minutes, the downpour became heavy, and the streets outside flooded with water. Tara, realizing that she couldn't walk in such weather, waited until the rain slowed. She glanced at her phone to check for messages but saw nothing urgent. So, she waited by the window for a while, letting the sound of the rain fill the room.

Finally, Tara decided to leave the campus. As she stepped outside, she spotted Aditya near the gates, holding his bag close and looking up at the sky, clearly waiting for the rain to let up. She walked toward him, and without a word, they both turned to take shelter under a small awning near the gates. The rain pelted down around them, but they were safe, standing close to each other, watching as the water rose around their feet.

Tara shivered slightly, and with a small laugh, she wrapped her arms around herself. "Well, this is just perfect," she said, glancing up at the sky with a playful smile. The rain made her hair stick to her face, but she didn't mind. It was one of those moments that felt like it could last forever, the kind where nothing else mattered.

Aditya, who had been unusually quiet for a while, turned to her. His expression was different—serious, almost nervous. Tara noticed the change in his demeanor. Her heart began to race as she looked at him, sensing that something was about to happen.

"Tara," he began, his voice soft but clear, "there's something I've been meaning to say."

Tara's smile faded, replaced by curiosity. She turned fully toward him, her eyes meeting his. "What is it?" she asked, her voice a little quieter now, as if the air between them had shifted.

Aditya hesitated for a moment, his hand tightening around the strap of his bag. Then, taking a deep breath, he spoke again. "I know I'm not the best with words," he said, his voice a little shaky, "but I... I love you, Tara. I think I've loved you since the moment we met. I just didn't know how to say it."

The words hung in the air between them, and for a moment, it felt like the world had stopped. Tara stood frozen, her heart beating so fast she could hear it in her ears. She didn't know what to say, didn't know how to respond. The rain continued to pour around them, but it felt as if time had slowed down, just for them.

Tara's breath caught in her throat, and all she could do was stare at him. She hadn't expected this, not in the rain, not in this moment. Her mind raced, trying to process what he had just said. She had always known, deep down, that there was something between them. But hearing him say it, hearing him confess it out loud, made everything real.

Before Tara could speak, Aditya reached into his bag, his hands trembling slightly. He pulled out something small, wrapped in cloth, and handed it to her. She looked down at the package, her curiosity growing. "Here," Aditya said softly, his voice barely above a whisper. "I've been working on this for a while. It's for you."

Tara looked up at him, her heart swelling with emotion. She carefully unwrapped the cloth to reveal a small photo album—just like the one she had been holding earlier. But this one was different. It was filled with pictures of their time together, moments that Aditya had captured. Every picture showed Tara in some way—whether she was laughing, thinking, or just being herself. Each photo held a story, a moment that was meaningful to him.

Tears welled up in Tara's eyes as she flipped through the pages. She had never seen something so thoughtful, so personal. "Aditya... this is..." she trailed off, unable to find the words to express how she felt.

Aditya smiled softly, his eyes filled with warmth. "It's my way of telling you how I feel," he said gently. "Every picture, every moment—it's all because of you."

Tara couldn't speak. The tears in her eyes were threatening to spill over, but she didn't care. She looked up at him, her heart full of love. She didn't need to say anything; the moment was enough. Without another word, she stepped forward and wrapped her arms around him, pulling him into a tight hug. The rain continued to fall around them, but in that moment, it didn't matter. All that mattered was the feeling of being close to him, of sharing something so real.

Aditya held her tightly, his arms around her, his heart racing. He had been waiting for this moment for so long, and now that it was finally here, he didn't want to let go. He whispered into her hair, his voice full of emotion. "I love you, Tara. I always have."

Tara pulled back slightly, her face flushed with tears and happiness. She looked into his eyes, her voice a little shaky but filled with sincerity. "I love you too," she whispered, "I've loved you all along."

The rain continued to pour, but they didn't notice. They stood there, holding each other, the world outside fading away. It was just them, together, at last.

7

Pages of Before

The next afternoon, Tara sat by her window, the soft rays of the sun filtering through the curtains. She had the small photo album in her hands, the one Aditya had given her the previous evening. She couldn't stop looking at the pictures, each one a snapshot of their time together. Her fingers traced the edges of the pages, her mind wandering back to the moments each photo captured.

Every picture seemed to take her back to a different place, a different time. She could feel the warmth of the sunlight in the photo where they had sat on the grass together, talking about everything and nothing at the same time. There was another picture of them at the café, Aditya laughing as Tara tried to explain something animatedly. She could almost hear his voice in her mind, as if he were right there beside her.

But it was the rain picture that kept drawing her in. The one where she and Aditya had stood together, sheltered under the small awning, the rain pouring down around them. Her heart fluttered at the memory. **"I love you, Tara,"** his words echoed in her ears, as clear as the moment itself. **"I think I've loved you since the moment we met."** She closed her eyes for a moment, letting the words wash over her like the rain had washed the world around them.

In her mind, the rain was still falling, and she could still feel the warmth of Aditya's arms around her. She could feel the soft beat of his heart against hers, and for the first time in a long time, her heart felt at peace.

Tara took a deep breath and opened her eyes, glancing at the picture again. The world outside seemed so distant, as if time itself had slowed down, leaving only the memory of that moment between them. It was as if Aditya's presence was still there with her, even though he wasn't physically beside her.

Her gaze lingered on the picture where Aditya had handed her the album. The shy, almost nervous look on his face as he handed it to her, the way he had seemed to hold his breath as she unwrapped it—it was all so real in her mind. It was a moment that would be etched into her heart forever.

Tara closed the album for a moment, pressing it against her chest. She sat there, silent, lost in thought. And for a second, it felt as though Aditya was whispering in her ear again, his voice low and tender, just as it had been the night before. **"I love you, Tara."**

Her chest tightened, and a small smile tugged at her lips. **"I love you too,"** she whispered to herself, as if the words were somehow more real when spoken aloud. Her heart swelled, full of emotion, full of a love she had hidden for so long but now could finally acknowledge.

The world around her seemed to blur as she sank deeper into the memory of that rainy evening. The sound of the rain, the feel of Aditya's arms around her, his words—everything felt so vivid, so close, like she was still there, in that perfect, fragile moment. Tara's fingers gently touched the photo of them in the rain, as if she could somehow reach into the image and pull Aditya back to her, feel his warmth once again.

She could almost hear his voice in her ear again, soft and loving, just like it had been when he confessed his feelings. **"Tara, I've loved you all along."**

she couldn't help but feel a sense of wonder wash over her. The rain, the moment, the words they had exchanged—it all felt too perfect to be a coincidence.

It was spring, the month of Phalgun, a time when the air was usually filled with the scent of blooming flowers and the promise of warmth. Tara had never experienced a spring like this one before. The weather was mild, the sun had been shining just the day before, and yet, out of nowhere, the rain had come, heavy and unrelenting.

She leaned against the window and looked outside. The rain had stopped for now, but the sky still held a deep gray hue, like the storm had just passed. Everything looked fresh and new, as if the world had been washed clean, ready for a new beginning.

Tara's mind wandered back to that night under the awning with Aditya. The rain had come so suddenly, almost as if it had been waiting for them. She closed her eyes for a moment, letting the memory of the stormy night flood her senses. It had been so surreal—like the rain itself had been a part of their story, falling just for them.

Sunddenly in next second

Tara was bubbling with excitement as she prepared for the gathering at her place. The whole group—Aditya, Meera, Shaan, Gaurav, Mita, and herself—was planning a special Holi celebration, and the anticipation of it all made her heart race with joy. It had been a while since they had all spent time together, and now, with the festival of colors just three weeks away, it was the perfect excuse to hang out and plan something memorable.

Tara had already started decorating her house, draping colorful fabrics over the furniture and arranging a few earthen pots filled with vibrant flowers. She was thinking about what they could do for the party—games, music, plenty of food, and, of course, the colors that would fill the air. The thought of how fun it would be to have everyone around made her smile.

Aditya, Meera, Shaan, Gaurav, and Mita were all coming over to discuss the party details. Tara was particularly excited about the idea of brainstorming with them. Shaan would probably suggest something fun and spontaneous, while Meera would have practical ideas, as always. Gaurav and Mita were the quieter ones, but they always had the best suggestions when it came to the little details.

Tara quickly prepared some snacks for everyone, hoping to keep everyone energized while they planned. She could already imagine the laughter and teasing that would fill the air when they all gathered together. As the afternoon sun began to set, she eagerly awaited their arrival. The countdown to the Holi celebration had begun, and Tara couldn't wait to see what ideas her friends would come up with.

The doorbell rang, breaking the moment, and Tara jumped up excitedly. She opened the door to find her friends—Aditya, Meera, Shaan, Gaurav, and Mita—standing there, chatting and laughing as usual. The atmosphere in the room instantly lifted with their energy.

"Hey! You're all finally here!" Tara greeted warmly, stepping aside to let them in.

"Of course we are," Shaan said with a grin, walking in first. "We've been looking forward to this all week."

The group made their way into the living room, where Tara had laid out snacks and drinks. Meera immediately moved toward the table, helping herself to the treats, while Shaan collapsed onto the couch with an exaggerated sigh. "You really outdid yourself this time, Tara," he said, grabbing a handful of chips. "This place looks amazing."

Tara laughed as she joined them, sitting down beside Aditya. "I'm glad you think so. I wanted everything to feel special for today's planning session."

Gaurav said softly, admiring the atmosphere. "I'm looking forward to Holi. It's been ages since we've all celebrated together."

Tara's eyes lit up with excitement. "Exactly! I'm thinking of organizing some games, maybe a little music, and, of course, a color fight! What do you all think?"

Aditya nodded, a smile tugging at his lips. "Sounds perfect. I was also thinking—maybe we should add a dance-off this year?"

"Yes!" Meera exclaimed. "And a big feast afterward. You know everyone loves a good meal after all the fun."

The conversation flowed easily, ideas bouncing around as they laughed and teased each other. They debated who would be in charge of organizing the colors and who would take care of the food.

The excitement for the upcoming Holi celebration grew with each passing minute.

Tara watched her friends, feeling a deep sense of gratitude. In this moment, surrounded by the people she cared about, she realized just how much she had grown to love them. The simple joy of being together, of planning this celebration, made everything feel right. The laughter, the warmth, the sense of belonging—it was something she would always cherish.

"We need to go all out this year," Gaurav said, his eyes sparkling with excitement. "I'm talking about colors, water balloons, and a proper *dhol* party."

Mita chuckled from across the room. "Of course, you'd want the loudest celebration, Gaurav. Knowing you, we'll end up in a full-on color war."

Shaan grinned mischievously. "I second that! Last year's Holi was tame. This year, no one should escape without being drenched in color."

Aditya, who had been quietly fiddling with his camera, looked up and gave a sly grin. "I don't think anyone's getting out of this unscathed, especially not Tara."

Tara raised an eyebrow, giving him a playful side-eye. "Oh really? And why am I the target?"

Shaan leaned back in his chair, a smirk on his face. "Because you're new to our group," he teased. "It's tradition. New members get the full Holi experience."

Tara crossed her arms and leaned in, her voice light but firm. "Fine, but don't think I'm going easy on any of you. By the end of the day, you'll all be unrecognizable."

Meera, who had been quietly watching the playful banter between Tara and Aditya, couldn't help but smile. It warmed her heart to see how easily Tara had become a part of their group. There was a lightness in the air whenever Tara was around—a certain spontaneity that made everything more fun. But as she watched Aditya and Tara interact, Meera couldn't ignore the familiar ache in her chest. She had loved Aditya for as long as she could remember, though she had never dared to speak of it. The friendship they shared was precious to her, and she never wanted to risk ruining it with the confession of her feelings.

Shaan, ever perceptive, caught the slight shift in Meera's expression. She quickly masked it with a smile, but he noticed the subtle sadness in her eyes. Nudging her gently, he asked, "What's on your mind, Meera? You're awfully quiet today."

Meera smiled, shaking her head as she recovered her composure. "Oh, nothing. Just trying to figure out how I'm going to survive this Holi with all of you troublemakers."

The group laughed, and Shaan gave a knowing look, but didn't press her further. He had been friends with Meera for years, and he knew that her feelings for Aditya were something she needed to handle in her own time. All he could do was offer her his support, like the rest of them always did.

As the evening wore on, the air filled with teasing, laughter, and the excitement of what was to come. Tara glanced at Aditya, who was still next to her, and smiled quietly. The connection between them was undeniable, and she couldn't wait to experience the fun and chaos of the upcoming Holi celebration. But more than that, she couldn't wait to continue making memories with him and the rest of their friends. This was just the beginning of many more beautiful moments to come.

As the evening came to a close, everyone slowly began to leave, promising to meet up again soon to finalize the details for the Holi celebration. Aditya, however, lingered for a moment, helping Tara with the last of the dishes before he and Meera decided to leave together.

The walk to Meera's home was quiet at first, with only the soft rustling of leaves in the breeze filling the space between them. Meera glanced at Aditya from time to time, sensing there was something different about the way he seemed today. There was an unfamiliar quietness to him—a subtle shift that she couldn't quite place.

As they walked along the quiet path, Meera spoke, breaking the silence. "Aditya," she began, her voice gentle, "You've been different lately. More... distracted."

Aditya looked at her, his expression softening. He smiled faintly, but there was a heaviness in his eyes. "I guess I've had a lot on my mind," he said, his tone hinting at something more.

Meera nodded, sensing he was holding back, but she didn't push. She had always respected Aditya's boundaries, knowing when to give him space and when to reach out. They had shared countless moments like this over the years—quiet walks, long conversations, and comforting silences that spoke more than words ever could.

They continued walking, the streetlights casting a warm glow on their path. As they neared Meera's house, Aditya finally spoke up again, his voice quieter this time. "Meera, I... I've been meaning to talk to you about something."

Meera turned to him, her heart beating a little faster. She could sense the weight of his words, the vulnerability that came with what he was about to say. Aditya, her best friend, the one she had always leaned on—he was about to share something important. Her curiosity piqued, but her heart also felt a little heavier, as if she already knew where this conversation was headed.

"I... It's about Tara," Aditya began, but before he could continue, a loud noise startled both of them.

A car screeched to a halt near the corner, and a figure stepped out hurriedly, breaking the quiet night. The moment was interrupted, and Meera glanced up at Aditya, her expression a mix of confusion and concern. Aditya seemed just as surprised, his words caught in his throat.

"Sorry, I was about to—" Aditya started, but then he saw the person who had appeared.

It was one of their old classmates, Ravi, who had been on the periphery of their friend group for a while but hadn't been around much lately. He waved and called out to them, walking over briskly. "Hey! Sorry to interrupt, but I need to talk to you both."

Aditya and Meera exchanged a brief look, the moment of honesty between them suddenly slipping away. Aditya gave a small, apologetic shrug to Meera. "Guess we'll have to talk later," he said, his tone light but his eyes apologetic.

Meera gave a small smile, though her heart wasn't fully in it. She nodded, trying to brush away the feeling of disappointment that lingered from the missed conversation. "No problem," she said, though she couldn't shake the feeling that this was one of those moments that could have changed everything.

Ravi, oblivious to the tension, continued with his erratic energy, and Aditya turned his attention to him, ready to shift gears. But as Meera watched them, she couldn't help but feel a small knot in her stomach, a quiet ache. Something told her that this conversation—this truth about Tara—was something she wouldn't want to hear.

The day of holi

The morning of Holi was filled with a special kind of magic. The sun rose slowly, casting a warm golden glow over the city, making everything feel alive. The streets were buzzing with excitement, and the air was filled with laughter and joy.

The smell of sweet treats like *gujiyas* and flowers mixed with the fresh morning air, making everything feel even more festive. Children ran down the streets, their faces already covered in bright colors, their eyes sparkling with mischief. Everywhere you looked, there were people getting ready to celebrate, filling the city with energy.

Homes were decorated with colorful banners, and the streets were alive with bright splashes of pink, blue, yellow, and green. The walls of buildings seemed to be painted in soft shades, and the roads were covered with colorful powder. It felt like the whole city had become a giant canvas of color.

The sound of *dhol* drums echoed from the distance, inviting everyone to join the fun. People danced and sang, their faces full of happiness and laughter. Today, no one cared about anything else. It was a day to come together, to forget the world, and celebrate the joy of life.

The city, bathed in all its bright colors, glowed under the warm sun. Holi made everything feel new and exciting. The streets were filled with love, laughter, and joy. It was a day when the world felt brighter, and everyone shared in the beauty of the celebration.

The morning of Holi felt like a dream for Tara. She stood in front of the mirror, looking at herself in her white dress. It was simple, but she loved how the colors of the day would turn it into something special. What made it even more exciting was the thought of what the day would bring, especially the moment she was hoping for—she wanted to be the first one to color Aditya. She had been waiting for this moment all day, wanting to surprise him with a splash of color, hoping that he would do the same for her.

Tara's heart raced as she walked downstairs, searching for Aditya among the crowd. His family, her brother Manav, and all their friends were there, but her eyes only searched for him. And then, their eyes met. He was standing with Gaurav near the door, laughing and talking. When he saw her, his face lit up, and Tara felt her heart skip a beat.

She smiled at him, and for a moment, it felt like the world around them didn't exist. It was just her and him. But before Tara could go to him, Meera called her over, and Tara found herself pulled into a conversation. But her mind was already on Aditya, wondering if he, too, was waiting for the same moment.

Finally, it was time. Tara was standing in the garden, the bags of colored powder and water balloons scattered around her. The excitement in the air was electric, but her focus was all on Aditya. As she picked up a handful of bright yellow powder, her heart was racing. She spotted him—his back turned, laughing with Shaan. This was it. This was the moment she'd been waiting for.

Tara took a deep breath and walked over to him. She stood right behind him, her heart pounding. For a second, she felt nervous, but she quickly shook it off. She had been dreaming of this moment all day, and there was no way she was going to let it slip by.

"Aditya," she said softly, her voice almost a whisper.

He turned around, a playful smile spreading across his face as soon as he saw her standing there, powder in her hand.

"Tara," he said, his eyes sparkling with mischief. "What's this? Are you going to color me?"

Without saying a word, Tara tossed the powder at him, laughing as it landed all over his shirt. The bright yellow color burst across his clothes, and he stood there for a moment, surprised by the sudden attack. Tara's eyes sparkled with happiness as she looked at him, feeling the playful energy between them.

Aditya reached out, brushing the powder from his hair, and stepped closer to her. His hand gently touched her arm, making her breath catch in her chest. He smiled at her, his touch soft and warm.

"I've been waiting for this moment too," he said, his voice low and full of meaning.

Tara smiled, her heart fluttering. "I wanted to be the first one to do this."

Without another word, Aditya took some powder from the bag and gently pressed it against her cheek. The color spread like a gentle kiss, and Tara's heart soared. She closed her eyes for a moment, feeling his fingers on her skin, and the world around them seemed to disappear.

"You look beautiful," he whispered, his hand lingering on her face for just a moment longer.

Tara smiled, her eyes meeting his. "You look beautiful too, Aditya. So full of color."

In that moment, everything felt perfect. The laughter of their friends, the music in the background, and the chaos of the celebration all faded away. It was just the two of them, standing together, surrounded by colors and warmth. Tara knew this moment would stay with her forever—the beginning of something new, something special.

As Aditya gently tucked a strand of her hair behind her ear, Tara felt her heart fill with happiness. She didn't need anything else in that moment—just him, and the colors they shared.

Just as Tara and Aditya stood there, lost in their moment, a sudden burst of color hit them both from behind. Shaan and Gaurav had launched an ambush, covering them in a rainbow of powders. Tara gasped, laughter escaping her lips as she tried to shield herself, but it was impossible. The air was filled with vibrant hues as the color explosion painted her skin and clothes.

"Gotcha!" Shaan shouted with a mischievous grin, his hands still holding a packet of blue powder. Gaurav stood beside him, his face covered in shades of pink and orange, grinning from ear to ear.

Tara looked at Aditya, both of them now completely covered in the chaos of color. Aditya, laughing, wiped a streak of yellow from his forehead and then turned to her, his smile wide and carefree. "I guess we're officially in the spirit of Holi now," he said, his voice full of amusement.

But before Tara could respond, the rest of their friends joined in, launching their own attacks. The whole group began shouting together, their voices echoing through the streets.

"Holi haiiiiiiii!"

The air was filled with joy, and the crowd around them cheered in excitement. The streets were a canvas of color—people dancing, laughing, and splashing water on each other. The scent of flowers and sweets hung in the air, mixing with the sound of dhols beating in the distance. Laughter and shouting filled the scene, making it feel like the entire world was celebrating together.

Tara and Aditya found themselves caught in the middle of it all, their faces painted with joy. As more and more people joined the celebration, the sound of "Holi haiii" became louder, reverberating around them. Gaurav and Shaan were already pulling Tara into the circle for a dance, while Meera and Mita laughed beside them, handing out water balloons to throw at each other.

Tara's heart swelled with happiness as she looked at the beautiful chaos around her. The love and joy of the festival had truly taken over, and she couldn't remember a time when she had felt more alive, more surrounded by people who cared. Aditya stood by her, his hand briefly touching hers as he grinned.

And in that moment, amidst the laughter, the colors, and the excitement of Holi, Tara knew she would cherish this day forever—especially the love that had bloomed between her and Aditya.

Tara, Aditya, Meera, Shaan, Gaurav, and Mita stood together in the heart of it all, laughing, dancing, and throwing colors at one another.

Shaan and Gaurav had taken charge of the music, and the thumping beats of the dhol could be heard in every direction. The sound pulled them all in, and soon enough, the entire group was dancing together in a circle, their laughter echoing through the streets. Each one of them, from Aditya's mischievous grin to Meera's twirling moves, seemed caught up in the same wave of pure joy.

Gaurav raised his hands, urging everyone to join in, and with that, a wild dance-off began. Tara, who had initially hesitated, found herself swept into the rhythm. She moved playfully, with a carefree energy she hadn't felt in ages. Aditya was right beside her, his movements matching hers, their eyes meeting between the bursts of color as they moved to the beat. They shared small smiles, their connection deepening with each shared glance.

Meanwhile, Shaan and Mita were in their own little world, throwing water balloons at each other and laughing like children. Shaan's carefree energy was infectious, and even Meera, who usually stayed on the sidelines, couldn't help but join in the fun. She hurled a balloon at Mita, hitting her squarely on the head.

"Got you!" Meera said, her laughter ringing out.

Mita wiped the water from her face, playfully narrowing her eyes. "You'll pay for that!" she threatened, before retaliating with a burst of color.

Tara laughed, her heart feeling lighter than it had in weeks. The whole day felt like a dream, filled with laughter and love, surrounded by friends who had become family. The celebration wasn't just about the colors or the games; it was the togetherness, the way they all came together to make this moment unforgettable.

As the sun began to set, painting the sky with a golden glow, they all gathered in a circle, out of breath but smiling. The street was filled with the joyful sounds of people from all walks of life, and in that moment, Tara realized how lucky she was to have found such a close-knit group of friends. She looked around at Aditya, at Meera, at Shaan, Gaurav, and Mita—and knew that this day would be one they'd remember forever.

"Best Holi ever," Aditya said, a grin still plastered across his face.

"Absolutely," Tara replied, her heart swelling with happiness as she looked at her friends, each one more colorful than the next, but all filled with warmth and laughter.

The world seemed perfect in that moment, as if everything had come together just as it was meant to be.

As the morning festivities started to wind down, Meera and Shaan found themselves sitting on the steps of the house, watching their friends from a distance. They had both managed to avoid the latest color attack and were taking a break to catch their breath.

"You've been quiet today," Shaan said, glancing over at Meera.

Meera shrugged and wiped some color from her forehead. "Just thinking."

"About what?" Shaan asked, his curiosity piqued.

She hesitated, unsure if she should say it aloud. "About everything, I guess. College, what's next, where we'll end up after graduation."

Shaan nodded, his expression thoughtful. "Yeah, I've been thinking about that too. It's like everything's changing so fast."

"It is," Meera agreed softly. "Look at us. In a few months, we'll be out in the real world. No more college. No more easy afternoons like this."

Shaan grinned. "We'll figure it out. We always do. And no matter what happens, this"—he waved his hand toward their group of friends—"this won't change."

Meera looked at him and smiled, her heart feeling lighter. "I hope you're right."

Shaan met her gaze, his eyes sincere. "I know I am. You're stronger than you think, Meera. And whatever happens, we'll face it together."

Her chest tightened at his words. Shaan had always been the one person she could rely on. He knew her better than anyone, and even though he was aware of her feelings for Aditya, he never made her feel awkward or out of place. Instead, he supported her—quietly, selflessly, without ever expecting anything in return.

"Thanks, Shaan," Meera said softly, her voice filled with warmth. "You've always had my back."

Shaan smiled, the bond between them unspoken but strong. "Always will, Meera."

Aditya, his face filled with a playful glint, gently pulled Tara aside, a mischievous smile tugging at the corners of his lips.

"Come with me," he said softly, his hand finding hers in the crowd.

Tara looked at him, curiosity lighting up her eyes, but she didn't ask any more questions. "Where are we going?" she asked, her voice filled with the excitement of something unknown.

"You'll see," Aditya replied, his eyes sparkling with a secret that made Tara's heart race a little faster.

Hand in hand, they walked away from the lively chaos of the Holi festival, moving toward the peaceful outskirts of the city. As they walked, the sounds of music and laughter faded into the distance, replaced by the soothing rustle of leaves and the gentle murmur of the river ahead. The air around them had cooled, and the sky above was a breathtaking blend of orange and pink, with the last rays of sunlight softly kissing the horizon as dusk began to fall.

When they reached the riverbank, Tara's breath caught in her throat. The sight before her seemed like something out of a dream.

Aditya had turned the quiet riverside into a place of magic. Strings of soft, twinkling fairy lights hung between the trees, casting a warm, gentle glow over everything. In the center of the space was a *jhula*—a swing made of smooth wood, decorated with delicate, fresh flowers in shades of white and pink. The swing swayed gently in the evening breeze, the scent of jasmine filling the air, creating an atmosphere of peace and beauty. Tara stood frozen for a moment, her eyes wide in wonder.

"Aditya..." she whispered, her voice filled with awe. "This is... beautiful. Did you do all of this?"

Aditya smiled, a soft, loving smile that seemed to make the entire world around them feel even more magical. He nodded, his eyes never leaving hers. "I wanted to do something special for you. Holi is a celebration of color and joy, and you, Tara... you bring that into my life. I wanted to create a moment that's just for us."

Tara felt her heart swell with emotion. She could feel the warmth of the moment, a warmth that wasn't just from the lights or the flowers but from the love that filled the space between them. Tears pricked at the corners of her eyes, but she didn't want to cry—she just wanted to soak in everything, every detail of this perfect, intimate moment.

Aditya's voice brought her back to reality as he gestured toward the swing. "Go on. It's yours."

Tara slowly walked toward the *jhula*, her heart fluttering in her chest. She sat down gently, her fingers brushing over the soft petals of the flowers that decorated the swing. The delicate touch of the petals seemed to match the tenderness in her heart. Aditya stood behind her, and with a gentle push, the swing began to sway. The motion was slow, peaceful, as if the whole world had slowed down just for them.

The river beside them whispered softly, its gentle flow adding to the calm atmosphere. The lights around them flickered gently, casting a soft, golden glow on their faces. Tara closed her eyes for a moment, taking in the magic of it all—the scent of the jasmine, the cool breeze, the peaceful sounds of the river, and the warmth of Aditya's presence beside her.

As the swing slowed, Aditya sat down next to her, his shoulder brushing against hers. They didn't need to speak. The silence between them was filled with everything they hadn't said out loud—the shared moments, the unspoken understanding, the feelings that had quietly built between them over time. It was a kind of silence that spoke louder than words, a language that only they seemed to understand.

Tara leaned her head gently on Aditya's shoulder, closing her eyes as she allowed herself to melt into the moment. "This is perfect," she whispered, her voice filled with a sense of peace. "I don't want this moment to end."

Aditya wrapped his arm around her, pulling her a little closer. "It doesn't have to," he murmured softly, his words like a promise.

They sat there for a long time, watching as the sky darkened and the first stars began to twinkle above them. Everything around them seemed to fade away—the world, the noise, the chaos—and there was only the quiet, comforting presence of each other. It was the most beautiful and peaceful moment either of them had ever experienced.

The world could have gone on without them, but in that moment, they didn't need anything else. There was just the love they shared, unspoken and pure, and the perfect peace of being together. The stars shone down on them, as if the universe itself was celebrating their connection. It felt like time stood still, just for them, and Tara knew in that moment that this was a memory she would carry with her forever.

When Tara finally returned home that night, her heart was still full of the beautiful evening she had spent with Aditya. The memory of the swing by the river, the fairy lights, and the peaceful moments they shared kept her warm inside. But as she walked through the door, she heard raised voices from the living room.

Her parents were arguing again. Their voices were sharp and angry, making the air tense and heavy. Tara's younger brother, Manav, was sitting on the stairs with his head down, looking upset. He was only three years younger than Tara, but the constant fighting had made him grow up faster than she liked.

Tara walked over to him and put a gentle hand on his shoulder. "Hey, are you okay?" she asked softly.

Manav nodded but didn't look up. "They've been arguing for a while," he said quietly.

Tara's heart broke as she glanced at their parents, who hadn't noticed her yet. She hated seeing them like this and hated even more how it affected Manav. He was just a kid, and he didn't deserve to be caught in their fights.

Then, their parents stopped arguing and looked at Tara and Manav. The tension in the room was thick, but there was also some guilt on their faces.

Tara looked at them calmly and said, "You don't have to do this in front of us. Please."

Her mother sighed and ran a hand through her hair. "We're sorry," she said, but it didn't sound like a real apology. It felt empty.

Tara nodded, taking Manav's hand and leading him upstairs. As they climbed the stairs, she couldn't help but think of the peaceful evening she'd had with Aditya, and how different it was from what she was coming back to at home.

She thought about the swing by the river, with flowers and fairy lights glowing softly. That moment felt magical and so different from the chaos in her house. It was like a beautiful memory that she could hold onto, even when everything else felt hard.

Once they reached the top of the stairs, Tara squeezed Manav's hand gently and smiled at him, hoping to comfort him. The two of them walked to their rooms in silence, leaving the arguing downstairs behind.

Tara stopped for a moment outside her room, looking back toward the living room where the fighting was still happening. But she felt a little better knowing that she had something beautiful to hold on to—the memory of her time with Aditya. It reminded her that even when things were tough at home, there was still love and peace in the world.

When she closed her bedroom door, Tara took a deep breath and let herself relax. The memories of her evening with Aditya made her feel safe and hopeful. She knew that no matter what was happening around her, the love she shared with Aditya would always be there, steady and strong.

8
Pages of Now

Sameer sits on the edge of his bed, the letters spread across his desk like fragments of a story still waiting to be told. He has read them over and over again, so many times that the words have become etched in his mind. But no matter how many times he reads them, something is missing. The letters tell half of the story—the happy half—the part that shows Tara and Aditya deeply in love. Yet, as he reads on, he wonders: if they were so happy together, why do some letters describe their separation?

Tara's love for Aditya is clear in every word, as are her fears and regrets. But something crucial, something deep and unspoken, seems to be hidden beneath the surface. Sameer feels a connection to their story, a connection that goes beyond just understanding their love. It's like their silence, their unsaid words, resonate within him. Why does he feel so drawn to their story? What is it about their fears and emotions that make him feel as though he knows them in a way he can't explain?

Sameer runs his hand through his hair, leaning back in frustration. He glances out of the window, the search for answers consuming him. It's been weeks, but he can't stop. He promised Rhea and Rohan he would take a break, but every time he tries to step away, something pulls him back. The search isn't just about uncovering the truth about Tara and Aditya anymore; it's about understanding why their story feels so deeply connected to his own.

His phone buzzes on the nightstand, pulling him from his thoughts. It's a call from his father—Baba.

"Baba?" Sameer answers, his voice soft, bracing himself for the familiar conversation. Baba has been calling more often lately, and though Sameer appreciates the check-ins, there's always a lingering feeling that something remains unsaid.

"Beta, how are you?" Baba's calming voice comes through the phone. "I was just thinking about you. You haven't called in a few days."

Sameer smiles, leaning back against the headboard. "I'm fine, Baba. Just... working on a few things."

"You sound tired," Baba observes. "You've been overworking yourself, haven't you? That exhibition is important, but it's not worth burning yourself out over."

"I know," Sameer replies, rubbing his forehead. "I just have a lot on my mind. You don't need to worry about me."

Baba chuckles lightly, a smile in his voice. "I'll always worry, Sameer. It's what parents do."

Sameer's smile falters a little. Baba always knows the right things to say. He offers support without fail, reminding Sameer to take care of himself. But there's always something distant in Baba's voice, a quiet space that Sameer can never quite understand. It's as if Baba has spent his whole life caring for Sameer and his mother but never for himself.

"Baba," Sameer starts, a little cautiously, "can I ask you something?"

"Of course," Baba replies. "What's on your mind?"

"Do you... ever feel like something is missing?" Sameer hesitates, trying to find the right words. "Like there's a part of your life that you don't talk about? You've always been there for me and Maa, but I feel like... I don't know, you never really talk about yourself."

There's a long pause on the other end of the line. Sameer can hear his father take a deep breath, as if he's considering how to answer.

"I guess I've always been like that," Baba says quietly. "After your mother passed away, I didn't think much about what I wanted or needed. My focus was always on you—on making sure you were okay."

Sameer feels a tightness in his chest. He's known for a long time that his father carried a heavy burden after his mother's death, but hearing Baba admit it so openly hits him harder than he expected.

"I miss her too, Baba," Sameer says softly. "But sometimes, I wonder if you miss more than just her. Like there's something else in your life that you gave up on."

There's a long pause before Baba speaks again, his voice tinged with sadness. "Maybe there is, Sameer. But it's hard to know anymore. Life has a way of moving on, even when we don't."

The words hang in the air between them, thick with unspoken truths. Sameer has always admired his father's strength, but now he realizes that strength is built on sacrifices and loneliness. Baba has given so much for his family, but in doing so, it seems he has lost something of himself along the way.

"Thanks, Baba," Sameer says quietly after a long silence. "I needed to hear that."

"I'm always here for you, beta," Baba replies gently. "Just remember, it's okay to take care of yourself too."

Sameer sits in silence for a few minutes after the call ends, his mind racing. Baba's words stir something in him—a feeling that he's been ignoring for a long time. It's so similar to what he's read in Tara's letters. Like Tara, Baba has chosen silence over vulnerability. He's hidden his pain, his desires, for the sake of those he loves. And in doing so, he's lost something along the way.

Sameer leans back, staring at the ceiling, trying to make sense of it all. His phone buzzes again, this time with a video call request. A smile tugs at his lips as he sees the name on the screen.

Siya.

Siya was someone who had always been there for him, even though they had never met in person. She was an Indian student studying in the U.S., and their friendship had begun online, purely by chance. Over time, their connection had deepened, and Sameer found himself confiding in her in ways he hadn't with anyone else. She had a way of understanding him that was both comforting and terrifying. Sometimes, he thought it might be more than friendship, but he wasn't sure if that was just his own wishful thinking.

He answered the call, and Siya's face appeared on the screen, her dark eyes lighting up as soon as she saw him.

"Sameer!" she exclaimed, smiling brightly. "It's been forever since we talked. What's going on?"

Sameer chuckled. "Hey, Siya. It hasn't been that long."

"It feels like it," she teased, adjusting her glasses. "You've been so caught up with this mystery you're chasing, I thought you forgot about me."

Sameer's smile softened. Siya had a way of cutting through the noise, of making him feel like everything would be okay, even when the world felt like it was spinning out of control.

"I could never forget about you," he said, the words slipping out before he could stop them.

Siya blinked, momentarily caught off guard, before laughing it off. "Well, I'm glad to hear that. So, how's the search going? Did you find anything?"

Sameer sighed, running a hand through his hair. "I'm getting close, I think. But it's frustrating. I've been hitting a lot of dead ends."

"Don't give up," Siya said, her tone encouraging. "You're smart, Sameer. You'll figure it out. Besides, it sounds like you're learning a lot about yourself along the way."

Sameer nodded, feeling a warmth in his chest that he couldn't quite explain. Siya always seemed to know the right thing to say, to make him feel understood in a way that even Rhea and Rohan couldn't. There was something about her—something that made him feel safe, even though they had only ever spoken through screens.

"I don't know what I'd do without you, Siya," he said quietly, his voice full of emotion.

Siya's smile softened. "You'd be just fine. But I'm glad to be here for you."

Before he could respond, there was a sudden knock on the door. Sameer glanced over his shoulder, realizing Rhea and Rohan had arrived earlier than expected.

"I've got to go," he said quickly, his heart racing. He hadn't told Rhea or Rohan about Siya, and for some reason, he wasn't ready for them to know yet. It felt like this connection was something he wanted to keep to himself for a little while longer.

"Okay," Siya said, her smile fading slightly. "Take care, Sameer. Call me when you can."

"I will," he promised before ending the call.

Rhea and Rohan barged into Sameer's apartment, laughing and chattering as they made themselves at home. Sameer welcomed the distraction, hoping they wouldn't notice the lingering emotions from his conversation with Siya.

"What's up, man?" Rohan asked, dropping onto the couch and grabbing one of the snacks Sameer had laid out. "You looked serious when we walked in."

Sameer shook his head, forcing a smile. "Just talking to a friend."

Rhea raised an eyebrow but didn't press him. Instead, she sat beside Rohan, pulling out her phone as if waiting for something. "My dad's been acting weird lately," she said after a moment, her tone suddenly more serious. "I think he's been working too hard, but he won't listen to me."

Sameer frowned, concern creeping into his expression. "What do you mean? Is he okay?"

"I don't know," Rhea admitted, biting her lip. "He's been complaining about chest pain, but he keeps brushing it off. I've been trying to get him to see a doctor, but you know how stubborn he is."

Just as she finished speaking, Rhea's phone buzzed in her hand. Her face paled as she read the message, and without a word, she stood up abruptly, her hands shaking.

"Rhea, what's wrong?" Sameer asked, standing up as well.

"It's my dad," she whispered, her voice barely audible. "He collapsed. They're taking him to the hospital."

....

The next few hours felt like a blur. Sameer and Rohan rushed to the hospital with Rhea, staying close by her side as they waited for any news about her father. The hospital waiting room was cold and sterile, its white walls only adding to the tension in the air. Rhea sat between them, her face pale and exhausted, her hands nervously wringing in her lap.

Sameer could see how scared she was. Without thinking, he placed a comforting hand on her shoulder, trying to offer some reassurance. "He's going to be okay, Rhea. We're here for you," he said, his voice soft but firm.

Rohan, usually the jokester, had grown quiet. His usual playful smile was gone, replaced by a serious look. "You're not alone in this," he added, his voice steady. "Whatever happens, we've got you."

Rhea glanced at both of them, her eyes shining with unshed tears. "Thank you," she whispered, her voice thick with emotion. "I don't know what I'd do without you guys."

Sameer and Rohan simply nodded, offering their silent support. They didn't say anything more, understanding that words weren't enough. They just stayed there, with her, as the minutes and hours slowly passed.

Finally, after what felt like an eternity, a doctor appeared. His face was calm, but there was a seriousness in his eyes.

"He's stable for now," the doctor said, looking directly at Rhea. "It was a minor heart attack, but we caught it in time. He'll need to rest and make some lifestyle changes, but he should recover."

Rhea let out a shaky breath of relief, her shoulders sagging as tears started to spill down her cheeks. "Thank you," she whispered, her voice breaking with emotion.

Sameer and Rohan exchanged a glance, a silent wave of relief passing between them. The tension they'd been holding onto for hours seemed to lift, but they knew the journey wasn't over yet. Rhea still needed them, and they were ready to be there for her.

Later That Evening

After Rhea's father was settled into the hospital and the doctors assured them he was in good hands, the three friends returned to Sameer's apartment. They were exhausted, physically and emotionally drained, but they were grateful that things hadn't turned out worse.

Rhea sat on the couch, her hands still trembling slightly as she sipped the cup of chai Sameer had made for her. She looked up at them both, her eyes full of gratitude and exhaustion.

"I don't know what I'd do without you two," Rhea said softly, her voice trembling.

Sameer sat beside her, wrapping his arm around her shoulders in a gesture of comfort. "You don't have to worry about that. We're here, always," he assured her, his words filled with sincerity.

Rohan, sitting across from them, gave a small nod. "We're not going anywhere, Rhea. You've always been the strong one for us. Now it's our turn to be strong for you."

Rhea smiled, her tears now mingling with a look of quiet relief. She leaned her head against Sameer's shoulder, finally letting herself relax as the weight of the day seemed to crash down on her. "I'm lucky to have you both," she whispered, her voice barely audible.

The three of them sat together in a quiet, comfortable silence, the bond between them stronger than ever. As the night wore on, Sameer's thoughts briefly wandered back to Siya. He couldn't help but wonder what it would be like if she were here with them—if she were a part of this tight-knit circle of friends. But for now, he kept those thoughts to himself, content with the love and support of the friends who had stood by him through everything.

9

Pages of Before

The following week, the calm of their routine was interrupted when Meera received an invitation to a college event that would require her to make a speech in front of a large crowd. Normally, she would have been thrilled about an opportunity like this, but the thought of speaking in front of so many people made her stomach churn.

"Are you okay?" Shaan asked, noticing her tense shoulders as they sat together on their usual bench by the banyan tree.

Meera let out a deep breath, trying to calm her nerves. "I'm fine... just nervous. It's a big deal, Shaan. I'm not sure I'm ready for this."

Shaan raised an eyebrow, his expression softening. "You've got this, Meera. I mean, you might overthink it a little, but you always rise to the occasion. Remember the presentation last month? You crushed it."

She nodded but still felt a tight knot in her chest. "That was different. This is... personal. It's about something I care deeply about."

Shaan didn't press her further. Instead, he just smiled his usual reassuring smile. "Well, whatever it is, I know you'll do great. And hey, if you need anything—ice cream, a pep talk, or just someone to scream at—I'm here."

Meera laughed, despite herself, the tension easing slightly. Shaan had a way of turning even the most nerve-wracking situations into something bearable.

Later that week, Meera found herself standing on the stage, the spotlight blinding her as she gazed out at the crowd of students and faculty. Her heart pounded in her chest, and she felt her throat dry up. She glanced to the side where Shaan was sitting in the front row, his thumbs up and a proud grin plastered on his face. His presence was the only thing that made her feel a little less like she was going to pass out.

Taking a deep breath, Meera began to speak. At first, her words stumbled, but then something clicked. With each sentence, she grew more comfortable, the words flowing with sincerity. She was speaking from the heart, and it didn't matter if her hands trembled or her voice wavered. What mattered was the message she was sharing.

By the time she finished, the room was quiet for a moment before the applause began. Meera stood there, stunned by the response, her cheeks flushed with a mix of relief and pride.

As she walked off the stage, Shaan was the first to reach her, enveloping her in a bear hug.

"Told you you'd crush it," he said with a grin. "You were amazing."

Meera laughed, feeling the weight lift off her shoulders. "Thanks for believing in me, even when I didn't."

"You don't need to thank me," Shaan replied. "I believe in you because you're capable of anything. Just don't go making a habit of getting all emotional up there. I might start crying, too."

Meera playfully shoved him. "Shut up, Shaan."

But even as she said it, she knew that she couldn't have done it without him. Shaan was her anchor, the one who helped her face her fears and push past her limits. And as they walked away from the event together, Meera realized just how lucky she was to have him in her life—her best friend, her rock.

And maybe, just maybe, there was more to their bond than she had been willing to admit.

Meera sat quietly in the corner of the small living room, feeling the weight of the last few days pressing down on her. Her mother had been sick for almost a week now, and it seemed like everything was slipping out of her control. She was trying to care for her mother while also dealing with her college assignments, but no matter how hard she tried, there was always something she was falling behind on. Her younger brother didn't understand what was happening, and her father was stressed too, doing his best but struggling to manage everything. Meera felt like the world was on her shoulders, and there was no one she could turn to for help.

Looking at the pile of assignments on the table, she felt a wave of anxiety. The deadlines were fast approaching, and she had no idea how she would finish everything. Her mind raced with worries, but before she could sink deeper into panic, she heard a knock on the door.

It wasn't a soft, polite knock. It was the kind of knock that was confident, familiar, and made her feel like it didn't even need an invitation. Meera didn't need to ask who it was—she already knew. She sighed and stood up to open the door.

To her surprise, it was Shaan, standing there with his usual grin. "Food delivery," he said with a wink, holding up a bag. "I bet you've been surviving on coffee and stress, haven't you?"

Before she could respond, Aditya stepped up behind him, holding a small bag. "I brought some cookies my father made. I thought you might need a little comfort."

Meera blinked, surprised. She hadn't realized how long it had been since she had eaten. "You guys didn't need to—" she started, but Shaan cut her off.

"We know we didn't," they said together, stepping past her into the house. "But you're too stubborn to take care of yourself, so we're doing it for you."

"Thanks," Meera mumbled, feeling a little lighter just seeing them. Shaan had a way of making everything seem easier, and he never made her feel guilty for needing help. He simply gave it, without question.

Aditya set the bag on the counter and began pulling out containers of food. "You really should eat, you know," he said, raising an eyebrow at her. "And I didn't just bring any food—I brought your favorite too. You have to treat yourself sometimes."

Meera couldn't help but smile, despite the weight she was carrying. She hadn't realized how much she had missed his easygoing nature until now. Shaan's and Aditya's lightness helped calm her mind, even if just for a moment. They didn't understand the full extent of her stress, but somehow their presence made everything feel just a little bit more bearable.

"I'm not really hungry," she said quietly. "I have too much to do."

"I'm sure you do," Shaan said, his tone playful but firm. "But you're clearly running on fumes. Trust me, you can't do your best work when you haven't eaten. And this—" he pointed to the food "—is non-negotiable."

Meera didn't have the energy to argue, so she pulled out a chair and sat down. As Shaan set everything up, she couldn't help but feel grateful. He didn't ask her to talk about her stress or try to cheer her up with words. He simply took care of things. That was enough for her.

As she started eating,she looked at her room. There were so many assignments piling up, and the thought of it all made her feel overwhelmed again. She looked at Shaan with a helpless expression.

Without missing a beat, Shaan said, "We'll take care of it. You've been doing enough already. You don't have to do it all yourself."

Aditya added with a smile, "Well, that's a dragon battle for me, but I'll try."

Meera shook her head, still feeling uncertain. "I can't ask you to do my work..."

"You didn't ask," they said in unison, giving her a wink. "We're offering. But you're taking a break. End of story."

Meera stared at them for a moment, then let out a small laugh. She should have felt embarrassed by how much they were stepping in, but instead, she just felt gratitude. There was no pretension with Shaan—he didn't need her to ask for help. He simply offered it, and that was one of the most comforting things in the world.

"I don't know what I'd do without you," Meera said softly, feeling the weight in her chest lift.

"You don't have to know," Aditya replied, taking a seat beside her. "Because I'm not going anywhere."

"Me neither," Shaan added with a grin.

It wasn't a grand declaration, but it didn't need to be. Meera understood perfectly what they meant. She didn't have to say anything more. She just let herself relax a little, feeling their presence as a reminder that she wasn't alone.

Later that night, when Meera finally went to bed, she was exhausted but strangely calm. Shaan and Aditya had stayed with her for hours, helping with the assignments and simply being there. It wasn't just the food or the work they had taken over—it was the fact that they had quietly supported her, never making her feel bad for needing help. She felt safe knowing they would always be there for her.

But just when she thought things might settle, an emergency changed everything.

In the middle of the night, it was her father's shout—her mother had been rushed to the hospital. Meera's heart dropped. She didn't even remember how she got to the hospital. Her mind was in a fog as she sat in the waiting room, staring at the door of the emergency room. Every minute felt like an hour. The beeping of heart monitors and the soft voices of nurses in the hallway didn't comfort her. All she could think about was her mother's health.

Her hands trembled as she sat on the plastic chair, holding onto her sweater, trying to keep it together. The pressure was overwhelming—how could she handle her mother's health, her family's needs, and school all at the same time? It felt impossible.

Suddenly, she felt a comforting presence beside her. It was Aditya. She didn't need to look up to know it was him. His voice, soft and reassuring, broke through the panic in her mind. "Meera, breathe. Take a deep breath. It's going to be okay."

She shook her head, her voice trembling. "What if something happens to her? What if I can't do enough?"

Aditya's eyes softened as he knelt beside her. "You don't have to do this alone, Meera. We're here with you. I'm not going anywhere. And neither is Shaan."

At the mention of Shaan, Meera turned to see him standing in the doorway. His face was full of worry, but his eyes were steady on her. He didn't speak much, but just seeing him there gave her a sense of calm.

Meera tried to hold back tears. "I don't know how to keep it together, Aditya. I feel like I'm breaking."

Aditya placed his hand on her shoulder, offering warmth and comfort. "You don't have to keep everything together, Meera. You're allowed to feel overwhelmed. You don't have to do this alone. We've got you."

For the first time that night, Meera allowed herself to lean into their support. Shaan held her hand, and Aditya's calm presence behind her felt like a shield—steady and unshakable.

"I'm scared," she whispered. "What if she doesn't make it?"

Shaan squeezed her hand. "You're doing everything you can, Meera. You don't have to have all the answers right now. And you don't have to carry this burden on your own. We're here. All of us."

Those words meant everything to Meera. She felt the weight on her shoulders lift just a little. With Shaan and Aditya by her side, she didn't feel as alone anymore. They were her anchors, grounding her in a storm of uncertainty.

As time passed, Meera started to feel a little less like she was drowning. Shaan and Aditya never left her side. They helped her with food, took turns sitting with her, and made sure she was okay in every way. They were her rock.

Finally, a doctor came out and told them her mother was stable for now. Meera felt the tension in her chest loosen a little, though she knew things weren't over yet. But with Aditya and Shaan there, she felt like she could face whatever came next.

Aditya looked at her with a soft smile. "It's going to be okay. You've got this."

Shaan gave his usual grin, even in such a heavy moment. "And we've got you. We'll be here for you, no matter what."

Meera smiled—tired, but grateful. She didn't know what the future held, but with her friends by her side, she knew she could handle it. They were her strength, and together, they could face anything.

....

Tara sat at the kitchen table, her eyes focused on the chipped edge of her cup, the sounds of her parents' argument ringing through the walls of their house. The raised voices, the bitter words—this had become a part of her reality, one she tried to ignore, but never fully could. It had been happening more frequently, and each time, it left her feeling more helpless.

Manav, her younger brother, sat across from her, his arms folded across his chest. He was only three years younger than her, but the fights had weighed heavily on him too. He rarely spoke about it, but Tara could see the strain in his eyes, the way he would tense up every time their parents argued.

"I wish they'd just stop," Manav mumbled, not looking at her. "Why can't they just... I don't know, talk to each other like normal people?"

Tara sighed, running her hand through her hair. "I don't know, Manav. I wish I had the answer."

Manav looked up at her, his gaze sharp. "At least you have Aditya."

Tara blinked, surprised by his sudden shift in tone. "What do you mean?"

"You have him," Manav repeated, his voice quieter now. "You can go to him when things get bad here. But what about me? I have no one."

Tara's heart ached at the sadness in his voice. "That's not true, Manav. You have me. You'll always have me."

Manav shook his head, his expression a mix of frustration and hurt. "It's not the same, Tara. You're in love with Aditya. You can leave this mess whenever you want. But I'm stuck here."

Tara felt a lump form in her throat. She knew Manav was right, to some extent. Aditya had become her refuge, the one place where she could forget about the chaos at home, even if just for a little while. But she hadn't realized how much it affected Manav—how much he felt left behind.

She reached across the table, placing her hand on his. "I'm sorry, Manav. I didn't mean to make you feel like that. I love you. You know that, right?"

Manav nodded, but he didn't say anything. Tara squeezed his hand, her mind racing with the weight of everything. She needed to fix this. She needed to be there for her brother, just as much as she was for Aditya.

....

Two days later, when Tara met up with Aditya for their usual coffee date, her mind was still heavy with thoughts of her family. They sat at their favorite café, the one tucked away on a quiet street, where they could talk without being interrupted by the world outside.

Aditya noticed her distraction immediately. "What's going on, Tara?"

Tara shook her head, trying to push the thoughts away. "It's just... my parents. They've been fighting again. And Manav, he's... he's taking it harder than I thought."

Aditya reached across the table, taking her hand in his. His touch was warm, comforting, and for a moment, Tara felt like she could breathe again. "I'm sorry, Tara. I wish I could do something to help."

"You being here helps," she said, giving him a small smile.

Aditya's eyes softened. "I'll always be here for you. You know that, right?"

Tara nodded, grateful for the steady presence he brought into her life. They didn't need to say much—their connection was beyond words. It was in the quiet moments, the way he looked at her, the way he held her hand, that she felt their love the most.

Later that evening, after their coffee date, Aditya surprised her with a bouquet of flowers—her favorite kind, lilacs. They walked through the park, the air cool and crisp, their fingers intertwined as they talked about everything and nothing.

"You always know how to make me feel better," Tara said softly, leaning into him as they walked.

Aditya smiled, pulling her closer. "That's because I love you."

Tara looked up at him, her heart swelling. "I love you too."

It was moments like this that made everything else fade away—the fights at home, the uncertainty of the future. With Aditya, everything felt right.

As they continued walking, Aditya suddenly turned to her, his expression serious. "Tara, there's something I need to tell you about Meera. She's... she's been going through some things lately, and I just want you to know how important she is to me."

Tara furrowed her brow, her concern growing. "What's been happening with Meera?"

Aditya sighed, his tone softening. "Meera's not just a friend, Tara. She's been there for me through everything. She's always supported me, been by my side no matter what, and right now, she's going through a tough time. I need to check on her, make sure she's okay."

Tara nodded, trying to understand. "Of course. I get it."

Aditya gave her a reassuring smile, squeezing her hand. "I'll go meet her, see how she's doing. Shaan's with her too, so she's not alone."

Tara's mind raced for a moment, processing everything. "You go, Aditya. I need to do something at home. But I'll join you in a bit. I just... need to take care of some things here."

Aditya hesitated for a moment, but then he nodded. "Alright. Take care of what you need to, and I'll be waiting."

Tara watched him go, feeling a mix of emotions. She understood why Aditya needed to be there for Meera, but a part of her couldn't shake the feeling of being left behind, even if just for a little while. Still, she knew that Meera was important to him, and she couldn't stand in the way of that. She just hoped that everything would be alright.

Meera sat in one of her favorite places to meet after classes—away from the noise and the distractions, a quiet corner in the park where they could just be. She had always loved this spot, hidden among the trees, with the soft rustle of leaves and the calm breeze that made everything feel peaceful. It was here that she and Aditya often met, a refuge from the chaos of their lives.

Today, however, there was a spark of tension in the air, something unspoken hanging between them. As she sat there, lost in her thoughts, Aditya suddenly gave her a playful strike, tapping her on the shoulder with an exaggerated swipe.

"Gotcha!" Aditya grinned mischievously, his usual spark of fun in his eyes.

Meera jumped, startled, before narrowing her eyes at him. "Seriously, Aditya?" she scolded, her voice tinged with mock annoyance. "Can't you just sit down without being an absolute terror?"

Aditya only laughed, leaning back in his seat with his usual easygoing demeanor. "What can I say? You make it too easy."

Meera rolled her eyes but couldn't suppress a smile. It was moments like these that made everything feel lighter, even if for a few minutes. They could just be themselves, without any complications.

"Your hair's a mess again," Meera teased, reaching over to tousle Aditya's already unruly locks.

Aditya swatted her hand away with a grin. "Is this what you do? Just sit here and judge my hair?"

"Well, someone has to keep you presentable," Meera replied, her tone playful as she adjusted his hair mockingly. "You can't go around looking like you just rolled out of bed all the time. What will Tara think?"

At the mention of Tara's name, a brief shift occurred in Aditya's expression. His smile softened, and he leaned back on his elbows, his gaze distant for a moment. Meera's heart clenched at the sight, but she quickly masked it with a playful smirk. She loved Aditya too much to let her feelings ruin the friendship they had.

"She likes me just the way I am," Aditya said, a smile returning to his face as he relaxed. "But you—" he teased, eyeing Meera with a mischievous look. "You should worry more about your own appearance, you know?"

Meera scoffed, pretending to be offended. "Please. I look fabulous, and you know it."

Aditya laughed, clearly enjoying their back-and-forth. For a moment, the tension of the day seemed to dissipate, replaced by the lighthearted ease they shared. Meera cherished these moments—moments where they could tease each other without the weight of everything else pressing down on them.

"I don't know how you do it," Aditya continued, his tone softening slightly. "How you always manage to stay so... calm and collected. Even when things around us get so messy."

Meera met his gaze, her smile fading just a little. "I'm not always calm, Aditya," she said, her voice quieter now. "But I try to be. For you, for everyone."

Aditya studied her for a moment, the playful light in his eyes dimming. He reached over, placing a hand on hers, his touch warm and reassuring. "I know. And I appreciate it more than you know. You've always been there for me, Meera. You don't have to pretend everything's okay when it's not."

Meera felt her heart flutter at his words, but she quickly suppressed the feeling. She had always been there for Aditya, supporting him without question. But sometimes, it was hard to ignore the ache in her chest—the ache that came with knowing that no matter how much she cared for him, he was with Tara. She was the one he truly loved.

"We all have our ways of coping," Meera said, offering him a small smile. "And this—" she gestured between the two of them, "this is mine. Just having these little moments with you. They help me forget everything else for a while."

Aditya smiled back, squeezing her hand gently. "Well, I'm glad I can be part of your coping mechanism. But remember, Meera, you're never alone in this."

Meera nodded, her heart swelling with warmth, though the underlying sadness remained. As much as she tried to keep their friendship light and carefree, there were days when the weight of her feelings for him was hard to carry. But for now, she was content to be there, to share these moments with him, even if it meant hiding her heartache behind laughter and teasing.

And so they sat there together, talking about everything and nothing, enjoying the comfort of each other's presence, while the world outside continued on, with its ups and downs.

As the laughter died down and the evening sky turned darker, a quiet silence settled between them. It wasn't uncomfortable, but it was heavy with the things Meera kept to herself. They sat side by side, gazing at the stars as they slowly began to appear, twinkling in the night sky. It was a peaceful moment, but in the back of Meera's mind, thoughts began to stir.

She often found herself wondering if Aditya could ever sense the feelings she kept hidden. Could he tell, in the quiet moments, just by the way she looked at him or the way she cared for him, how deeply she loved him? There were times when she almost thought he might, but then she quickly pushed the thought aside. She had never said it out loud, and maybe he didn't need to know.

Meera had learned to live with these feelings quietly. She loved Aditya in a way that didn't ask for anything in return. She wanted him to be happy, even if that happiness wasn't with her. And deep down, she knew that his happiness with Tara was the best thing for him. That's all that mattered. She could stand on the sidelines, watching him be with someone else, because as long as he was happy, she was content.

That was the kind of love Meera had—selfless. It didn't come with expectations or demands. She never asked for more than their friendship, because she cherished it too much to risk losing it. If she confessed her feelings and things changed, she wasn't sure if she could handle it. So, she kept her emotions buried, valuing the bond they shared more than anything else.

Her heart ached at times, but she was willing to carry that ache in silence, for as long as it meant keeping Aditya in her life, even if it was only as a friend.

As the evening wore on, everyone slowly gathered around Meera and Aditya. Tara, Shaan, and Gaurav joined them, each settling into the small, cozy spot under the stars. The air was thick with unspoken thoughts, and the atmosphere felt heavier than usual. It was as if everyone could sense that something was about to change, but no one knew exactly how to say it.

Gaurav, as usual, was the first to speak up. He looked around at all of them with a thoughtful expression, his voice steady but serious. "Meeta and I have been talking a lot lately about our future," he began, glancing at Meeta, who nodded in agreement. "We've decided to take different paths in our careers. It's not going to be easy, but it's something we need to do for ourselves."

There was a pause as everyone took in his words. Tara looked at Meera, her expression thoughtful, while Aditya leaned forward slightly, clearly listening intently. Shaan was unusually quiet, his face unreadable.

Gaurav continued, his eyes on Meeta now, as though trying to seek her reassurance. "It's going to be tough, no doubt. The distance, the challenges... It's not the kind of thing we can just ignore. But we both know it's the right choice for us. It's something we have to pursue, even if it puts a strain on us."

Meera felt a lump form in her throat as she watched Gaurav and Meeta's faces. She understood what they were saying all too well. She had seen Aditya and Tara's relationship go through its own ups and downs. She had always feared that pursuing dreams and passions might eventually pull them all in different directions, and Gaurav and Meeta's words seemed to confirm that fear.

A silent, collective thought passed through each of their minds: maybe it was time for them to think about their own paths too. Perhaps, like Gaurav and Meeta, they needed to focus on their futures, even if it meant choosing separate paths, just as their friends had done.

Tara caught Aditya's gaze, her mind racing with the possibilities. Aditya, too, seemed lost in thought, as if weighing the idea of balancing their relationship with their dreams. Shaan, who had always been a quiet observer, glanced at Meera, then at Tara, his eyes flickering with a deep understanding.

They all sat there in silence for a moment, the weight of Gaurav and Meeta's words sinking in. It was a bittersweet realization: to grow, sometimes you had to let go of things you loved, even if only for a while. It wasn't going to be easy, but maybe they, too, had to choose their paths carefully and see where it led them.

10

Pages of Before

———♡———

The final days of college were a whirlwind of emotions. The campus buzzed with excitement, laughter, and a touch of sadness as everyone prepared to step into the next phase of their lives. For Aditya, Meera, Shaan, Tara, Gaurav, and Mita, these last days felt even more meaningful. Their lives had been deeply connected through years of friendship, shared dreams, and countless memories. Now, they stood on the brink of change, each one preparing to walk their own path.

Aditya had always dreamed big, his ambition driving him to aim for a career that would challenge his mind and spirit. He was focused, yet he often found himself thinking about how much he would miss these moments of carefree laughter with his friends. Tara, on the other hand, had chosen a quieter but equally passionate path. Her love for art and writing was leading her toward a future filled with creativity. Despite her excitement, she couldn't ignore the pang of bittersweet feelings as she realized she wouldn't see Aditya every day anymore.

Shaan was as cheerful as ever, hiding his own uncertainties behind his usual humor. He had decided to take a chance on a career in event management, knowing it wouldn't be easy but excited about the possibilities ahead. Meera, ever practical and determined, was stepping into a field she had long aspired to join, ready to prove herself in a world she had been preparing for. Gaurav and Mita had their own challenges to face. Gaurav was pursuing a corporate career, driven to succeed despite the intense competition, while Mita was venturing into a completely different field of social work, hoping to bring change and help others.

Aditya's apartment was a mess, as usual. Photographs, both framed and unframed, leaned against walls, camera equipment occupied every available surface, and travel brochures peeked out from under books. Amidst the chaos sat Meera, cross-legged on the floor, sifting through a stack of his latest photos. The images were stunning, as always, but they also told a story of someone who rarely stopped moving.

"You've been busy," Meera said, glancing up at him with a knowing smile.

Aditya, sitting on the couch and fiddling with his camera, gave her a sheepish look. "Yeah, you could say that. Been all over the place lately. But hey, I'm here now, aren't I?"

Meera raised an eyebrow, her tone light but her words weighted with meaning. "Physically, maybe. But your mind? Pretty sure it's still on your next assignment."

Aditya chuckled, leaning back with a sigh. "Guilty. There's just so much to do, you know? So many stories I want to tell, so many places I haven't been yet."

Meera set the photographs down and looked at him, her expression soft but firm. "I know, Adi. But while you're out there chasing stories, don't forget the ones happening here. Life's not just what's in front of the lens."

Aditya paused, her words settling over him. Meera had always had this way of cutting through the noise in his head, grounding him in ways no one else could. "I don't mean to lose track," he admitted quietly. "Sometimes it's just... hard to find the balance."

Meera's smile was gentle. "I get that. I'm not saying you shouldn't chase your dreams. I'm just saying, don't let them pull you so far away that you forget what's right in front of you."

Aditya's eyes softened as he looked at her. "You know, you're probably the only person who can call me out like this and not make me feel guilty."

"That's what best friends are for," Meera teased, her eyes sparkling. "Now, enough about you. How's work for me? Fantastic, thanks for asking."

Aditya laughed, throwing a pillow at her. "Okay, okay, tell me. What's this big project you've been working on?"

Meera's face lit up, her passion shining through as she spoke. "The NGO I'm with is expanding. We're launching this education initiative for underprivileged kids. It's been chaotic—meetings, fundraisers, you name it—but seeing it all come together? Totally worth it."

Aditya leaned forward, genuinely impressed. "That's incredible, Meera. You're out here changing lives, and I'm just snapping pictures of sunsets."

Meera rolled her eyes. "Don't sell yourself short, Adi. Your photos make people see the world differently. You capture what most people overlook. That's powerful."

Aditya smiled, warmth spreading through him. "Thanks, Meera. I don't say it enough, but... I'm lucky to have you in my life. You keep me sane."

Meera shrugged, though her eyes glistened with emotion. "Someone has to. Otherwise, you'd be lost in your chaos forever."

They laughed together, the sound filling the room like a familiar melody. Despite the differences in their lives, the bond between them remained unshaken—a quiet, steadfast friendship that thrived amidst the chaos. And in moments like this, they both knew that no matter where life took them, they'd always have each other to lean on.

Shaan and Tara had built a special kind of friendship over time. While it wasn't as deep as Tara's bond with Aditya, it was light and refreshing in its own way. Shaan had this rare ability to make Tara laugh, even when she felt low. Their dynamic was simple—he brought the fun, and she balanced it with her thoughtful nature. They understood each other without trying too hard, and that's what made their friendship easy and genuine.

One bright afternoon, they decided to explore the city's famous bazaar. It was a lively place, packed with colors, sounds, and delicious smells. The air was filled with the scent of spices, flowers, and freshly cooked food. Everywhere they looked, there were stalls selling vibrant fabrics, shiny jewelry, handmade pottery, and mouth-watering snacks. The bazaar felt alive, buzzing with energy and endless possibilities.

"This is so beautiful," Tara said, her eyes lighting up as she turned her head to take it all in. "I don't think I've been anywhere like this before."

Shaan grinned and gave her a playful nudge. "That's because you're always with Aditya. He's cool and all, but come on—he's not the 'let's explore a random market' type. You need to hang out with me more. I'll show you the real fun places."

Tara rolled her eyes but couldn't help laughing. "I'm not that boring, you know! I just like things to be... organized."

"Exactly!" Shaan said, pretending to be very serious. "And I like things messy and fun. That's why we're the perfect team."

She shook her head, laughing at his antics, as they continued to walk through the crowded market. Every corner of the bazaar seemed like a treasure chest, full of unique and colorful items. They stopped at different stalls to admire the handmade jewelry, vibrant scarves, and pottery with beautiful designs. Tara was amazed by the creativity on display, and Shaan, as usual, kept the mood light with his funny comments.

Soon, a small stall caught Tara's attention. It looked cozy and inviting, with strings of colorful trinkets hanging at the entrance. Inside, shelves were packed with beautiful necklaces, bracelets, and wooden carvings. The shopkeeper, an older man with a big mustache and kind eyes, stood outside, calling to them with a cheerful voice.

"Come in, come in! You won't find treasures like these anywhere else," he said, waving them over. "Everything here has a story."

Tara smiled and stepped inside, with Shaan following her. She picked up a delicate necklace, admiring the intricate carvings. Just then, the shopkeeper's voice softened, taking on a more serious tone.

"Do you believe in love stories?" he asked, looking at Tara. She paused, startled by the question, as he continued.

"This necklace," he said, holding it up gently, "was made by a man who loved a woman deeply. But she was someone he could never have. He put all his feelings into making this for her, hoping one day she would wear it. But she never did."

The words hit Tara like a wave. Her hand froze as she stared at the necklace. The story felt too close to home. She thought of Aditya, the unspoken feelings she had for him, and all the fears that had kept her silent. Her chest tightened with emotions she hadn't let herself feel in a long time.

Shaan, who had been watching her, noticed the change in her expression. His usual playful tone softened. "Hey, are you okay?" he asked, stepping closer to her.

Tara forced a small smile and nodded. "Yeah, I'm fine. Just... thinking."

Shaan didn't push. He had a way of knowing when not to say anything. Instead, he pointed to a colorful wind chime hanging nearby. "Look at that! Imagine how ridiculous that would look in your super-organized room," he joked.

Tara let out a soft laugh, grateful for his effort to distract her. They left the stall together, walking side by side through the busy bazaar. The sounds of vendors shouting and people laughing filled the air, but Tara's mind kept going back to the necklace and the story behind it.

She glanced at Shaan, feeling thankful for him. He had a gift for making things easier, even when her thoughts felt heavy. He didn't ask her to share more than she wanted to; he simply stayed by her side and made her laugh when she needed it most.

And though she didn't say it aloud, Tara silently appreciated how Shaan had unknowingly made her day just a little lighter.

As they walked through the bazaar, Shaan noticed Tara had gone quiet. Her usual spark seemed dimmed, and her smile wasn't reaching her eyes. He decided to break the silence, his tone soft yet curious.

"So… what's the plan with you and Aditya?" Shaan asked, glancing sideways at her. "I mean, you two are like magnets—always drawn to each other."

Tara blinked, startled by the question. She let out a small laugh, but it sounded hollow. "Plan? There's no plan. We're just… us."

Shaan raised an eyebrow. "Come on, Tara. You're not fooling me. Everyone can see how you feel about him. So, what's stopping you?"

Tara sighed and slowed her steps, her eyes fixed on the cobblestone path beneath her feet. "It's not that simple, Shaan. I… I do love him, but there's so much in my head right now. So much I can't figure out."

Shaan stopped walking and turned to face her, his expression serious for once. "What's going on, Tara? You know you can talk to me."

She hesitated, but something about Shaan's steady gaze encouraged her to open up. "It's my parents," she finally said, her voice quiet. "They've been fighting a lot lately. It's like they're completely different people now. They used to be so happy, so… in love. But now, it's just arguments and silence."

Shaan frowned. "I'm sorry, Tara. That sounds really tough. But what does that have to do with you and Aditya?"

Tara's eyes filled with unshed tears as she looked up at him. "Because I'm scared, Shaan. I've always believed in love, in forever. But watching my parents fall apart… it's shaken me. What if love isn't enough? What if we end up like them?"

Her voice cracked, and she quickly looked away, embarrassed by her emotions. But Shaan gently placed a hand on her shoulder, stopping her.

"Tara, listen to me," he said, his voice firm yet kind. "You're not your parents. Their story doesn't have to be yours. You and Aditya have something real, something people spend their whole lives looking for. Don't let fear take that away from you."

Tara shook her head, wiping her eyes. "It's not just fear, Shaan. It's... everything. I've been so caught up in their fights, trying to fix things, trying to keep it all together, that I haven't even had time to think about my own future. I feel like I'm stuck in this endless loop of 'what ifs.'"

Shaan softened, his voice almost a whisper now. "You've been carrying so much, Tara. But you don't have to do it alone. Aditya cares about you more than anything—I see it every time he looks at you. And you have me too. You don't always have to have it all figured out."

Tara smiled faintly, her heart heavy but a little lighter after hearing his words. "Thanks, Shaan. I guess I just need time to sort through everything."

Shaan nodded, giving her a reassuring pat on the back. "Take all the time you need. But don't let time steal what your heart already knows. Sometimes, the scariest risks are the ones worth taking."

Tara looked at him, her eyes full of gratitude. "You're a good friend, Shaan."

He grinned, his playful tone returning. "I know. Now, let's go find some samosas before I get all emotional too."

She laughed softly, and together they walked further into the bazaar, the weight on her heart feeling just a little less heavy.

Tara arrived at Aditya's place just as the sun was beginning to set, painting the sky in hues of orange and pink. She was greeted by the familiar scent of his home—a mix of freshly brewed coffee and the faint aroma of jasmine flowers from his mother's garden. Aditya opened the door with his usual warm smile.

"Hey," Tara said, stepping inside. "I had such a nice time with Shaan today. We talked a lot, and it felt good to share things with him. He's a great listener."

Aditya's smile widened as he closed the door behind her. "I'm glad. I always thought you two would get along well. He has this way of making people feel comfortable. I'm happy you've found that connection with him."

Tara nodded, her eyes soft with gratitude. "Yeah, it was easy talking to him. It's nice having someone who listens without judgment."

Aditya gestured for her to sit on the couch, but before she did, she added, "Oh, and by the way, Manav and I will be staying here tonight. I hope it's okay. Manav really needs to relax, and he always feels so much better when he's around your parents. Your mom has this magic touch, you know?"

Aditya chuckled, leaning against the armrest. "Of course it's okay. Manav is family. My parents will love having him here, and honestly, it'll be good for him. They always seem to know how to make people feel at home."

Tara's face lit up. "Thanks, Aditya. I knew you'd understand. He's been a little overwhelmed lately, and I think some time here will really help."

"Absolutely," Aditya said, his tone warm. Then, with a mischievous glint in his eyes, he added, "By the way, I have something special planned for you tonight."

Tara tilted her head, her curiosity piqued. "Special? What kind of special?"

Aditya grinned but didn't give anything away. "You'll see. Just trust me."

She narrowed her eyes playfully. "Wait a second. Does your mom know what you're up to? Or your dad, for that matter? Don't they ever wonder what's going on with us?"

Aditya leaned forward, resting his elbows on his knees, his voice steady but filled with affection. "Tara, my parents know. And so do yours."

Tara's eyes widened. "What? How? When did that happen?"

Aditya leaned back, clearly enjoying her reaction. "I told my mom a while ago. She told your parents. Simple as that."

Her mouth fell open slightly in surprise. "And... they're okay with it? No questions, no concerns?"

He shrugged casually, a teasing smile on his face. "Why would they have a problem? They know we love each other. Besides, they trust us."

Tara blinked, still trying to process the ease with which he'd handled something she had spent months worrying about. "You really didn't think to mention this to me before?"

Aditya chuckled, standing up and offering her his hand. "No more questions, Tara. Now, get ready for your surprise."

She took his hand, shaking her head but smiling. "You're impossible, you know that?"

"And you love it," he quipped, leading her towards the door.

As they walked out, Tara couldn't help but feel a sense of calm she hadn't experienced in a while. Aditya's confidence, his way of making everything seem so simple, was something she deeply admired. Whatever he had planned for the evening, she knew it would be special—because with Aditya, it always was.

After dinner, Tara and Manav stayed back to help Aditya's parents clear the table and tidy up the kitchen. The house was filled with laughter and warmth, the kind that only came from being surrounded by people who cared deeply for one another. Manav seemed relaxed, chatting animatedly with Aditya's father, while Tara helped his mother stack plates and wipe down the counters.

"You two are such a blessing," Aditya's mother said with a kind smile, patting Tara on the shoulder. "It's nice to have young energy in the house."

Tara blushed slightly and smiled back. "It's nothing, Aunty. You make us feel so at home here."

Once everything was done, Tara stretched her arms with a sigh. "Well, I guess it's time to head to bed. Thank you for dinner. It was amazing, as always."

She made her way to the guest room and opened the door, expecting to find it just as she'd left it. Instead, her eyes fell on a small package sitting on the bed, wrapped neatly with a note attached to it. Curiosity piqued, she picked up the note, and a grin spread across her face as she read Aditya's familiar handwriting:

"Meet me at the rooftop at 11.

P.S. Don't take forever to get ready—you know what I mean!"

Laughing to herself, she set the note aside and opened the package. Inside was a stunning white full-length dress with intricate embroidery along the hem and neckline, paired with a vibrant red dupatta. Tara's breath hitched at the sight—it was beautiful, elegant, and so very thoughtful.

She glanced at the clock. 10:30. "Alright, Aditya," she muttered to herself, "challenge accepted."

Tara quickly freshened up and slipped into the dress. The fabric felt soft against her skin, and the dupatta added a graceful touch. She took a quick glance in the mirror, adjusted her hair, and smiled. She looked and felt... different. Special.

By the time Tara stepped onto the rooftop, her heart was racing—not from the climb, but from the fluttering anticipation building in her chest. The cool night air kissed her skin as she took in the breathtaking sight before her. The rooftop was transformed into a wonderland of soft golden fairy lights, their gentle glow blending harmoniously with the infinite sparkle of the stars above. Scattered flower petals formed a delicate trail, leading to a wooden bench that stood at the heart of the setup.

And there he was—Aditya. Dressed in a crisp white shirt that seemed to shimmer in the dreamy light, he looked effortlessly handsome. He stood with his hands tucked casually into his pockets, but the warmth in his gaze as he turned to her was anything but casual. It sent a wave of emotion coursing through her.

"You're late," he teased, his lips curving into that familiar smile that always made her heart skip a beat.

Tara rolled her eyes, a soft laugh escaping her lips as she walked toward him. "Well, I wasn't going to risk rushing and ruining this beautiful dress, was I?"

She reached him, and he gestured to the bench with a small, secretive smile. "Sit," he said gently.

Tara giggled, lowering herself onto the bench. "What's all this, Aditya? What's going on?"

Instead of answering, Aditya knelt before her, and Tara's laughter faltered. Her breath caught as she watched him take one of her feet delicately in his hands. His touch was warm and careful, sending a shiver up her spine.

He reached into his pocket and pulled out a small velvet box, opening it to reveal a pair of intricate silver anklets. The tiny bells adorning them shimmered under the lights, their beauty matching the moment's quiet intimacy.

"Aditya..." she started, her voice barely a whisper, but he stopped her with a soft shake of his head.

"Just let me," he said, his voice low and tender.

With painstaking care, he secured one anklet around her ankle. His fingers brushed against her skin as he worked, and Tara found herself holding her breath. The softness of his touch, the reverence in his movements—it felt as though he were performing a sacred ritual. She couldn't tear her eyes away from him, her heart swelling with emotions she couldn't name.

The faint jingling of the anklet filled the silence as Aditya moved to her other foot, repeating the gesture with the same devotion. Time seemed to slow, every movement heightened, every touch leaving a lasting impression on her soul. When he was done, he remained on his knees, his hands still cradling her foot, as he lifted his gaze to hers.

"Tara," he began, his voice steady yet heavy with emotion, "do you know how much you mean to me?"

Her heart skipped a beat. She couldn't look away from his eyes—so full of love, so full of truth.

"I knew from the moment I met you that you were someone extraordinary," he continued. "You've brought light into my life in ways I never imagined. You've made me see the world differently, feel things more deeply. And every single day, I fall more in love with you."

A tear slipped down Tara's cheek as she listened, her heart overwhelmed by the sincerity in his voice.

"You're not just someone I love," Aditya said, his voice softening. "You're someone I revere. To me, you're divine. You're like a goddess, Tara."

The words took her breath away. She couldn't stop the tears that followed, but they weren't tears of sadness—they were tears of gratitude, of love, of being seen in a way she had never been before.

Aditya reached up and gently brushed her tears away with his thumb. "Hey," he murmured, his smile warm and reassuring. "Why are you crying?"

Tara shook her head, her voice trembling. "Because... no one's ever said anything like that to me before. I don't even know if I deserve it."

Aditya's smile deepened, his eyes shining with certainty. "You deserve this and so much more, Tara. And I'll spend my whole life proving that to you."

Slowly, he stood, his face now level with hers. Their eyes met, and for a moment, it felt as if the entire universe had paused to witness their connection. The stars above seemed to shine brighter, the fairy lights casting a magical glow around them.

Aditya took her hands in his, his grip firm yet gentle. "You're my everything, Tara. I don't just see my today with you—I see my forever. You're the one I want to share my dreams with, the one I want to grow old with."

Unable to hold back any longer, Tara threw her arms around him, burying her face in his chest as sobs escaped her. Aditya held her close, one hand cradling the back of her head, the other wrapped around her protectively.

When they finally pulled apart, he cupped her face, his thumbs brushing away the last traces of her tears. "No more crying," he said softly, his tone teasing but filled with love. "I have one more surprise for you."

Tara laughed, her cheeks flushed. "Another one? You're really outdoing yourself tonight."

"You deserve nothing less," he replied with a grin.

As Tara wiped away her last tear, still feeling overwhelmed by everything Aditya had said and done, he smiled at her with a warmth that melted her heart. "No more tears," he whispered softly, gently taking her hand. "Come with me."

Her curiosity growing, Tara let him lead her toward the other side of the rooftop. The night air was sweet with the smell of flowers, and the soft sound of her anklets tinkling as she walked made everything feel even more magical. The fairy lights that twinkled around them seemed to grow brighter with each step, filling the rooftop with a golden glow, as if the night itself was smiling upon them.

Aditya stopped by a small table and, with a graceful movement, flipped a switch. The lights around them brightened, casting an even warmer glow, and suddenly, the entire rooftop felt like a dream. It wasn't just the lights, but the whole atmosphere—soft, romantic, and glowing with a magic that seemed to exist only for the two of them.

He smiled, glancing back at Tara, before walking over to a little tape player on the table. With a simple motion, he pressed play, and a soft, romantic song began to play. The music was slow and sweet, like a melody made just for them, and Tara's heart skipped a beat when she realized it was a song they'd shared once before. The same song they had listened to on a quiet evening together. As the soft notes filled the air, everything seemed to fade away except the two of them, lost in the melody.

Aditya turned to her, his eyes full of tenderness and mischief. He reached out his hand, pulling her gently toward him. "May I have this dance?" he asked, his voice low and full of warmth.

Tara's heart raced in her chest, but she didn't hesitate. "Of course," she whispered, a soft smile tugging at her lips.

With a smile that lit up his face, Aditya placed one hand on her waist, guiding her close, while she rested her hands on his shoulder. Their bodies moved slowly, swaying to the gentle rhythm of the music. Each step was light, like they were floating on air, and Tara couldn't help but close her eyes for a moment, letting herself be carried away by the soft beat of the song. It was as though nothing else mattered—just her and Aditya, moving together in perfect harmony.

The soft flicker of the lights danced around them, casting shadows that only seemed to make the moment more special. It felt like they were the only two people in the world, and for those few moments, time didn't seem to exist. Everything was still and perfect.

Aditya moved her gently in his arms, guiding her with a confidence that made Tara feel completely safe. His touch was tender but strong, each movement filled with care. He twirled her around once, her dress spinning out like a soft cloud, and Tara couldn't help but laugh, her heart light with happiness. When he pulled her back into his arms, she felt her breath catch, his warmth surrounding her as they continued to move together, perfectly in tune.

His hands gently held her closer, his fingers brushing the back of her neck, sending a wave of shivers down her spine. They moved in a slow circle, as if the whole world had stopped for them. Tara rested her head against his chest, hearing the steady beat of his heart as they swayed, lost in the music and in each other. There was no need for words, no need for anything except the way they felt in that moment.

As the song swelled, Aditya lifted her into a gentle spin once more, his hands steady on her waist. Tara's laughter rang out, bright and pure, as she twirled in the soft glow of the lights. When he pulled her back into his arms, he held her tighter than before, as if he never wanted to let go.

Tara's hands moved from his shoulder to gently cup his face, her thumb brushing over his cheek as she looked into his eyes. There was so much emotion in his gaze, so much love that it took her breath away. "You mean everything to me," he whispered, his voice thick with feeling.

Tara's heart swelled with emotion, and without thinking, she whispered back, "And you mean everything to me."

He smiled, a smile full of warmth and certainty. With a gentle pull, he brought her closer, their bodies fitting together perfectly. The music played on, the notes wrapping around them like a soft, comforting blanket, and they moved together without any care for time, without thinking of anything but the love between them.

For what felt like forever, they danced, the world outside the rooftop disappearing. There was only them, lost in the rhythm of the song, their hearts beating as one. When the song began to slow, Aditya pulled her into a final embrace, his hands holding her close as the last notes played softly in the background.

They stood like that for a moment, wrapped in each other's arms, with the fairy lights flickering around them and the night air cool against their skin. Tara rested her head on Aditya's chest, feeling the warmth of his embrace and the steady beat of his heart. In that moment, she knew that this was where she was meant to be. With him. Forever.

The music faded into silence, but the love between them lingered in the air, soft and everlasting.

As the music slowed down and the last notes faded away, Tara stayed in Aditya's arms, feeling completely lost in the moment. The soft glow from the fairy lights around them mixed with the quiet night air, creating a warm, peaceful atmosphere. Tara was so happy, but just as she was about to speak, Aditya smiled at her with a mischievous gleam in his eyes.

"Close your eyes," he said, his voice playful and full of excitement.

Tara raised an eyebrow, still feeling the excitement from their dance. "Why? Another surprise?" she asked, smiling.

Aditya smiled even more and nodded. "Just trust me. Close your eyes."

Tara couldn't resist, so she gently shut her eyes. The cool night air brushed against her skin as she stood still, listening to the quiet sounds around her. She felt Aditya's presence near her, his warmth surrounding her. Every moment felt like something magical was about to happen, and her heart raced with excitement.

She stayed like that for a few moments, feeling his hand gently covering her eyes. His touch was soft, like he was protecting her from something special. Tara stood still, curious about what was coming next.

After a few seconds, she felt Aditya's hand slip away from her eyes. Slowly, she opened them, blinking against the sudden light. As her eyes adjusted, she was surprised to see that she wasn't alone anymore.

Around her, under the soft fairy lights, were all her friends and family. Their laughter filled the air as they stood with huge smiles on their faces. Tara's mouth dropped open in shock as she looked around. She had completely forgotten—it was her birthday.

"Surprise!" they all shouted together, their voices full of happiness. "Happy Birthday, Tara!"

Tara's hands went to her mouth in disbelief. She had no idea that everyone had come together for her. She'd been so caught up in the magic of the evening that the date had slipped her mind.

She looked around, taking in the sight of everyone she loved standing there. Manav , Meera , Shaan , mita everyone was there , holding his hands out as if to say, "I told you this would be great!" Her heart swelled with joy. Aditya's parents were there , beaming with pride and warmth. Tara's eyes filled with happy tears. Aditya had invited everyone who meant something to her.

Aditya stood beside her, gently guiding her into the center of the group. "Happy Birthday, Tara," he said softly, his voice full of love.

Tara smiled up at him, her heart full. "Aditya... this is amazing. I didn't expect this at all."

The crowd cheered again, some of them clapping and others laughing with joy. Manav came up to her with a small cake, decorated with flowers and candles flickering in the night air. "Make a wish, Tara!" he said, his grin wide. "You have to make a wish!"

Tara smiled and closed her eyes for a moment, silently making her wish. When she opened her eyes again, she blew out the candles, the soft flames disappearing with a gentle puff. The crowd cheered once more, and Tara laughed with pure joy.

Aditya squeezed her hand. "I think your wish is already coming true," he said softly.

Tara looked up at him, a big smile on her face. "Maybe it already has."

The night continued with music, laughter, and love. Tara's friends and family talked and laughed, enjoying the celebration. Aditya's parents spoke warmly of her, telling her how happy they were to see her with their son. Manav and the others kept the mood light, teasing Tara with jokes, and even her friends joined in the fun.

Aditya stayed by her side the entire time, his presence making her feel safe and loved. Tara looked around at the people she cared about, feeling completely happy. The twinkling lights, the laughter, and the music made everything feel perfect.

For Tara, this wasn't just a birthday. It was a celebration of everything she loved—friends, family, love, and a night full of unforgettable moments. It was a sign of the wonderful future she had with Aditya, one full of magic and love.

As Tara looked around, soaking in all the love and joy of the surprise birthday party, she felt so happy, like her heart was about to burst. Meera, Mita, and Shaan were all there, smiling brightly and wishing Tara a wonderful birthday. Their warm wishes filled the air, and Tara could feel the love in every hug and every smile. But as she turned toward Aditya, standing beside her, her heart skipped a beat.

It was the way Aditya looked at Tara—so full of love and warmth. Tara's happiness shone so brightly, and Aditya's eyes sparkled in a way that made Tara feel like she was the center of his world. For a moment, Meera felt her own heart ache. It wasn't jealousy. No, she wasn't jealous of Tara at all. She was happy for her, truly. But seeing them together, so perfect, made her remember all the dreams she had once had. Dreams of a life with Aditya. A life where she was the one standing beside him, where he looked at her with the same love and devotion.

She stood there, smiling, but the pain in her chest was hard to ignore. She had spent so many years imagining this moment—dreaming of one day becoming Aditya's wife, having their own little family, a baby boy, just like she had always imagined. And now, seeing Tara there, in Aditya's arms, all of Meera's old dreams felt distant.

But Meera wasn't angry. She didn't feel bitter. She was happy for Tara, truly. But inside, a part of her felt like it was breaking. She had never told anyone, not even Shaan, how much she had hoped for this life with Aditya. And now, watching them together, it was hard to keep those feelings buried.

Shaan noticed the look in Meera's eyes, the way she had become quiet, her smile slightly forced as she watched Tara and Aditya. He stepped closer to her, his concern evident. "Meera, are you okay?" he asked, his voice gentle.

Meera tried to smile again, but it felt so difficult. "I'm fine, Shaan," she said softly, though her voice wavered just a little. "I just... I just never thought it would be like this."

Shaan gave her a worried look, his eyes soft with understanding. He knew Meera had been close to Aditya for years, and he could guess the feelings she was hiding. "You've always dreamed of being with him, haven't you?" Shaan asked, his tone gentle but full of care.

Meera nodded slowly, her eyes not leaving Tara and Aditya. "Since we were kids, I always thought it would be me. I thought... I thought one day, Aditya would look at me the way he looks at Tara now. I even imagined having a little boy with him, a family of our own. And now..." Meera's voice faltered, and she swallowed hard. "Now I see Tara, and it feels like all my dreams are slipping away."

Shaan could see the pain in Meera's eyes, even though she was smiling. "Meera," he said softly, reaching out to take her hand. "You don't need to hide your feelings. I know this is hard for you, but you're a wonderful person. Tara is lucky to have you as a friend. And Aditya, he's always cared for you, too. Just not in the way you wanted."

Tears welled up in Meera's eyes, but she quickly blinked them away, trying to hold herself together. She looked at Shaan, her voice breaking just a little. "I just wanted to be the one. I wanted to be the one to make him smile like that. To build a future with him. But I guess that's just not meant to be."

Shaan squeezed her hand gently, not knowing exactly what to say to make her feel better. He knew it was a pain only time could heal. "I understand, Meera. I really do. But you're not alone. You have your friends, your family, and me. And if you ever need to talk, I'm always here."

Meera nodded, trying to smile through the pain. But just as she was about to say something, she suddenly felt dizzy. Her vision blurred slightly, and a wave of exhaustion washed over her. She swayed on her feet, her breath catching in her throat.

Shaan noticed immediately. "Meera? Hey, are you okay?" His voice was full of concern as he gently reached out to steady her. "You don't look well."

"I... I'm fine," Meera whispered, but her voice was weak, and she couldn't seem to stand still. The dizziness was getting worse.

Shaan didn't hesitate. He gently guided her toward the door of the house, away from the party. "Come on, Meera. Let's get you to a room to rest," he said softly, helping her walk.

As they moved toward the room, Meera felt the weight of everything—her unspoken love for Aditya, the dreams she had, and the hurt she had hidden for so long. But there was also comfort in Shaan's presence. He was there for her, always, even when her heart ached in ways she couldn't explain.

When they finally reached the room, Shaan helped her sit on the bed, his concern never leaving his face. "Rest here. You'll feel better soon," he said, sitting beside her for a moment to make sure she was comfortable.

Meera smiled faintly. "Thank you, Shaan," she whispered, feeling the tears she had been holding back threatening to fall.

Shaan nodded. "Take care of yourself, Meera. You deserve happiness too."

As Meera lay down, the sound of laughter and music from the party seemed so far away. But in that quiet moment, she knew her heart needed time to heal. And maybe, just maybe, the pain would ease with each passing day.

The chapter ended there, with Meera resting in the room, still processing everything, and Shaan sitting by her side, silently offering his support.

11

Pages of Now

Sameer stands at the hospital entrance, feeling the weight of the last few days pressing down on him. He had been running on empty, his thoughts a constant swirl of concern for Rhea and the situation with her dad.

Rhea's dad had suffered a mild heart attack earlier . It had shaken them all, and though he was stable now, the fear still lingered in the air. Sameer had been spending as much time as possible at the hospital, trying to ease Rhea's worries, while Rohan was doing his best to support them both. It was a tough time, but they were sticking together.

His phone buzzes in his pocket. It's a message from Siya, asking how Rhea's dad is doing. Sameer hesitates for a moment before replying. He doesn't want to worry her, but he knows Siya always cares.

"Yeah, Rhea's dad had a heart attack. It was mild, but it still scared her. We've been at the hospital a lot lately, just trying to keep her spirits up," he types.

The message goes through, and almost immediately, Siya responds. "Poor Rhea. Is she holding up okay?"

He runs a hand through his hair, a tired sigh escaping him. "She's trying. Rhea's strong, but this has really shaken her. Rohan and I are doing what we can to help."

The reply is quick again. "You're a good friend, Sameer. She's lucky to have you."

Sameer smiles at the screen, the warmth in her words making him feel lighter, even if just for a moment. Siya has a way of grounding him, of reminding him of the good even when everything else feels overwhelming.

They chat for a little longer, switching topics to lighter things—the letters Sameer has been reading, his father's health, and Siya's recent adventures in New York. For a few minutes, the world feels normal again, but the sound of a knock on the door pulls Sameer back to reality.

"Rhea and Rohan are here," he says, glancing toward the door. "I've got to go, but I'll call you later, okay?"

Siya's response is soft but sincere. "Take care, Sameer. And don't forget—if you ever need to talk, I'm just a call away."

"I know," he replies, his voice carrying a quiet appreciation. "Thanks, Siya."

He ends the call just as Rhea and Rohan step into the room. Rhea looks exhausted, but there's a quiet strength in her eyes that Sameer admires. Rohan, ever the support system, follows closely behind, offering a reassuring smile to Sameer.

"We brought you some coffee," Rhea says, though she looks more tired than usual. Her smile is there, but it's a little forced, a little faded.

Sameer stands up from where he's been sitting. "Thanks," he says, taking the cup Rhea hands him. "How's your dad doing?"

Rhea exhales deeply, rubbing her eyes. "He's stable. But it's hard, Sameer. I can't stop thinking about it. I hate seeing him like this."

Sameer gives her a sympathetic look. He knows the feeling. "I understand. It's not easy, but you've got to keep yourself strong too. Your dad needs you to stay strong."

Rhea nods, her eyes welling up. "I know. It's just... tough." She takes a deep breath and forces a smile. "But I'm okay. Just a little tired."

Rohan looks at Sameer, his expression serious. "We're all in this together. Right?"

Sameer nods. "Right." He takes a sip of the coffee, the warmth of it comforting, even if it can't fully replace the emotional exhaustion he feels.

As they sit together, the weight of everything hangs over them, but there's a silent understanding between the three of them. They don't need to say much. They all know how important it is to stick together during times like this. Sameer watches Rhea, his heart heavy for her.

Despite the difficult circumstances, the bond between them feels unbreakable.

Rohan looked at Sameer. "What's up, man? You look like you've been deep in thought."

Sameer shrugged, trying to shake off the heaviness of everything that had been weighing on his mind. "Just talking to Siya. You know, the usual."

Rhea, who had been unusually quiet since they arrived, sat down beside Sameer. She fiddled with her phone, her fingers tapping absent-mindedly on the screen. "I'm just glad you're here," she said softly, her voice tired. "I don't think I could handle all of this on my own."

Sameer gave her a reassuring smile and placed a comforting hand on her shoulder. "You don't have to. We're here for you, Rhea. Always."

Rohan nodded in agreement. But unlike his usual playful self, there was a serious look on his face. "Your dad's a tough guy. He's going to pull through this, no question."

Rhea managed a weak smile, though it didn't quite reach her eyes. The worry in her gaze was hard to miss. "I know he is. But it's still hard. Seeing him in that hospital bed... it made me realize how much I've taken for granted. He's always been the strong one, taking care of everything—our schooling, our careers, even our stupid love lives," she added, throwing a teasing look at Rohan.

Rohan grinned, though the sadness in his eyes was still evident. "Hey, speak for yourself. My love life is thriving, thank you very much."

Rhea raised an eyebrow. "Oh, really? I'll ask Baba about that."

Sameer chuckled, the sound lightening the atmosphere a little. "Yeah, right. Your dad's been there for everything—our schooling, careers, all the ups and downs. He's always looking out for us, even when we're too stubborn to listen."

Rhea nodded, her thoughts turning back to her father. "He really is the best, isn't he? I just hate seeing him like this. He's always been my rock, you know? And now I feel like the roles have reversed." Her voice trembled slightly, and she blinked back the tears threatening to fall.

Rohan leaned forward, his expression softening. Though he tried to lighten the mood, there was a genuine warmth in his words. "That's what family's about, Rhea. We take care of each other when it counts. Your dad's going to be fine because he's got you."

Rhea took a deep breath, her shoulders slumping in exhaustion. "I hope you're right, Rohan," she murmured. "I just feel so helpless."

"You're not helpless," Sameer said gently. "You're doing exactly what you need to do right now. Being here, supporting him, keeping your head up. It's all going to make a difference."

The three of them sat in a comfortable silence for a moment, the weight of the situation still heavy but slightly more bearable.

Sameer watched the exchange quietly, feeling grateful for the small moments of connection, even in the middle of such a difficult time. They were all in this together, and as hard as it was, they would make it through.

....

Later that evening, Sameer and Rohan accompanied Rhea back to the hospital to check on her father, who was due to be discharged soon. As they entered the hospital room, Rhea's father, was sitting up in bed, looking much better than he had the day before.

"Ah, there's my favorite idiots," he greeted them, a mischievous glint in his eyes.

"Hey, we're not your only idiots, right?" Rohan joked, pulling up a chair. "So, Shaan, did the doctors give you good food? Made any new friends?"

Shaan scowled playfully, shaking his head. "Shut up, you idiot. Just because I'm in a hospital doesn't mean I've forgotten how to knock some sense into you."

Rhea laughed, her eyes brightening for the first time in days. "See, Dad? You're already back to your old self."

Shaan grinned, but his expression softened as he looked at his daughter. "You worry too much, Rhea. I'm fine. But thank you for being here."

Rohan, ever the joker, leaned over and whispered loudly to Sameer, "You think he's going to go easy on us after this? I doubt it."

Sameer smirked. "Yeah, right. He'll probably be even tougher on us now."

Shaan pointed a finger at both of them, laughing. "You boys better behave, or I'll call your mothers."

"You mean Meera?" Rhea chimed in, referring to the late Meera who had been such a pivotal figure in all their

lives.

Shaan's smile softened at the mention of Meera's name. "Meera would've had all of you wrapped around her finger, no doubt."

Shaan was just looked at three of them how Sameer and Rohan is there for Rhea like some back memories on his head

The room fell into a comfortable silence, the shared memories of Meera bringing a sense of peace to the moment. For a while, they simply enjoyed each other's company, grateful for the bonds that held them together even through the toughest of times.

....

The next morning, sunlight streamed through the large windows of the hospital room, casting a warm glow over the scene. Sameer, Rhea, and Rohan had arrived early, determined to keep Rhea's father company while he recovered from his mild heart attack. Despite everything that had happened, Shaan seemed to be in high spirits. The room was filled with laughter and conversation, as his energy remained just as vibrant as always.

Shaan looked much better than he had the day before, sitting up in bed with a playful spark in his eyes. As usual, he started teasing Rohan about his love life, making jokes that kept the mood light. Sameer sat back in his chair, watching them with a smile. Even though they were all concerned about Shaan's health, being together in this moment brought a sense of comfort. There was peace in knowing they were surrounded by people who truly cared about each other.

"I swear, Shaan," Rohan said dramatically, stretching out his words, "one of these days, I'll find the love of my life, and you'll all be shocked. And seriously, why aren't they discharging you yet? What is it, Shaan, are you charming the nurses or something?"

Shaan raised an eyebrow and grinned widely. "Charming? You bet, Rohan. Well, if you keep up this 'shut up and get to work' attitude, you might as well marry your career, huh?"

Rhea laughed, shaking her head as she turned to her father. "Please, Dad, don't encourage him. He's already unbearable as it is. If you keep feeding his delusions, we'll never hear the end of it."

Rohan acted hurt, placing a hand over his heart. "Delusions? I'm a catch, okay? You'll see!" he declared.

Sameer chuckled, shaking his head at the back-and-forth between Rhea and Rohan. It was familiar, comforting even, and the lighthearted banter helped ease the tension that had lingered since Shaan's health scare. For a moment, they were able to forget the worries and just be together as friends.

But as the morning went on, the conversation took an unexpected turn. Rhea, who had been scrolling through her phone absently, suddenly looked up with a spark of realization. "Oh, I almost forgot! Sameer's been totally hooked on this crazy mystery. He found these old love letters, and now he's obsessed with figuring out who wrote them."

Shaan, who had been lazily sipping water, raised an eyebrow, intrigued. "Old letters? Love letters, you say?"

Rohan grinned, happy to jump in. "Yeah, it's all he talks about now. He found them in this old house he's renting. They're from some woman named Tara, written to a guy named Aditya. Sameer's convinced there's a huge love story hidden in those letters."

Sameer felt himself blush a little under the attention. "It's not that big of a deal," he said, trying to downplay it. "It's just... there's something about their story that keeps bothering me. I don't know why, but it's like I need to know what happened between them."

Shaan's expression shifted slightly, and there was something in his eyes that Sameer couldn't quite place. It wasn't exactly surprise, more like... recognition?

"Well," Shaan said slowly, his voice thoughtful, "love stories have a way of haunting us. Especially the unfinished ones."

Sameer looked at Shaan, a sense of curiosity stirring inside him. Before he could ask more, a nurse entered the room to check on Shaan's vitals, interrupting the moment. The conversation shifted away, but the way Shaan had spoken left a mark in Sameer's mind. There was something about his words, the way he looked at him, that made Sameer feel like there was more to the story than just old letters.

The nurse moved around the room, but Sameer's thoughts were elsewhere, his mind replaying the conversation, wondering what Shaan had meant. Something was nagging at him, something bigger than just the letters or the love story he was unraveling. He knew he had to dig deeper, but for now, he kept quiet, letting the day unfold as it would.

....

Later that evening, after Shaan was discharged from the hospital and safely back home, the group decided to throw a small get-together to celebrate his recovery. It wasn't anything grand—just a cozy evening with close friends and family in Rhea's house. Shaan had insisted on keeping it low-key, but that didn't stop everyone from showing up with food, drinks, and stories to share.

The atmosphere in the house was warm and cheerful, with laughter filling every corner. Rhea had set up a small table in the living room, piled high with snacks and drinks, and the sound of music played softly in the background. Shaan, now looking even better than before, was comfortably settled on the couch, surrounded by the people he cared about. His usual playful energy was back, and he didn't waste any time teasing Rohan, who had brought his "latest creation"—a batch of homemade snacks that no one was quite sure how to describe.

"You know, Rohan," Shaan said with a grin, holding up one of Rohan's snacks, "you might want to consider a career change. These could be classified as 'hazardous to health.'"

Rohan chuckled, shrugging. "Hey, I'm still perfecting my skills! It's a work in progress!"

Rhea rolled her eyes but couldn't help but smile. "You're a disaster in the kitchen, but I love you anyway."

Sameer, leaning against the wall with a drink in hand, watched the playful banter with a smile. It was moments like this that made everything feel right again. They had all been through so much together, and now, in this moment, they were just friends enjoying each other's company.

As the evening went on, the group settled into easy conversations. Shaan and Rhea shared funny stories from their past, reminding everyone of the times they had spent growing up together. Laughter filled the room, and even though there was a certain heaviness from everything Shaan had been through, there was a sense of joy in the air that couldn't be ignored.

At one point, Shaan turned to Sameer, his expression softening. "I meant to ask you earlier," he began, his tone more serious, "how's that mystery of yours going? The one with the letters?"

Sameer paused, a little caught off guard by the question. He had almost forgotten about the conversation from earlier that morning. "Oh, yeah, I'm still trying to figure it out," he said, his voice thoughtful. "I don't know, there's just something about these letters that doesn't sit right with me. I feel like there's more to the story, like something important was left unsaid."

Shaan felt a shiver run down his spine as Sameer spoke. But before he could ask anything further, Rhea jumped in, bringing the conversation back to lighter topics.

"Alright, enough about mysteries and love stories for one night!" she declared, grinning. "Let's play a game. Who's up for a little fun?"

Everyone immediately agreed, and the rest of the evening was filled with laughter, jokes, and friendly competition.

The house buzzed with warmth and laughter as old friends gathered in the living room. Sameer found himself sitting on the couch, sipping tea while watching the interactions around him. Rohan's parents had come over too, and the room was filled with the familiar sounds of family banter.

"You know," Rohan's father, Mr. Sharma, said with a sigh as he settled into a chair next to Shaan, "it's moments like these when I really miss Rhea's mother and Meera."

Rohan's mother nodded in agreement, her eyes soft with nostalgia. "Yes, they were the heart of these gatherings. Always the life of the party."

Sameer's heart tightened at the mention of his mother, Meera. It had been years since she had passed, but the ache of her absence never truly went away. He caught Rhea's eye, and she gave him a small, understanding smile. They had both lost their mothers, and the shared grief between them was something they rarely talked about but always felt.

"Your mother, Meera," Rohan's father said, turning to Sameer, "was the kind of woman who could light up a room just by walking in. I've never met anyone like her."

Sameer nodded, swallowing the lump in his throat. "Yeah, she was."

As the conversation moved on, Rhea's father, Shaan, chuckled softly and turned to Mr. Sharma. "By the way, where's Shiva? He should've been here."

Rhea looked up from her drink, shaking her head. "Oh, Dad, Baba's been busy with some things. You know how he is."

Shaan nodded thoughtfully, but before anyone could ask more, Sameer's phone buzzed. It was a video call—from his father, Shiva.

Sameer glanced around the room, realizing everyone was watching him. With a deep breath, he answered the call. His father's familiar face appeared on the screen, a tired but warm smile on his lips.

"Baba," Sameer greeted, trying to keep his tone light.

"Sameer, beta! I was just thinking about you," his father said, his voice as calm as ever. "I hope I'm not interrupting anything."

"You're fine," Sameer replied, glancing at Shaan, who waved at the camera with a grin. "Actually, Shaan uncle's here. Everyone's here, actually."

"Ah, Shaan!" Shiva exclaimed, recognizing his old friend. "How are you, my old friend? Still causing trouble, I'm sure."

Shaan laughed, his eyes twinkling. "Trouble? Me? Never."

The two older men exchanged a few more lighthearted words, and soon the entire room was engaged in conversation. Sameer's father seemed to blend right into the gathering, despite being miles away on a screen. But even as he spoke with ease, Sameer couldn't shake the feeling that something was off. The weight of their earlier conversation—the one about his father's unspoken loneliness—still hung in the air.

After a few minutes, Shiva turned his attention back to Sameer, his voice quieter now. "How are you, beta? You seemed distracted the last time we spoke."

Sameer hesitated, not wanting to burden his father with the confusion he was feeling. "I'm okay, Baba. Just... busy."

"You know you can talk to me," Shiva said gently. "About anything."

"I know," Sameer replied, though he didn't feel ready to share the whole story about the letters just yet.

Shiva smiled, though there was a flicker of sadness in his eyes. "Alright, beta. Just take care of yourself."

As the call ended and the night went on, Sameer's mind kept circling back to the letters—to the mystery of Tara and Aditya, and to his father's quiet strength. He was so lost in thought that he barely noticed when Shaan pulled him aside, leading him to the quiet of the kitchen.

Shaan closed the kitchen door behind them, cutting off the sounds of laughter from the living room. He turned to Sameer, his expression serious but not unkind.

"You've got a lot on your mind, don't you?" Shaan asked, leaning against the counter.

Sameer nodded, unsure of how to explain the turmoil inside him. "It's... it's these letters, uncle. I can't stop thinking about them. About Tara and Aditya. I don't even know why I'm so invested in their story, but I am. I feel like it's taking over my life."

Shaan crossed his arms, his eyes narrowing thoughtfully. "You're searching for something, Sameer. And I don't think it's just about the letters."

Sameer looked up, startled by the accuracy of Shaan's words. "What do you mean?"

Shaan sighed, running a hand through his graying hair. "I think you're looking for answers, not just about Tara and Aditya, but about your own life. About the things you haven't said, the feelings you've buried."

Sameer swallowed hard, the truth of Shaan's words hitting him like a wave. He hadn't realized it before, but Shaan was right. His obsession with the letters was tied to something deeper—something unresolved in his own life.

"There's something you need to know," Shaan said quietly, his eyes never leaving Sameer's. "I wasn't sure if I should tell you, but I think it's time."

Sameer's heart raced. "What is it?"

Shaan glanced around the room, as if checking to make sure they were alone. "I know where Tara is."

Sameer's eyes widened in shock. "What? How... how do you know that?"

Shaan's expression was unreadable, but there was a flicker of something in his eyes—something that hinted at secrets long kept. "It doesn't matter how I know. What matters is that I can tell you where to find her. But you need to be ready for the answers you're searching for."

Sameer felt his pulse quicken. The idea that he might finally get answers, that he might finally unravel the mystery that had consumed him for so long, was overwhelming.

"Are you sure?" Sameer asked, his voice barely above a whisper.

Shaan nodded, his gaze steady. "I'm sure. But you need to go to her, Sameer. This isn't something you can figure out by sitting in a library or reading letters. You need to hear the truth from her."

Sameer's mind raced with possibilities. He had been searching for weeks, feeling as though he were stumbling around in the dark. And now, here was Shaan, offering him the key to the answers he had been seeking.

"I'll give you the address," Shaan said, pulling a small slip of paper from his pocket. "When you're ready, go and meet her. You'll find all your answers there."

Sameer took the paper with trembling hands, the weight of the moment pressing down on him. He didn't know what to say—didn't know how to process the flood of emotions rushing through him.

"Thank you," Sameer whispered, his voice hoarse.

Shaan smiled, placing a reassuring hand on Sameer's shoulder. "Sometimes, the hardest part is not finding the answers, but being ready to face them."

....

As the evening drew to a close, the friends and family gathered once more in the living room, laughing and sharing stories. But Sameer's mind was elsewhere, his thoughts consumed by the address in his pocket and the weight of the decision he now had to make.

Rhea, noticing the shift in Sameer's mood, came over and placed a hand on his arm. "You okay?"

Sameer smiled, though it didn't quite reach his eyes. "Yeah. Just thinking."

Rhea nodded, sensing there was more going on but not pushing him. "Whenever you're ready to talk, we're here."

Sameer nodded, grateful for her friendship, but knowing that the next step in his journey was something he had to take alone.

As the night wound down and the guests began to leave, Sameer stood by the window, staring out into the quiet night. The address in his pocket felt heavy, and the weight of the unanswered questions hung over him like a cloud.

But now, for the first time, he felt like he was finally on the verge of understanding. He was ready to take the next step—to face whatever truth awaited him, no matter how difficult it might be.

And with that thought, Sameer knew that his journey was far from over.

12
Pages of Before

It was a late afternoon, and the soft, golden sunlight stretched lazily across the sky. The warm glow touched everything around, creating a peaceful, almost magical atmosphere. Aditya and Tara were walking together towards a small mandir (temple) on the edge of the city. This temple was a special place, known for its calm, quiet surroundings, tucked away among tall trees and lush greenery. The air felt different today, almost as if it carried a kind of magic that made Tara's heart feel light, full of warmth, and contentment as she walked beside Aditya.

They had been planning this visit for days, hoping to escape the noise and rush of their everyday lives. Both of them wanted to find a moment of peace, a time when they could simply be together without the distractions of the world. But for Aditya, this visit held a deeper meaning. It wasn't just about spending time with Tara in a beautiful place; he had something important on his mind, something he wanted to share with her. But for now, he was content with just being beside her. The serenity of the place felt perfect for the feelings he carried in his heart.

The temple was small, with stone steps leading up to it. As they reached the entrance, Aditya looked at Tara with a playful smile on his face, the twinkle in his eyes showing that he was up to something.

"Do you know what people say about this place?" he asked, his voice filled with mischief.

Tara, curious, raised an eyebrow. "What?" she asked, a smile already tugging at the corners of her lips.

"They say that anyone who exchanges garlands here is bound to be together forever," Aditya said, his eyes glimmering as if he were telling her a secret. "It's like an unspoken promise of love."

Tara laughed, shaking her head. "Are you serious? That sounds like something you just made up to make this trip even more fun!"

Aditya raised his hands in mock defense. "Hey, I'm not making it up! It's a real tradition. And anyway, I think we should try it." His smile grew wider, clearly enjoying the fun of it all.

Tara looked at him, amused and slightly confused. "What do you mean 'try it'? You want us to pretend to get married?" She teased, her voice light with laughter.

Aditya's smile deepened, and with a playful wink, he pulled out two garlands made of **Genda Phool** (marigold flowers) from his bag. The bright orange and yellow petals shimmered in the light, as if glowing with their own inner warmth. The garlands looked fresh and beautiful, their sweet scent filling the air.

"Why not?" Aditya said, his tone teasing yet soft. "Let's act like we're getting married, just for today. Just for fun."

Tara stared at the garlands for a moment. There was something about Aditya's spontaneous, romantic nature that was both endearing and charming. Despite herself, she felt a flutter in her chest. She had never imagined something so playful could feel so meaningful.

"Okay," she said with a soft laugh, her voice a little more tender now. "Let's do it."

They walked together to the front of the temple. The temple was almost empty, with only a few devotees praying quietly in the corners. The place felt calm and sacred, the perfect setting for their little act of pretend love.

As they stood in front of the deities, the playful mood between them softened. The lightness of their banter faded, and they found themselves facing each other in a quiet, peaceful silence. For a moment, Tara forgot that they were only pretending. Everything around them seemed to fade away, and it was just the two of them, standing in the presence of the sacred deities, as if they were part of something much bigger than themselves.

"Here," Aditya said, handing her one of the garlands. His voice was gentle now, less teasing, more sincere. "You go first."

Tara took the garland, her fingers brushing over the smooth petals as she stepped closer to him. She could feel her heart race just a little, and her hands trembled ever so slightly. There was something about the moment that felt more real than she had expected. She slowly lifted the garland over his head, her fingers gently brushing against his skin as it settled around his neck. The garland felt heavier than she had thought, as if it carried with it an unspoken promise. When she looked up at Aditya, their eyes met for a brief, intense moment. There was no teasing now, just a deep connection that neither of them could deny.

Aditya grinned softly, his eyes warm, as he took the other garland. His fingers brushed against her neck as he placed it over her head, and for a second, Tara felt as if time itself had slowed down.

"See?" Aditya said, his voice low and intimate. "Now we're officially bound for eternity."

For a moment, Tara couldn't find the words to respond. Her heart fluttered, a strange mix of joy and something deeper rising within her. They stood there together, in front of Radha and Krishna, with the garlands resting around their necks. The marigold flowers, bright and alive, seemed to echo the energy between them, a bond that felt more than just playful or temporary.

"This is ridiculous," Tara whispered, though her smile gave away the joy she was feeling.

"Maybe," Aditya said, stepping a little closer, his voice soft. "But it's the best kind of ridiculous."

They stood there for what felt like hours, but in reality, it was only a few minutes. The playful act of pretending to get married had slowly turned into something more meaningful, something symbolic. It was as if, in that moment, they were making a quiet promise to each other, one that went beyond words. Tara could feel it in the way Aditya's gaze held hers, the way his hand lingered on her arm as they stood together, their hearts quietly intertwined.

The light around them seemed warmer, the air sweeter. Their love so pure and eternal. It was as if the gods themselves were watching over them, blessing this small, fleeting moment of happiness.

For that brief, magical moment, it didn't matter that they were only pretending. It didn't matter that it was just a game. Because in their hearts, they knew that this was something real, something that could last far beyond the game they were playing.

In their hearts, it felt like they were married—not in the way the world understood marriage, but in the most important way possible: in love. And for Tara, standing there with Aditya, with the garland of marigolds around her neck, it was as if their love had already been promised.

After leaving the temple, the air felt cooler as the sun began to set, painting the sky with shades of pink, orange, and gold. The fading light bathed the streets in a soft, gentle glow, and the world around them seemed to slow down, as if the universe was taking a deep breath and holding it, allowing the two of them a moment of peace. The hum of the busy city seemed distant now, the bustling sounds of the day replaced by the quiet evening calm. It was like walking through a dream—a dream where nothing else mattered but the two of them, side by side, in this magical moment.

The streets, now quieter, gave them the space to walk in comfortable silence, letting their thoughts wander freely. Tara could hear the faint rustle of leaves in the trees as a breeze danced through the air. The world felt suspended in time, and it made her feel connected to something larger than just the two of them.

After a long stretch of silence, Aditya spoke, his voice soft yet steady, breaking the tranquility. "Tara," he began, and she instinctively turned to look at him, sensing something different in his tone.

"What is it?" Tara asked, her voice barely above a whisper.

Aditya stopped walking, his hand brushing against hers as he turned to face her fully. For the first time all evening, his expression was not playful or teasing but serious—more serious than she had expected. Tara felt a flutter of unease in her chest.

"I got an opportunity. A big one," Aditya said, his words hanging in the air like a promise.

Tara's heart skipped a beat, and her mind raced, trying to make sense of what he meant. "An opportunity for what?" she asked, her voice a mix of curiosity and concern.

Aditya took a deep breath, his excitement evident even through his calm demeanor. "It's a photography gig. In a big city. I've been invited to work with a well-known photographer there, someone who can really help me take my career to the next level. It's... it's everything I've been working towards," he explained, his eyes shining with a mix of excitement and disbelief.

Tara felt a rush of pride for him—Aditya had always been incredibly talented, and she knew he deserved this chance. But along with that pride, there was an undercurrent of something else, something she couldn't quite put into words. The thought of him leaving, even if it was just for a while, made her heart ache in a way she hadn't expected.

"That's amazing, Aditya," Tara said, forcing a smile, her voice filled with genuine happiness. She placed a hand on his arm, feeling a warm sense of pride and admiration for him. "I'm so proud of you."

Aditya's face brightened with the weight of her words, his smile widening. "But it's not just about me. I've been thinking about our future—about what we want," he said, his voice lowering slightly as if he were sharing a secret with her. "If this works out, I can finally build the life I've always dreamed of. And you... you can be a part of that. We could move to the city together, start fresh. We could be happy, Tara."

The words "our future" lingered in the air, and Tara's heart swelled with a mix of hope and fear. She felt her breath catch, her thoughts racing. Could this be the beginning of something beautiful? Could they really build a life together, just like he said? The idea of a fresh start, of a new chapter in a new city, seemed like a dream come true, one she had imagined many times before. But the reality of it was both thrilling and daunting.

She let herself imagine it for a moment: Aditya chasing his dreams in photography, creating beautiful images and making a name for himself. And her—finding her own path, whatever it might be, standing beside him as his partner. The thought made her feel light and hopeful, as if the possibilities were endless.

Tara looked at him, her gaze soft yet steady. "That sounds beautiful, Aditya," she said, her voice quiet, filled with wonder. "I've always believed in you, and I know you're going to do great things." She paused, feeling the weight of the decision settling in. "But... are you sure? I mean, what about everything here? About us?"

Aditya smiled gently, reaching out to take her hand in his. "I'm sure," he said, his voice reassuring. "I've thought about it a lot. And I want you by my side, Tara. I want us to have the life we both deserve. If this opportunity works out, we could build that life together. We could be happy, just like we've always dreamed."

The warmth of his hand in hers was comforting, grounding her as she processed the enormity of what he was saying. It felt like the kind of decision that could change everything, the kind of decision that could bring them closer or tear them apart. But for now, in this moment, she allowed herself to imagine it—to believe in the possibility of it.

Aditya squeezed her hand gently, as if sensing her hesitation. "I know it's a lot to take in," he said softly. "But I need you to know that no matter what, I want us to build this future together. I don't want to do it without you, Tara."

Tara's heart swelled with emotion at his words. She had always known that Aditya was someone who would chase his dreams with all his heart, but to hear him say he wanted her with him on that journey filled her with warmth. It was the kind of love that made her believe in fairy tales, in the possibility of two souls intertwining and building something beautiful together.

For a moment, she simply stood there, looking at him, taking it all in. The soft glow of the setting sun, the promise of the future, and the quiet certainty that, no matter where life took them, they would always be there for each other.

"I'll be with you," she said finally, her voice steady and full of love. "I don't know what the future holds, but as long as we're together, I'm ready to face it. We can build our life, Aditya. Together."

Aditya's eyes softened, and his smile grew even wider. He leaned in, pressing a gentle kiss to her forehead, a silent promise that everything would be okay, no matter what.

And as the last rays of the sun dipped below the horizon, the world around them seemed to fade away, leaving only the two of them in their shared moment—two people, in love, ready to take on the future side by side.

But as the excitement began to build in her chest, Meera and Shaan appeared, their faces tense.

"Tara," Meera said urgently, "Manav is looking for you. It seems important—he looked really scared."

Shaan nodded, adding, "He told us to tell you, 'Come home, Di. It's important.'"

Tara frowned, her heart sinking. Something about the message felt wrong—urgent in a way that made her stomach twist.

"Is everything okay?" Aditya asked, noticing the change in her expression.

Tara nodded, though her mind was already elsewhere. "Yeah, I just... I need to go home. Manav needs me."

Aditya's smile faltered, concern creasing his brow. "Do you want me to come with you?"

"No, it's fine," Tara said quickly, forcing a smile. "I'll see you later."

As they parted ways, the warmth of their earlier moment began to fade, replaced by a growing sense of dread. Tara hurried home, her mind racing with all the possibilities of what could be wrong.

....

When Tara arrived home, the atmosphere was heavy, suffocating. The usual warmth of the house, filled with laughter and the comforting hum of daily life, had vanished, replaced by a silence so stark that it echoed. The living room felt unwelcoming, its familiar corners somehow foreign in the dim light of the evening. Tara noticed how everything seemed out of place—her father's favorite book lay discarded on the coffee table, her mother's knitting kit untouched in the corner. It was as though the house itself bore the weight of whatever had happened.

Her gaze landed on Manav, who sat hunched on the couch, his shoulders slumped as if he carried the weight of the world. His face was pale, his eyes downcast, and his hands were clenched tightly in his lap. Tara's heart clenched at the sight of her usually cheerful younger brother reduced to this state.

"Manav," she called softly, dropping to her knees in front of him. Her voice was gentle, though fear rippled beneath her calm tone. "What's wrong? Tell me."

Manav looked up slowly, his eyes meeting hers. They were filled with fear, sadness, and something else—helplessness. The sight made Tara's stomach twist.

"Di..." he began, his voice barely above a whisper. "It's Mom and Dad. They've been fighting. It's bad. Really bad."

Tara blinked, the words taking a moment to sink in. Her parents? Fighting? Of course, they'd had arguments in the past, but they had always resolved them quickly, their love shining through even in moments of disagreement.

"What do you mean, fighting?" she asked, her voice steady but laced with concern.

Manav swallowed hard, as though the words he was about to say physically hurt him. "I mean... they're talking about divorce."

The word hung in the air like a thunderclap, sending shockwaves through Tara. She froze, staring at her brother as if he'd just spoken in a language she didn't understand. Divorce. The idea seemed impossible, unimaginable.

"No," she said, shaking her head instinctively. "That can't be true. Mom and Dad... they love each other. They've always been happy."

Manav looked down, his trembling hands clutching at the fabric of his jeans. "I heard them, Di. They were yelling about it. I didn't mean to listen, but I couldn't help it. They were saying things I've never heard them say before. Blaming each other. It's like..." His voice cracked, and he wiped at his eyes hastily, as though ashamed of his tears. "It's like they've stopped caring."

Tara's chest tightened. Her parents had always been her role models, the couple she looked up to when she dreamed of her own future with someone like Aditya. They were the reason she believed in love—the kind of love that lasted through thick and thin, that grew stronger with time. The idea of them considering divorce felt like the foundation of her world was crumbling beneath her.

"How long has this been going on?" she asked, her voice quiet, almost afraid of the answer.

"very long ," Manav admitted, his voice trembling. "I noticed the arguments getting worse, but I didn't think it was... this serious. I tried to talk to them, but they just told me to stay out of it. It's like they don't even care how this is affecting us."

Tara reached out, pulling Manav into a tight hug. He leaned into her, his frame shaking with suppressed sobs. She stroked his back gently, her own emotions threatening to overwhelm her.

"It's going to be okay," she whispered, though she didn't entirely believe her own words. How could it be okay when the two people she thought would always be there for each other were falling apart?

As she held Manav, her mind raced. She tried to piece together every interaction she'd had with her parents over the past few weeks. Had she missed the signs? Had there been subtle clues in their voices, their expressions, the way they looked at each other?

Her parents had always seemed so perfect. She had taken for granted the way her father would always refill her mother's tea before she asked, or how her mother would laugh at his jokes, even the ones that weren't funny. They had shared a rhythm, an unspoken understanding that she had admired for as long as she could remember.

Now, that rhythm was gone.

"What do we do, Di?" Manav's voice broke into her thoughts. "How do we stop them?"

Tara pulled back slightly, looking into his tear-filled eyes. She didn't have an answer, and the weight of that realization was crushing. But she knew she had to be strong for him, even if she didn't feel strong herself.

"We'll figure it out," she said, her voice firmer now. "We'll talk to them. Together."

Manav nodded hesitantly, his trust in her evident despite his fear.

But as Tara sat there, holding her brother and trying to project a calm she didn't feel, a darker thought crept into her mind. If her parents—her role models—couldn't make their love work, what did that mean for her and Aditya? Was love, no matter how strong, always destined to fade?

She pushed the thought aside, focusing instead on the immediate task at hand. She needed to talk to her parents, to understand what had brought them to this breaking point. And more than that, she needed to remind them of the love they had once shared—the love that had been the foundation of their family.

For now, though, she simply held Manav, drawing strength from the bond they shared. Whatever lay ahead, they would face it together.

...

Meanwhile, across town, Aditya was sitting with Meera at their favorite spot in the local park. The two of them had been best friends since childhood, their bond unbreakable despite

all the changes life had thrown their way. As they sat together, Aditya couldn't help but gush about Tara, his excitement about their future bubbling over.

"I think she's the one," Aditya said with a grin, his eyes bright with happiness. "I mean, I've never felt this way about anyone before. We're planning our future together, Meera. Can you believe it?"

Meera smiled, though her heart ached with every word he said. She had always known that her feelings for Aditya would remain unspoken, tucked away in the quiet corners of her heart. But hearing him talk about Tara—about the life he wanted to build with her—made it all the more real. He was happy, and that was all that mattered to Meera, even if it meant swallowing her own feelings.

"I'm happy for you, Aditya," Meera said softly, her smile genuine despite the lump in her throat. "Tara's lucky to have you."

Aditya laughed, oblivious to the turmoil inside Meera. "I'm lucky to have her. She's incredible. I don't know how I got so lucky."

Meera nodded, her heart breaking a little more with each word. But she had always known that her love for Aditya would remain one-sided, and she had come to terms with it. Their friendship meant more to her than anything else, and she would never let her feelings get in the way of that.

Just then, Shaan appeared, grinning as he approached the two of them. "What are you two lovebirds talking about?"

Aditya rolled his eyes. "Lovebirds? Meera and I? Come on, Shaan."

Meera laughed, grateful for the distraction. "He's right, Shaan. We're best friends, nothing more."

Shaan raised an eyebrow, teasing them. "Sure, sure. But have you ever wondered what it would be like if our kids became best friends, just like us?"

Meera " you people are still kids and you are talking about your kids hahaah. "

Aditya chuckled, leaning back on the bench. "If I have a daughter, I'll name her Meera. After all, you've been there for me since childhood. You always means a lot to me. I know I kinded avoid you because even after I got so wrapped up in Tara, you never left my side. You're special to me, Meera, and I've told Tara that too and she agreed because Tara also knows how much you guys mean to me."

Meera's breath caught in her throat, and for a moment, she couldn't speak. She smiled, blinking back tears. "You don't know how much that means to me." (in head of Tara all memories get rewind write all those memory)

Shaan, sensing the shift in tone, tried to lighten the mood. "Look at me, sitting here like a third wheel. Do I have no value in this friendship anymore?"

Both Aditya and Meera laughed, the tension easing. "Shut up, Shaan," they said in unison, playfully pushing him.

Just then, their other friends, Gaurav and Mita, arrived, joining the conversation with ease. The group spent the rest of the afternoon laughing, teasing each other, and making plans for the future. But even as the laughter filled the air, Meera couldn't shake the feeling that something was shifting—something that would change everything.

....

That evening, after spending the day with friends, Aditya met up with Tara as planned. But as soon as he saw her, he knew something was terribly wrong. Her shoulders sagged under an invisible weight, her face pale and drawn. Her eyes, rimmed with red, told him she had been crying—crying more than he'd ever seen her before.

"Tara," Aditya said, his voice soft yet laced with urgency. "What's going on? What happened?"

Tara lifted her gaze to him, her lips trembling as she tried to form the words. "It's my parents," she finally managed, her voice cracking under the strain. "They're talking about divorce."

The words hung between them, heavy and suffocating, like a dark storm cloud that refused to dissipate.

"I tried to talk to them," Tara continued, her voice trembling as tears welled up again. "I begged them to explain, to think about us—about Manav and me—but they wouldn't listen. They just kept arguing. They don't care how much it's hurting us."

Aditya's heart broke in her pain. He stepped forward and pulled her into his arms, holding her as tightly as he could without saying a word. Her sobs racked her body, each one more anguished than the last.

"I'm so sorry, Tara," he whispered, his voice thick with emotion. "I had no idea... I can't imagine what you're going through."

Tara clung to him, her hands gripping his shirt as though he were the only solid thing in the world that was falling apart. "I don't understand," she whispered through her tears. "They were supposed to be forever. They've always been so in love. They were my example, Aditya—the reason I believed in love. How could they just... throw it all away? How could it all come to this?"

Aditya felt a lump form in his throat. What could he say to her? There were no words that could fix this, no promises he could make that would undo the pain she was feeling. He held her tighter, his heart aching as her sobs echoed in the quiet night.

As the minutes passed, Tara's tears subsided into soft hiccups, but the weight of her words lingered. Aditya had always admired the way she looked at her parents—with a mix of admiration and certainty that love could conquer anything. But now, that certainty had been shattered.

The next morning, as the sun rose over the city, Aditya stood by his packed bag, staring at the train ticket in his hand. Today was supposed to be the day—the day he would leave for the city to chase his dreams of becoming a renowned photographer. This opportunity was everything he had worked for, everything he had dreamed of.

But as his mind drifted back to Tara—her tears, her trembling voice, her fragile state—he felt an overwhelming sense of guilt. How could he leave her like this? How could he focus on his dreams knowing she was breaking apart, struggling to keep her world from crumbling around her?

Without a second thought, Aditya tore the ticket in half. The sharp rip echoed in the silent room, and he tore it again, and again, until the pieces were too small to fit back together. He let the scraps fall from his hands like confetti, watching as they fluttered to the floor.

Tara and Manav needed him. Right now, they are more important than any dream or opportunity.

From the doorway, Manav stood watching, his face a mixture of understanding and worry. He had seen it all—Tara's anguish, Aditya's sacrifice. And though he admired Aditya's selflessness, a gnawing fear took root in his heart.

He could see it in his sister's eyes, even when she tried to hide it. Her parents' crumbling marriage had shaken her to her core, forcing her to question everything she believed about love, trust, and forever. Manav feared she would start doubting her own relationship with Aditya as well.

Would she begin to think that love was temporary, fleeting? Would she pull away from Aditya, convincing herself that their story would end the same way her parents' story was ending? Manav's chest tightened at the thought.

He didn't want to lose his sister to her fears. He didn't want her to lose Aditya, who loved her more than anything. But as he watched the tension build in the house, the shadows growing darker with every passing moment, Manav couldn't shake the feeling that something irreversible was coming.

The house itself seemed to absorb the unease, its walls whispering with memories of love and laughter now overshadowed by arguments and broken trust. And for the first time, Manav felt truly afraid—not just for his family, but for what these cracks in their foundation might do to all of them.

In the days that followed, the air remained thick with dread. Tara wandered the house in a daze, her mind a storm of emotions she couldn't tame. Aditya stayed close, offering comfort whenever she needed it, but even his presence couldn't completely ward off the creeping fear that threatened to consume her.

For Tara, the question that loomed largest in her mind was the one she didn't dare voice aloud: If her parents couldn't make it, what chance did she and Aditya have?

13

Pages of Now

Sameer stood at the station, the cool evening breeze brushing against his face. The weight of the bag on his shoulder felt heavier than usual, but it wasn't the kind of weight that came from exhaustion. It was the kind that came from anticipation, a sense of purpose. This wasn't just another train journey for work or a random escape to shake off boredom. No—this trip was different. It felt like he was chasing something far more meaningful, something that had quietly but powerfully intertwined with his life.

This wasn't just about uncovering Tara and Aditya's story anymore. Somehow, their emotions, struggles, and love had become his own. It was as if their tale had spilled into his heart, pushing him to uncover every fragment of their lives, as though doing so would help him piece together something missing within himself.

As the train whistle blew, Sameer adjusted the strap of his bag and climbed aboard. His heart thudded in his chest, partly from excitement and partly from an inexplicable nervousness. He found his seat by the window and sank into it, placing his bag on the floor beside him. The platform outside buzzed with life—vendors shouting, passengers hurrying, families exchanging goodbyes. He stared out of the window, momentarily lost in the chaos outside, before turning his focus inward.

Unzipping his bag, Sameer pulled out his camera. His fingers traced its edges with a sense of familiarity. It had been his trusted companion for years, capturing moments that others often overlooked. Lately, though, he had been so consumed by Tara and Aditya's story that he'd forgotten what it felt like to see the world through the lens of wonder. Now, on this journey, something stirred within him—a yearning to rediscover that joy.

The train jolted forward, its wheels screeching as it slowly began to leave the station. Sameer raised his camera and looked through the viewfinder. The bustling platform was still visible, filled with strangers living their own lives, each carrying their own stories. He adjusted the focus and clicked, capturing the moment as it faded into the distance.

As the train picked up speed, Sameer shifted his gaze to the world beyond the station. He snapped another photo—a young woman saying goodbye to her family, tears brimming in her eyes. Then another—an elderly couple leaning on each other for support as they walked along the platform. He captured a man reading a book, his brow furrowed in concentration, and a child laughing as she tugged at her father's hand.

Each image spoke to him, carrying the essence of life's quiet, unspoken connections. These were the moments Sameer loved to freeze in time. The raw emotions, the fleeting glimpses of joy, sadness, love, and hope that so many people overlooked in their rush to move forward.

As the train sped into the night, Sameer lowered his camera and smiled softly. This journey wasn't just about solving a mystery or finding answers anymore. It was about feeling life in all its beauty, one snapshot at a time. For the first time in weeks, he felt a sense of peace—a quiet confidence that whatever awaited him at the end of this journey, he was ready to face it.

As the train moved through the countryside, the scenery outside began to change. The bustling cityscape gave way to endless green fields, dotted with tall trees and small, quaint villages. Sameer leaned against the window, feeling a sense of calm settle over him. There was something about watching the world glide by that slowed everything down, making each passing moment feel deeper, more reflective.

At one point, he noticed an elderly man sitting across the aisle. The man gazed out of the window with a serene smile, his expression radiating a quiet peace. He looked like someone who had lived through countless stories, now content to simply watch the world unfold. Intrigued, Sameer instinctively raised his camera and clicked, capturing the man lost in his thoughts.

The soft shutter sound made the man turn his head. His smile grew wider as his eyes met Sameer's. "First time on this route?" he asked in a warm, calm voice.

Sameer lowered his camera and nodded. "Yeah, it's my first time on this journey, at least."

The man chuckled, the sound rich and comforting. "I've taken this train many times. It's special, you know. The places you pass, the people you meet—it always feels like you're discovering something new. Even if you're just passing through."

Sameer smiled, intrigued by the man's words. "What about you? Why do you travel?"

The man, who later introduced himself as Prakash, tilted his head slightly, his smile turning wistful. "I used to be a schoolteacher. Spent most of my life in one town, teaching the same lessons, living the same routine. After I retired, I realized how much of the world I'd never seen. So now I travel. I meet people, listen to their stories, and remind myself how much bigger life is than the little corners we live in."

Sameer found himself nodding, surprised by how much he resonated with the sentiment. "That's what I do too, in a way. I'm a photographer. I try to capture those moments—the ones that tell stories people might not notice otherwise."

Prakash's eyes twinkled as he leaned forward slightly. "Then you're already doing something special, young man. But let me tell you something. Sometimes the most important stories aren't the ones we're looking for—they're the ones that find us."

Sameer let the words sink in as the train chugged along its journey. Every face he saw, every stretch of land that rolled past the window, suddenly felt like a story waiting to unfold. With his camera in hand and Prakash's words in his heart, he knew this journey was only just beginning.

....

Later in the afternoon, the train made a stop at a small, quiet station. Sameer stepped off, eager to stretch his legs and breathe in the fresh air. The platform was peaceful, with only a handful of passengers milling about. The aroma of freshly brewed chai wafted through the air, drawing Sameer's attention to a small tea stall.

He walked over, bought a cup of chai, and leaned against a nearby post, sipping the warm, fragrant tea. As he stood there, the steam curling up from the cup, his thoughts began to drift.

"Why does this feel so complicated?" he muttered to himself, staring at the distant horizon. He wasn't just chasing a story anymore; he was tangled in something much deeper. The mystery of Tara and Aditya wasn't just about uncovering their past—it had become a reflection of his own questions about love, destiny, and the paths people choose.

Taking another sip, Sameer let his mind wander. "Why do we always think the answers will fix everything?" he mused, watching a pair of birds fly off into the open sky. "Maybe... it's not about the answers at all. Maybe it's just about understanding the journey."

The thought hung in the air, and for a moment, Sameer felt a strange sense of peace. He had been so focused on finding every missing piece of the puzzle that he hadn't paused to appreciate the beauty of the process itself—the train rides, the strangers he met, the emotions that stirred within him.

As the train whistle blew, signaling it was time to leave, Sameer took one last sip of his chai, savoring its warmth. He tossed the empty cup into a nearby bin and walked back to his compartment, his thoughts quieter now, but no less profound.

Settling into his seat, he gazed out the window as the train pulled away from the station. The world outside moved again, but inside, Sameer felt the motion slow. Perhaps, he thought, the tea seller's words—or rather, his own musings—were right. Sometimes, the answers didn't matter as much as the journey to find them.

.....

As the train rolled closer to his destination, Sameer felt a growing sense of anticipation. The letters from Tara had haunted him for weeks, and now, he was finally going to meet the woman who had written them. What would she be like? Would she be the same Tara whose love for Aditya had spilled across the pages, or had time and life changed her into someone different? He reached into his bag and pulled out the final letter—the one that had struck him the hardest. It was Tara's goodbye to Aditya, a letter filled with love but also with a deep, heartbreaking sadness.

"Dear Aditya,"

This is the hardest thing I've ever had to do. By the time you read this, I'll be gone. I don't know if I have the right words to explain why I'm leaving, or if they even exist. My heart feels like it's breaking into a million pieces, but somehow, I know this is what I need to do.

Aditya, I love you. I love you in ways I didn't even know were possible. You have been my calm in chaos, my light in the darkest moments, and my safe place when the world felt too much. Loving you has been the most beautiful part of my life, and it terrifies me to walk away from that. But something inside me is telling me I must.

I don't think love is supposed to feel this way. This scared me. This heavy. I thought it was simple—something that would just work if it was real. But love is more than just two people wanting to be together, isn't it? It's messy. It's fragile. And sometimes, it demands things of us that we're not ready to give.

I've tried to fight this fear, Aditya. I've tried to push it down, to ignore it, to tell myself that if I love you enough, everything will be okay. But it's still there, whispering in the back of my mind, telling me that I'm not enough for you. That I'll hold you back. That the beautiful thing we have will eventually turn into something that hurts us both.

I've spent sleepless nights trying to understand why I feel this way. Is it because of my parents? Because I've seen what love can do when it breaks apart? Or is it something broken inside me, something I can't fix no matter how much I want to? I don't know, Aditya. I wish I did.

All I know is that I can't stay. Not like this. I don't want to be the reason you stop chasing your dreams, the weight that pulls you down when you should be flying. I can't bear the thought of us becoming strangers someday, or worse—two people who resent what we once had. I'd rather leave now, while everything between us is still beautiful and pure, than risk watching it crumble under the weight of my fears.

Please don't think this is your fault. You are everything good, everything right in this world. You deserve someone who can love you without hesitation, without doubts, without the fears that I carry. You deserve a love that feels like freedom, not like chains.

I will always carry you with me, Aditya. Every smile, every laugh, every moment we shared—it's etched into my heart, and it always will be. Even as I say goodbye, I know I will love you for the rest of my life. But sometimes, love means knowing when to let go, even when it hurts more than anything.

Goodbye, Aditya. Please be happy. Please chase your dreams. Please find someone who can give you the love you deserve.

With all my heart,

Tara.

Sameer carefully folded the letter, his heart heavy with the emotions Tara had poured into her words. He tried to imagine what it must have been like for her—to love someone so deeply yet believe that the only way to protect that love was to walk away. It was a kind of pain he couldn't fully grasp, but her words made him feel as if he was carrying a piece of it himself.

The train slowed as it approached the final station, the wheels screeching softly against the rails. Sameer gathered his belongings, his thoughts racing. What lay ahead of him? What would he find when he rang the bell at Tara's house? Would she have answers that tied everything together, or would he leave with even more questions swirling in his mind?

As he stepped off the train, the cool evening air brushed against his skin, bringing with it a mix of calm and anticipation. The small town stretched out before him, bathed in the warm, golden light of the setting sun. It felt peaceful, almost timeless, with cobblestone streets winding between houses that looked as though they had been plucked from a forgotten era.

The streets were quiet, lined with trees whose leaves rustled softly in the breeze. The houses looked quaint and lived-in, their gardens bursting with colors—roses, lilies, and marigolds in full bloom. Vines of ivy climbed gracefully up the stone walls, giving the town a serene, storybook charm.

Following the directions Shaan had given him, Sameer walked through the narrow lanes, his steps quick but uncertain. His heart pounded harder with every turn, the weight of anticipation growing heavier with each passing moment. Finally, he found himself standing in front of the house.

It was an old, charming home with a small white gate and a narrow path lined with bright marigolds leading to the front door. The windows glowed faintly with the light of the setting sun, and the air carried the faint, sweet scent of flowers.

Sameer hesitated, his hand hovering over the doorbell. He stood there for a moment, his breath catching as he thought of everything that had led him to this point. The letters, the stories, the faces he had imagined—all of it had brought him here. Taking a deep breath, he steadied himself and pressed the doorbell.

The sound of the doorbell echoed softly, and after a few moments, the door opened with a gentle creak. Standing there was a young girl, probably around sixteen years old, with curious eyes and a bright, friendly smile.

"Hi," Sameer said, suddenly feeling unsure of himself. "I'm looking for... I'm Sameer. Is Tara here?"

The girl's smile widened. "Hi, Sameer. I'm Meera."

Sameer froze for a moment, his heart skipping a beat. Meera. Hearing that name here, in this house, felt like a twist he hadn't seen coming.

"Come on in," Meera said warmly, stepping aside and pointing toward the garden. "You can wait there while I call my mom."

Sameer nodded and followed her outside. The garden was beautiful, full of life and color. Bright flowers swayed gently in the breeze, tall trees provided cool shade, and a small fountain trickled softly in the corner. The peacefulness of the place made Sameer feel as if he had stepped into a different world.

He sat on a wooden bench under a blooming tree, but his mind was far from calm. Thoughts raced through his head, each one raising more questions than the last. If Tara had a daughter named Meera, did that mean she had moved on? Had she found someone else to share her life with? Or... had she married Aditya after all?

And if Tara and Aditya had been together, then why were there letters filled with such pain and longing? What had happened between them?

The story in his mind, the great love story he had imagined, was becoming more confusing with every moment. Maybe this wasn't the love story he thought it was. Maybe it was something entirely different.

Lost in his thoughts, Sameer didn't notice the soft sound of footsteps behind him.

"Excuse me?"

The gentle voice pulled him from his thoughts. He turned quickly, and his heart skipped a beat.

Standing there, just a few feet away, was Tara.

.....

Tara stood in front of Sameer, and although she had aged, her beauty was still powerful. Her hair, now touched with gray, seemed even more beautiful, like silver threads woven into her life's story. It was as if every strand carried a memory, showing the years, she had lived, filled with both joy and hardship.

Her face, with lines that came with time, looked softer, calmer, and wiser. The wrinkles around her eyes didn't take away from her beauty; instead, they made her seem peaceful, as if she had experienced and understood life deeply. She was not just older, but more graceful, as if the passage of time had only made her more serene.

Her eyes, though they showed signs of age, still held warmth and kindness. When they met Sameer's, there was a deep connection between them, as though all the years had vanished for a moment. They were eyes that had seen love, pain, and life, but still held a quiet hope.

She wore a red dupatta that was old and worn, but it added to her beauty. The bright color stood out against the calm surroundings. The fabric of the dupatta, although soft from age, seemed to carry memories of her past—of love and moments that she had cherished, even if those times had faded over the years.

In her old age, Tara was still beautiful, but it was a different kind of beauty. It came not just from her looks but from her strength and her gentle spirit. Sameer felt as though he was in the presence of something truly special, something that had lasted through time. Tara's beauty was not only in how she looked but in how she had lived, loved, and grown, and it shone through in everything about her.

For a moment, neither of them spoke, the air heavy with unspoken words. Tara stood there, her eyes welling up with tears that she tried to keep hidden, blinking rapidly to keep them from falling. Sameer, too, felt his heart ache as he watched her, feeling an unexpected rush of emotions. He had traveled so far, seeking answers, but this moment—this raw, emotional encounter—was something entirely different. It felt like the weight of everything that had happened, everything that was still unsaid, was pressing down on them both.

Tara's voice, when it came, was soft and trembling, full of emotion. "You look... so much like him."

Sameer's chest tightened at the words, a feeling of confusion clouding his mind. "Like who?" he asked, not understanding.

Tara didn't immediately answer. She blinked, and a tear escaped down her cheek, which she quickly wiped away, but it seemed to only make the sadness in her eyes more evident. "Aditya," she whispered, her voice barely audible.

The mention of Aditya's name was like a sharp blow to Sameer's chest. It was as if the world around him paused, and all the questions he had been carrying—questions about Tara, about love, about the letters—suddenly became much more real, much more intense. Tara wasn't just a woman who had written letters; she was someone who had lived a life tied deeply to Aditya, and now Sameer was standing in the middle of that past, feeling the enormity of the connection.

"I... I don't understand," Sameer stammered, his mind struggling to piece everything together. "Why did you—"

But Tara shook her head gently, her expression soft yet filled with sorrow. She raised a hand as if to ask for silence, and her voice broke through the air, filled with years of unspoken grief. "I'll tell you everything," she said, her words weighed with the kind of history Sameer could only begin to grasp. "But first... I need a moment."

Sameer's heart raced as he nodded, sitting back down on the bench. He could feel the tension in the air, the space between them thick with emotions that neither of them knew how to express. Tara slowly turned, her movements slow and deliberate, as though she were carrying the weight of all her past with her. She walked towards the edge of the garden, her steps quiet on the grass, and stood there for a moment, her hands gripping the railing.

She didn't look at Sameer as she stared out at the garden, her gaze lost in the sea of flowers, as if she were searching for something in the distance—something or someone long gone. For a moment, Sameer could almost see it: the way her eyes softened, the way her lips parted in a silent whisper of a name—Aditya. It was as if, for those few seconds, Tara was no longer standing before him. She had drifted back in time, to a place where Aditya was alive in her heart, where their love had once been all-encompassing and perfect. He could feel her longing for him, as if Aditya was still out there, still waiting for her in some far-off memory.

Sameer watched her, his heart aching with a mixture of empathy and confusion. He knew that there was more to this story than he had anticipated. The pain Tara carried was not just the pain of leaving Aditya—it was the kind of ache that had lived inside her for years, a constant companion that had never truly left. Sameer's chest tightened as he realized how much Aditya had meant to her, how deep their love had been, and how much of it had remained unresolved.

The quiet stretched on, filled with the weight of memories, of things left unsaid, of hearts that had loved and lost. Sameer couldn't interrupt her now. He couldn't rush her. He could only wait, as she had asked, for Tara to find the words that had been locked inside her for so long.

And in that silence, Tara seemed to be looking for the strength to finally share everything she had kept buried. It wasn't just a story of love and heartbreak—it was the story of a woman who had lived through the impossible, who had tried to hold onto love that had slipped through her fingers, and who had made decisions that had haunted her ever since.

14
Pages of Before

The day Tara's parents told her and Manav about their divorce felt like a moment suspended in time, one that would stay with her forever. It was as if the world she had always known was being shattered in front of her, and she couldn't find a way to stop it. Tara sat on the edge of the sofa, her eyes fixed on her parents, her heart pounding in her chest. The living room, which had once been filled with laughter and warmth, now felt cold, distant. The walls seemed to close in on her, amplifying the silence between her family.

Her father, who had always been her rock, now seemed small. His usually confident demeanor was gone, replaced by an exhaustion she had never seen before. His shoulders slumped, and his hands trembled slightly as he spoke, as if each word was dragging him further into a space he couldn't escape. "We've tried everything," he said, his voice low and heavy with regret. "But... it's better this way. For all of us."

Tara felt like the ground beneath her was slipping away, as if the earth itself was crumbling under the weight of her parents' words. How could this be happening? She had always believed in the idea of family, the idea that no matter what, they would stick together. But now, that belief was being torn apart. The arguments she had overheard, the occasional distance between them—it all suddenly made sense. But she never imagined it would come to this, that her parents would actually say the words that broke everything.

Beside her, Manav, only three years younger but already wise beyond his years, sat rigid. His hands were clenched so tightly that Tara could see the white knuckles. His usually carefree face was now pale, his lips pressed tightly together in a line. He wasn't the one who usually showed fear, or confusion, but now, he looked lost. Tara could almost feel his heart racing, echoing her own.

Their mother's voice cut through the thick silence, soft but filled with sorrow. "We don't want to force you into anything," she said, her eyes glistening with unshed tears. "You... you both have a choice. You can decide who you want to live with. But whatever you choose, we'll make sure you're cared for."

The words hung in the air like a cruel joke. A choice? How could they ask her to choose between the two people she loved most in the world? How could they expect her to split her heart in half, to pick one over the other? It felt impossible, unfair—like a punishment she didn't deserve. And what about Manav? He was still a child, trying to make sense of the world. How could he possibly carry the weight of this decision?

Tara's throat tightened, and she opened her mouth to say something, but no words came out. Her hands reached out instinctively, and she grasped Manav's hand in hers. He squeezed it back, his grip tight, his fingers cold. It was as though he was holding onto her for dear life, as if their hands could somehow make everything okay.

Manav was the first to break the silence, his voice barely more than a whisper. "We don't want to choose."

Their parents exchanged glances, their faces showing surprise and a hint of relief. They had expected tears, anger, maybe shouting—but not this. Not this quiet defiance, this refusal to pick a side. Tara felt a mixture of guilt and strength flood her chest. She wasn't sure how this would work—how they would manage to divide their lives between two homes, two hearts—but she knew she couldn't betray either of them. She wouldn't.

Tara found her voice, though it shook with emotion. "We can't choose between you. We... we won't."

Her father sighed deeply, his eyes weary. He rubbed his temples as if the weight of the decision was taking everything from him. "We understand, Tara," he said softly, his voice distant. "But things are going to change. You'll have to split your time between us."

Her mother nodded, tears streaming down her face now, but she said nothing more. Tara's heart sank as the reality of their words set in. This wasn't just a bad dream; this was real, and she had to face it. How would she manage? How would they all survive this? Tara didn't have the answers, but she knew she couldn't let her family fall apart completely.

As her father's words echoed in the room, Tara felt the immense responsibility that had just been placed on her shoulders. She was no longer just a daughter; she was someone who had to protect Manav, hold the family together, and try to be strong when she felt like everything was falling apart. And yet, as she sat there, she could feel a small flicker of something inside her—something that whispered she would find a way, even if it took everything she had.

The days ahead would be hard. They would be filled with moments of confusion, sadness, and uncertainty. But Tara made a vow at that moment, sitting beside her brother, holding his hand. She would not let this decision break them. They would face it together. She would find a way to hold her family up, even if she didn't know how yet. The cracks might be there, but she would try to glue them back together, one small piece at a time.

In the days that followed, Tara's life took on a new rhythm, one that revolved around keeping Manav safe from the pain they both felt but could never quite name. He was young—too young to understand the complexities of what had happened—and his world had shattered in a way that no child should ever have to experience. Tara became his shield, the one who absorbed the brunt of the emotional fallout. Every moment she wasn't with him felt like she was abandoning him to his own confusion and anger.

Their home, once a place of laughter and comfort, now felt like a series of disconnected spaces. When they stayed with their mother, the house was quiet—too quiet—almost as if the very walls had absorbed the sadness that hung heavy in the air. It lacked the warmth it once had, the vibrant energy that Tara had grown accustomed to. It was just... stillness, with an undercurrent of grief that she couldn't escape, no matter how hard she tried.

The days with their father weren't much better. He tried to keep the mood light, cracking jokes, making attempts at normalcy, but there was a sadness in his eyes that Tara could never ignore. He was broken, too, in his own way, and Tara could see it in the way his shoulders sagged as he tried to act cheerful for their sake. But his efforts only highlighted the cracks in the family, the gaping emptiness that no amount of pretending could fill.

Tara felt like a stranger in both homes, constantly adjusting to a new rhythm, trying to balance the emotions of both parents, all while desperately trying to keep her own emotions in check. But she couldn't help but feel that she was slowly losing herself, that she was becoming someone she didn't recognize. She had to be strong, for Manav, for their parents, for everyone else. But where was her own strength supposed to come from when she felt like she was sinking beneath the weight of it all?

Manav, in his confusion, withdrew deeper into himself. He didn't want to talk about their parents, didn't want to acknowledge that their lives had changed in a way that couldn't be undone. Instead, he became a shell of the bright, energetic boy Tara once knew. He would retreat into his room, his door closed tightly, shutting her out from the world he was trying to escape. He'd stare blankly at his homework or scribble violently in his notebook, his thoughts spilling out in angry, messy words. It was as though he was trying to write away the hurt, to somehow make it all disappear.

Tara would sit beside him, always calm, always patient, even when her own heart ached to see him like this. She'd gently try to coax him out of his shell, to talk, to share his feelings, but Manav had built a wall that was nearly impenetrable. He didn't want her pity, didn't want her sympathy—he just wanted everything to go back to how it had been. And every time Tara tried to reach him, to help him understand that things would be okay in time, it felt like she was speaking to someone who couldn't hear her, someone too far gone in their own pain to see the love she was offering.

It broke Tara's heart to see her brother like this. He was so lost, so angry, and Tara wasn't sure how to bring him back from the edge. She was his protector, his safe place, and yet, for the first time in her life, she felt powerless. There was no magic solution to make things better, no easy way to fix the wreckage their parents' divorce had caused. It was a slow, painful process, one that she couldn't control.

But despite the darkness that hung over them, Tara knew she couldn't give up on him. She had to keep trying, even when every attempt to break through his walls seemed futile. She couldn't let him slip away into the anger and confusion that threatened to consume him.

So she kept fighting—fighting for him, fighting for herself, and fighting for the family she still believed could be healed, even if it seemed impossible. Every tear, every sleepless night, every painful conversation—it all became a small step in the journey of trying to make things right again. And though she couldn't see it yet, Tara believed that somehow, some way, things would eventually fall into place. She just had to hold on long enough to see it through.

Aditya became her rock during this time, always there when she needed someone to lean on. He didn't try to fix things—he knew that wasn't possible. Instead, he simply sat with her, listened to her, and held her when she needed to cry. His presence was a quiet reassurance that she wasn't facing this storm alone.

They spent hours together, often in silence, their bond deepening in those moments when words weren't necessary. Tara found solace in Aditya's company; in the way he made her feel safe even when everything else felt uncertain. He never pressured her to talk about her parents or the divorce unless she wanted to. Instead, he provided her with the space to breathe, to feel, without the weight of expectations.

On days when Manav's anger threatened to boil over, Aditya would be there, offering a calm presence that helped to ground Tara. Sometimes, he'd bring along his camera, and they would walk through the park, Aditya snapping photos while Tara simply existed beside him, grateful for the escape.

While Tara found strength in Aditya during one of the most difficult times of her life, Aditya too sought comfort in his best friend, Meera. Their friendship was a long-standing one, forged through years of shared memories, laughter, and deep trust. Meera was the one Aditya could always turn to, no matter what was happening in his life. Whether it was about his fears, his hopes, or, more recently, his growing feelings for Tara, Meera was there to listen without judgment. She had been his confidante since childhood, and in the midst of the emotional turmoil surrounding Tara and the changes in their lives, Meera's steady presence was a constant source of reassurance for Aditya.

But while Aditya's heart brimmed with love for Tara, Meera's heart quietly ached in the background. It was a pain she had carried for as long as she could remember—the quiet, unspoken love she felt for Aditya. This love wasn't loud or demanding, and it wasn't the kind that expected anything in return. It was simply a part of who Meera was, woven into the fabric of her being. She had never voiced it, never allowed it to interrupt their friendship, but it lingered in the quiet corners of her heart, a silent companion she learned to live with.

Even with the pain of her unspoken love, Meera never let it come between her and Aditya. She supported him wholeheartedly, listening to him talk about Tara with a genuine smile, her heart sometimes tightening in response. She was truly happy for him—she wanted nothing more than for him to find happiness, to find someone who could make him feel as alive and loved as Tara did. But there were nights when the world was quieter, and the weight of everything seemed heavier, when the loneliness crept into Meera's heart. It was in these moments, when she was alone with her thoughts, that she couldn't help but wonder what might have been if things had unfolded differently—if her love had been returned, if Aditya had ever seen her in the same way she had always seen him.

Shaan, their ever-loyal friend, saw the quiet pain in Meera's eyes, even though she never spoke of it. Shaan knew her better than anyone else—he understood the subtle ways she hid her emotions, the way her gaze softened whenever Aditya was near, and how her smile would falter just a little when he spoke of Tara. But despite recognizing the sadness in her, Shaan never pushed Meera to confront it. He respected her silence, understanding that sometimes, people need space to carry their burdens in their own way. Instead, Shaan was simply there for her, just as she had always been there for everyone else. He offered his presence, his quiet understanding, knowing that Meera, in her own time, would find a way to navigate the quiet ache in her heart.

One evening, as Aditya and Shaan walked through the park, the evening sun casting long shadows on the path before them, Shaan couldn't help but notice how tense Aditya had become. The weight of his thoughts seemed to press down on him more than usual, and Shaan had known him long enough to understand that something was troubling his best friend.

"You're quiet today," Shaan said, nudging Aditya's shoulder playfully. "What's going on? You've been distant lately."

Aditya glanced at Shaan, his mind swirling with conflicting thoughts. He took a deep breath, trying to find the right words. "I've been thinking about the photography opportunity," he said, his voice a little hesitant. "It's the break I've been waiting for, you know? A chance to go professional, to really make something of this."

Shaan nodded, sensing the internal struggle in Aditya's voice. Photography had always been Aditya's dream, and this opportunity—an internship with a top photography firm—was a dream come true. Everyone around him, including Shaan, had been encouraging him to seize it. It was his moment, and Shaan had no doubt that Aditya had the talent to make it big.

"So, what's holding you back?" Shaan asked, knowing full well that Aditya wasn't the type to second-guess himself unless something deeper was going on.

Aditya paused, glancing at the ground as they walked. His mind drifted to Tara, and he felt a wave of concern wash over him. "It's Tara," he finally said, his voice quieter now. "She needs me right now, Shaan. More than anything. With everything going on at home, I can't just leave her."

Shaan stopped walking, his brow furrowed in confusion. "But Aditya, this is *your* chance. You've worked so hard for this. Photography is everything you've dreamed about. Tara would never want you to give up on your career for her. You know that."

Aditya's gaze turned inward, and for a moment, he looked like a man torn between two worlds. "I know, Shaan. But right now, Tara's struggling more than anyone realizes. She's keeping it all together for her brother, for her family, but I can see it. She's falling apart. I don't know how much longer she can hold it together. And I—" he stopped himself, the weight of his words sinking in. "I can't leave her when she needs me the most."

Shaan stood there for a moment, studying Aditya, understanding the depth of his friend's loyalty and love for Tara. He had always admired Aditya's selflessness, but this was different. This was a choice that would affect the course of Aditya's life, and Shaan knew it wasn't easy for him.

"Look," Shaan said, his voice softening, "I get it. Tara means the world to you. But you've got to think about yourself too. You've spent so many years dreaming of this career. If you don't take this opportunity, you might regret it. It's not about leaving Tara behind—it's about doing what's best for you, for your future."

Aditya met Shaan's eyes, his resolve firm despite the conflict within him. "I know what you're saying, Shaan. But I can't be the person who's not there for her when she needs me the most. I've already been letting her down for too long. I can't do that anymore. I have to stay."

Shaan's face softened as he nodded slowly, understanding the choice Aditya had made. "I know, man. I just want what's best for you. But I know you'll figure it out. Tara's lucky to have someone like you in her corner."

Aditya gave a small, grateful smile, though there was a heaviness in his heart. "I hope I'm doing the right thing."

Shaan clapped him on the back. "You always do."

Aditya's voice was firm, though the weight of his words made his heart ache. "Tara's already lost so much, Shaan," he said, his eyes meeting his friend's with a quiet intensity. "Her family, her sense of stability, everything she thought she knew about love. She's holding it all together, but I can see it—she's on the edge, and I can't just walk away from her now. She's already lost enough, and I won't be the one who leaves her behind."

Shaan looked at Aditya, sensing the deep conviction in his friend's words. He had always known how much Tara meant to Aditya, but hearing it like this, seeing the pain in his eyes, made him realize just how much weight Aditya was carrying.

"I get it," Shaan said softly, the frustration in his voice giving way to understanding. "But you've got to take care of yourself too, man. If you don't follow your dreams, it'll eat away at you. Tara would never want that for you. You deserve this, Aditya."

Aditya shook his head slightly, his resolve unwavering. "I know, Shaan. But this moment right here—Tara needs me more than anything. I'm not leaving her, not now. Not after everything she's been through."

Shaan didn't respond immediately, allowing the silence to settle between them. He could see how torn Aditya was, but there was no changing his mind. And despite everything, Shaan respected his decision.

"You're doing what feels right to you," Shaan finally said, his voice low but supportive. "And I can't fault you for that."

Aditya gave a small nod, grateful for Shaan's understanding. "Thanks, man." He sighed deeply, his thoughts drifting back to Tara, the weight of his choice settling in his chest. "I just hope I'm not making a mistake."

....

It had been a few weeks since Mita and Gaurav had left, and life in their circle had slowly returned to a kind of normalcy. But for

Shaan, something felt different. He had been paying close attention to Meera, noticing that she wasn't her usual self. Meera had always been the one who brought energy into the room. She was the type of person who could light up a space with her laughter, the one who made everything feel like an adventure, even on the dullest days. She was full of life, always the first to come up with spontaneous plans and to share a funny story that would make everyone smile.

But lately, Shaan had noticed a subtle shift in her. She was quieter than usual, more withdrawn. Where once her eyes had sparkled with excitement, they now seemed distant, as if she were somewhere far away, lost in her own thoughts. Her usual enthusiasm was replaced by an eerie calm. She had stopped reaching out for group activities or suggesting things to do. When they would all hang out, Meera would sit at the edge, her thoughts seemingly elsewhere. Shaan didn't want to believe it at first, thinking that maybe she was just going through something personal or perhaps needed space to adjust to the changes in their friend group, especially with Aditya and Tara's growing relationship.

But one evening, everything became clearer. Shaan was walking through the park, trying to clear his head after a busy day. As he passed by a quiet corner near the fountain, he spotted Meera sitting alone on a bench. At first, he thought she was just resting, but then he saw it—her hands were trembling slightly as she clutched a small piece of paper in her lap. Her face was turned down, and though the light from the streetlamps softly illuminated her features, it couldn't hide the tears that streamed down her face. Meera, the girl who was always so full of life and strength, was crying—alone, in silence.

Shaan's heart sank as he approached her, unsure of what to say or how to comfort her. He stopped a few steps away, not wanting to startle her, but also unable to just walk away. He had seen her vulnerable before, but this felt different. This was something deep, something Shaan hadn't been able to understand before now. The paper in her hand, the tears on her cheeks, they all spoke volumes that he hadn't been ready to hear. Something was hurting her, something she hadn't shared with anyone—not even with him, her closest friend.

He stood there for a long moment, unsure if he should speak or just wait for her to notice him. The silence between them stretched out, thick and heavy, filled with unspoken words. Finally, Meera looked up, her eyes meeting his, and in that moment, Shaan knew something had changed forever.

Shaan approached quietly, his heart pounding as he saw the pain clearly etched across Meera's features. She sat there, alone in the dim light, her shoulders hunched, as though the weight of something unbearable was pressing down on her. Without a word, he sat beside her, careful not to interrupt the silence. He wasn't sure what to say, but he didn't need to. He just wanted her to know that he was there, that she wasn't alone in this moment of hurt.

Meera wiped her eyes quickly, almost ashamed, and her voice came out as a soft whisper, barely audible. "I didn't want anyone to know."

Shaan frowned, looking at the piece of paper she held in her hands, her fingers gripping it tightly, as though it might slip away if she wasn't careful. He glanced back at her, his concern growing. "What is it, Meera? What's going on?"

She hesitated for a long moment, her breath catching in her throat, before she slowly handed him the paper. Shaan unfolded it with gentle fingers, his heart sinking as he read the words written there. The paper felt heavier than it should have, and the reality of what it said hit him hard—like a punch to the gut that left him gasping for breath.

Meera was sick. And not just sick, but seriously, devastatingly sick. The doctors had given her a diagnosis—an illness that would shorten her life, leaving her with only few years at most to live. The words blurred before his eyes, but the meaning was clear. Meera had known for some time now, and instead of turning to her friends, instead of sharing this heavy burden, she had kept it to herself. She didn't want anyone to carry her pain with her.

Meera's voice trembled as she spoke softly, "I just... I wanted to keep things normal for as long as I could."

Shaan felt his throat tighten, a lump forming that made it hard to swallow. His eyes burned with unshed tears as he looked at her, struggling to find the right words. "Meera, why didn't you tell us?"

Her eyes were downcast, her hands wringing the edges of the paper. "I didn't want anyone to feel sorry for me," she said, her voice barely a whisper. "Especially not Aditya. He's so happy right now... with Tara. They've got so much going on between them. I didn't want to ruin that."

Shaan's heart broke for her. He couldn't imagine the weight she had been carrying alone, how much strength it must have taken to keep it all inside. Without thinking, he reached out and pulled her into a tight hug, holding her close as her tears soaked into his shirt. There were no words that could fix this, no magic phrase that could make it better. But in that moment, he made a promise to her—to be the friend she needed, no matter what.

"I'm scared," Meera whispered, her voice shaking with the rawness of her emotion. "The doctor said they can't really say how long I've got. It could be five months or five years, but... I just need to take care of things. I don't want to go. Not yet."

Shaan closed his eyes, holding her even tighter, as though he could shield her from the fear and the pain that threatened to overwhelm her. "You're not going anywhere, Meera. Not for a long time. And whatever happens, we'll face it together. You're not alone in this."

The two of them sat there in the fading light of the evening, the weight of Meera's secret heavy between them. It was a quiet moment, filled with the unspoken understanding that things would never be the same. But in that moment, Shaan knew one thing for sure—he would be there for her. He wouldn't let her face this fight alone, not now, not ever.

15
Pages of Before

Tara sat by the window, staring blankly at the rain that had begun to pour outside. It had been one of those days where everything felt too heavy to carry—too much weight, too much emotion, too many thoughts swirling around her mind, making her feel like she was sinking deeper and deeper into herself. She had never thought that she could feel this lost, but today, with the way things were unraveling, she was truly uncertain of where she was headed.

Her parents' divorce had shattered something inside her—a belief, a hope, a dream that she had held on to for as long as she could remember. She had always believed in love. Love was supposed to be the force that held everything together. It was supposed to be the reason you stayed, even when life got tough. It was supposed to carry you through the darkest days and the brightest ones. Love was supposed to be enough.

But now, sitting alone in the quiet of her room, listening to the gentle patter of raindrops, she couldn't help but feel that love had failed her parents. It hadn't been enough to save them. It hadn't been enough to hold them together when things started falling apart. And now, the most devastating truth of all settled deep into her heart—if love wasn't enough for them, then how could it possibly be enough for her and Aditya?

She had always believed that she and Aditya were different—that their love was something unique, something special.

She had believed in their future, in their dreams together. But now, she wasn't so sure. Every time she thought about the life she wanted to build with him, she couldn't shake the image of her parents, who had once been as deeply in love as she and Aditya were. Yet, even with all the love they had for each other, they couldn't make it work.

The thought of ending up like them—broken and lost—terrified her. She couldn't bear the thought of being in the same place as they were, especially not with Aditya. She loved him too much to put him through the same pain. She loved him too much to risk destroying everything for him, just as her parents had done.

Tara heard the faint sound of footsteps approaching her room. Her younger brother, Manav, had been quietly observing her for weeks. He had seen the way she had withdrawn from everything, even from Aditya, though he knew that deep down, her feelings for him hadn't changed. He could see it in her eyes—there was something broken inside her, something that she wasn't allowing herself to confront. But Manav was determined to make her face it. He couldn't stand seeing her this way, so lost and afraid.

"Tara," he called softly, knocking once before opening the door to find her sitting by the window, staring into the rain.

She didn't turn around. She couldn't.

"Don't shut yourself off like this," Manav said, his voice gentle but firm as he approached her. "You can't push everyone away just because Mom and Dad couldn't make it work."

Tara's body stiffened at his words, and for a moment, she didn't know how to respond. She wanted to tell him how much it hurt to watch her parents fall apart, how much it hurt to feel like love wasn't enough. But she couldn't bring herself to say it. The tears were already threatening to spill, and she wasn't sure if she could hold them back much longer.

"Love isn't enough, Manav," she whispered, her voice barely audible. "It wasn't enough for them. It won't be enough for me and Aditya either."

Manav's eyes widened in shock. He had never heard her speak like this before. Tara had always been the strong one, the one who believed in love's power to heal, to fix, to endure. To hear her speak with such resignation in her voice broke his heart. But he couldn't just stand there and let her believe that love wasn't worth fighting for. He couldn't let her throw away the one thing that had always been her strength.

"That's not true," he argued fiercely, kneeling down beside her. "You and Aditya are different. You're not like Mom and Dad. Their problems were their own. They made their choices. But you and Aditya... you're stronger than that."

Tara shook her head slowly, her heart aching with the weight of her own fear. "I used to think that," she whispered, "but now... I don't know anymore. Look at what happened to them, Manav. They had it all—love, a family, everything. But in the end, it wasn't enough. I don't want to end up like that. I don't want to hurt him."

Manav didn't know how to help her. He could see that she was in deep pain, a pain that ran much deeper than just the divorce. This was about something fundamental—a fear that she couldn't quite articulate but that she felt in her bones. She was scared, terrified, that the love she had with Aditya would end in the same way as her parents'. That one day, despite everything, they would fall apart, and it would leave her shattered.

He reached out and gently took her hand, squeezing it in a way that was meant to comfort her. "Tara, you can't think like that. You and Aditya are not your parents. Your love isn't like theirs. You've fought for each other, you've been through so much together. You've already shown that your love is worth it."

Tara squeezed her eyes shut, trying to push the tears back. But it was no use. The floodgates had opened, and she let them fall freely. "I don't want to risk it, Manav. I don't want to risk hurting him. I love him too much to let him down, and if I stay with him, I'm just going to hurt him in the end. I can't be the reason he ends up like them."

She pulled her hand away from his gently, her fingers trembling with the weight of the decision she had already made in her heart.

Manav watched her, his heart breaking at the sight of his older sister so vulnerable, so lost. He knew that she was scared—that the idea of loving Aditya for the rest of her life and then watching it slip away in a way she couldn't control was more than she could bear. But he also knew that Tara's decision wasn't just about her fear. It was about protecting Aditya, about protecting herself from the pain that she was convinced would come. She didn't want to give everything to someone and lose it all in the end.

"You can't make that decision for him, Tara," Manav said softly, his voice filled with urgency. "You can't just walk away because you're scared of what might happen. That's not fair to you, and it's not fair to him. He deserves a chance, just like you do. You have to trust in your love, trust that it's strong enough to face whatever comes your way."

But Tara's resolve had already hardened. She loved Aditya more than anything, but she wasn't willing to put him through what her parents had gone through. She wasn't willing to be the one who pulled him into a future full of uncertainty, pain, and heartache. She didn't want to be the reason his life wasn't everything he had hoped for.

"I love him, Manav," Tara said softly, tears still streaking down her face. "But I can't let him love me. Not like this. Not if it's going to end like them."

Manav sat there, unsure of what to say. He wanted to fix it, to make everything better for her, but he knew that wasn't possible. Sometimes, the hardest battles were the ones we fought inside ourselves, and Tara was fighting one of the hardest battles of all.

The silence between them grew thick, heavy with the weight of everything unsaid. Manav could see the love Tara had for Aditya, but he also saw the fear that was consuming her. She was so afraid of losing him that she was willing to walk away to prevent it from happening. And that, Manav knew, was the most painful kind of love—one that was too afraid to fight for itself.

In that moment, Tara made her decision. She would never marry anyone. Not even Aditya. No matter how deeply she loved him, she couldn't risk it. She couldn't face the possibility of love failing her again.

And so, she resolved to pull away. She would keep her heart guarded, shielded from the love that she had once believed would save her. She would never allow herself to love again—not with the same abandon, not with the same hope that had once made her believe in happily ever after.

As the rain continued to fall outside, Tara sat alone with her decision, knowing deep down that it was the right one—though the ache in her heart told her otherwise.

....

Tara had always believed that love was a force that could conquer anything—anything except fear. And her fear now was as tangible as the walls closing in around her. Each time she saw Aditya, something inside her broke a little more. It wasn't just his unwavering love for her that tore at her heart, but the reality that he was sacrificing too much for her. She saw it in his eyes every time they were together, the way he held back his dreams, his career, his life—all because of her. His future, his ambitions, everything that was once so clear to him, now seemed uncertain. And Tara couldn't let that be because of her.

They sat on the roof, just as they always did. The same spot where they shared their first kiss, where they laughed together until their stomachs ached, where they dreamed of a future that seemed so simple, so certain. The stars stretched out across the sky, cold and distant, a mirror to the emptiness that Tara felt inside her. The world around them had never seemed so quiet, so heavy.

Tara had hoped that the silence would speak for them, that perhaps the quiet night air would carry their unspoken words and fill the space between them. But it didn't. It only deepened the chasm that had slowly started to widen between them. Tara felt it—a weight pressing down on her chest, making it hard to breathe. Aditya was no longer the same. He had been holding back for her, for the love he still had, but Tara knew it was only a matter of time before it all unraveled.

And that's when it happened. Without even looking at him, she spoke, her voice barely above a whisper. "I don't think I can do this anymore."

Aditya froze beside her, his heart hammering in his chest. He had sensed the change in her long before she spoke. The way she'd become quieter, more distant. The way her eyes lost the spark they once had when they were together. It wasn't like the Tara he knew. And now, hearing her say those words, it felt as if his world had been shattered in an instant. He had always feared that this day might come, but he had never imagined it would hurt this much.

"What do you mean?" he asked, keeping his voice calm, though inside, everything was unraveling.

Tara's gaze remained fixed on the sky, her hands trembling as she clasped them tightly in her lap. "I'm holding you back, Aditya," she said, her voice cracking. "I'm… I'm not the person you think I am. You deserve someone who believes in love, someone who isn't broken like me."

Aditya's heart clenched at her words. He wanted to pull her into his arms, to tell her that she wasn't broken, that she was everything he ever wanted. But he stayed silent, the words caught in his throat. He couldn't bring himself to argue, not yet. He had to understand what was happening.

"Tara, don't say that," he said softly, his hand reaching for hers, grasping it gently. "You're not broken."

But Tara pulled her hand back, her eyes swimming with tears. "But I am, Aditya," she whispered, the weight of her words almost too much to bear. "I'm so afraid of losing you, of us becoming like my parents, that I'm ruining everything. You deserve more than that."

Aditya shook his head, desperate to reach her, to make her understand. "I don't want more, Tara. I want you. I've always wanted you. And if that means waiting a lifetime for you to believe in us again, then I'll wait. I'm not going anywhere."

His words hung in the air, heavy and sincere. But Tara's heart broke all over again. He loved her—she knew that. He loved her in a way that made her feel like the most cherished person in the world. And yet, she couldn't escape the fear that was suffocating her.

Tara wiped away a stray tear, her voice barely audible as she spoke again, "You're too good for me. And that's why I have to let you go."

Aditya's breath caught in his throat. He couldn't believe what she was saying. Was this really happening? Was she really going to walk away from everything they had, everything they could have been?

"No," he said firmly, shaking his head. "I'm not going anywhere, Tara. You're my future. If you need time, I'll give you time. If you need space, I'll give you space. But I'm not giving up on us."

His words echoed in the night, and for a moment, it seemed as though the world had paused, holding its breath. Tara leaned in closer, her heart aching as she rested her head on his shoulder. She closed her eyes, wishing that the moment would last forever. But she knew it couldn't.

She couldn't be the reason he gave up his dreams. She couldn't be the one to hold him back. And as much as it tore at her soul, she knew that the best thing she could do for him was to let him go. To set him free.

Tara's chest tightened, the weight of her decision suffocating her. She loved him—more than she could ever express. But love wasn't always enough. And this time, it wouldn't be.

She closed her eyes, trying to push away the tears that were threatening to spill over. "I love you, Aditya," she whispered, barely audible. "But I can't keep holding you back. You deserve to live your life. And I'm not the one who can give that to you."

Aditya's throat tightened, the words she spoke breaking him inside. He wanted to argue, to tell her that he would wait forever, that he would never leave her. But he knew that the words wouldn't change anything. Tara had already made up her mind. She had already decided that this was the end.

"I'll always love you," he whispered, his voice breaking. "I will never forget you."

Tara turned to face him, her eyes full of sorrow. She leaned forward, her lips pressing softly against his. The kiss was gentle, a silent goodbye, a moment of tenderness before everything they shared came to an end. It was a kiss that spoke volumes, one that conveyed all the love, the regret, the pain, and the unspoken goodbye that neither of them could bear to say aloud.

As their lips parted, Tara pulled away, her heart breaking into a thousand pieces. She didn't want to leave him, didn't want to walk away from the love they had built, but she knew that it was the only way. She had to let go. For him.

Aditya watched her, helpless, as she stood up and turned away. He wanted to stop her, to beg her to stay, but the words wouldn't come. Instead, he watched as she walked away, the night swallowing her up. And in that moment, he knew—he knew that this was the end.

Tara walked away without looking back, her heart shattered into pieces, but her steps steady, resolute. She had made her choice. And though every fiber of her being screamed for her to turn back, to call out to him, to beg him to stay, she kept walking. Because she loved him too much to watch him give up his future for her.

As she disappeared into the distance, Aditya sat alone on the roof, his heart heavy with the weight of her decision

16

Pages of Before

Aditya's steps were slow, each one heavier than the last, as he walked down the dimly lit street. His heart still ached with the pain of the night—of Tara's departure. He couldn't understand why it had to end this way. He didn't know if he would ever come to terms with it. The world felt too still, too silent. His mind was clouded with so many thoughts, so many questions, that it was hard to focus on anything other than the crushing emptiness in his chest.

He had to see someone. He needed to talk to someone. And there was one person who had always been there—Shaan. His best friend, the one person who had witnessed every moment of his life, every heartbreak, every joy. He needed Shaan now, more than ever.

As he arrived at Shaan's apartment, he felt a cold shiver run through him. The door was slightly ajar, which was unusual. He pushed it open gently, his mind still reeling from the events that had unfolded in the last few hours.

Inside, the apartment was eerily quiet. The faint sound of muffled sobs reached Aditya's ears. He froze, not sure if he was imagining it. His heart raced, and he stepped further inside, following the sound of the crying.

It was Shaan.

Shaan sat on the couch, his hands covering his face, his body shaking with sobs. The sight was so unlike Shaan that it stopped Aditya in his tracks. Shaan, the one who always had a solution, the one who never let anything get to him, was now broken. Aditya stood there, watching his friend cry, unsure of what to do.

"Shaan?" Aditya finally whispered, his voice barely audible.

Shaan's head jerked up, his eyes red and swollen. He looked at Aditya as though he hadn't noticed him enter. For a long moment, neither of them said anything. The air between them was thick with unspoken words, with confusion, with grief.

Aditya took a tentative step forward. "What happened, man?" he asked, his voice low, filled with concern. "What's going on?"

Shaan wiped his eyes, trying to compose himself, but the tears just kept coming. "Aditya... I don't know how to say this, but... it's Meera... she..." His voice broke, and he had to pause, taking a deep breath to steady himself. "She's sick, Aditya. Really sick."

Aditya's heart skipped a beat, his confusion growing. He had heard about Meera's health before—her occasional fatigue, her bouts of weakness—but he never imagined it was anything serious. "What do you mean? What's going on with her? Is she okay?"

Shaan let out a shaky laugh, but it was hollow, empty. "No, Aditya, she's not okay. She hasn't been okay for a while now. The doctors... they say she doesn't have much time left."

The words hit Aditya like a punch to the stomach. He felt his world tilt, his head spinning as he tried to process what Shaan was saying. "What? No, no. That can't be... she's..." He stopped, unable to find the words. Meera—strong, vibrant, full of life—couldn't possibly be in that condition. It didn't make sense.

Shaan looked at him, his eyes filled with a mixture of sorrow and guilt. "I didn't want to tell you like this, Aditya, but you need to know. I couldn't just keep it from you anymore." He paused, as if weighing the next words carefully. "She's been fighting this illness for months. No one knew—not even her family. She didn't want to burden anyone. Not with her work, not with her charity, not even with her own health. She always put everyone else first. The doctors... they said she doesn't have much time left. Maybe a few weeks at best."

Aditya was paralyzed. His mind raced, trying to comprehend what Shaan was saying. "I... I don't believe this. Meera... she can't be..."

Shaan shook his head, his voice softening with emotion. "She never lived for herself, Aditya. Not once. Her whole life was about everyone else—her family, her NGO, the kids she helped. She never gave herself a chance to live for herself, to be happy. She always put everything and everyone before her. And now... now it's too late."

Aditya stared at his friend, still trying to piece it all together. It didn't make sense. Meera, the woman who had been the heart and soul of everything good in his life, couldn't be on the brink of death. She was too strong for this. She had too much to offer.

Shaan let out a breath, his voice trembling as he spoke again. "Aditya, there's something else I need to tell you. Something I didn't want to say. Something I never thought I'd have to say." He hesitated for a moment, his hands gripping the edge of the couch. "Meera... she never really lived her life. Not like she wanted to. Not the way she dreamed. All she ever wanted, Aditya... was a happy, peaceful life with you. She always loved you, more than just a friend. More than anyone could understand. She loved you with everything she had."

Aditya felt like the ground had been ripped out from under him. His mind was spinning, his heart racing. Meera... loved him? For years, they had been friends, but he had never seen her in that way. He had never known that she harbored such deep feelings for him. The revelation shook him to his core.

"What are you saying, Shaan?" Aditya whispered, his voice barely audible.

Shaan's eyes filled with tears again, and he looked away, unable to meet Aditya's gaze. "I never thought it was right to tell you, not until now. But you need to know, Aditya. She... she always wanted to be with you. She always hoped that one day, you'd see her the way she saw you. That you'd both be happy, together. She never stopped loving you, even when she tried to move on, even when she fought with everything she had. She loved you... more than anyone else in this world."

Aditya's heart sank as the weight of Shaan's words settled over him. He couldn't breathe. His mind was a whirlwind of emotions—shock, disbelief, guilt, confusion. Meera had always been there, by his side, supporting him in every way, and he had never realized the depth of her feelings. He had been so consumed by his own world, by his own heartbreak, that he had missed it all.

"Why didn't she ever tell me?" Aditya asked, his voice trembling. "Why didn't she say anything?"

Shaan looked at him, his expression pained. "Because she didn't want to ruin everything, Aditya. She didn't want to put any more pressure on you. She saw how much you were struggling, how you were holding back for Tara. She couldn't bear to see you torn between them. So she kept her feelings to herself, always."

Aditya sat there in stunned silence, his heart heavy with a mixture of grief and regret. He had always thought that his heart belonged to Tara, and now Meera's love for him had changed everything. It felt like the pieces of his life were slipping away, one by one, and he couldn't catch them fast enough.

Shaan's voice broke through his thoughts, soft and full of sorrow. "She never stopped loving you, Aditya. She wanted to be with you, more than anything else. And now..." He choked on his words, unable to continue.

Aditya's chest tightened, the pain of it all too much to bear. He stood up abruptly, pacing back and forth in the small apartment. "I... I don't know what to do with all this. I never knew... I never knew she felt like that. I never knew what she was going through."

Shaan stood up too, his face pale. "I'm sorry, Aditya. I should have told you sooner. But it's too late now. She doesn't have much time left."

Aditya turned to Shaan, his eyes wide with disbelief. "What do you mean? What can I do? Is there anything I can do for her? Is she in the hospital?"

Shaan shook his head, his expression grim. "There's nothing anyone can do, Aditya. The doctors have already done everything they can. All we can do now is be there for her. She's in a lot of pain, but she's holding on. For now."

Aditya's heart shattered as he stood there, unable to move. Meera was dying, and he had no idea how to process it. He had missed his chance to love her, to give her everything she had always wanted. And now it was too late.

Tears filled his eyes as he looked at Shaan, his voice barely a whisper. "I... I never knew, Shaan. I never knew."

Shaan's face softened with sympathy. "I know, man. I know."

....

The silence that lingered in the room was thick, as Aditya's heart continued to race, caught in the storm of emotions, the guilt of not realizing Meera's feelings for him, and the pain of knowing the truth now—too late. He stood there, frozen, his mind still processing the devastating conversation with Shaan. He wanted to ask more, to beg for answers, but the weight of it all left him speechless. Shaan, standing beside him, was equally lost in thought, his face pale from the burden of everything they had just shared.

But before either of them could say anything more, the door creaked open.

A soft voice broke the tension. "Shaan? Aditya?"

They both turned to see Meera standing at the doorway, her frail figure framed in the dim light from the hallway. There was no sign of the pain she had been fighting, no trace of the illness that Shaan had just revealed. She looked... *normal*. Strong. The Meera they both knew and loved. Her face held that familiar smile, a warm, radiant expression that didn't betray any of the turmoil she had been enduring.

For a moment, both Aditya and Shaan just stared at her, their eyes wide, unable to move.

"Meera..." Shaan said, his voice almost a whisper. His emotions were evident on his face—confusion, worry, and a touch of relief.

Meera's smile faded as she stepped closer into the room, noticing the silence that hung between them. "What's going on? Why do you both look like you've seen a ghost?" She glanced at Shaan, and then at Aditya, her brow furrowing slightly. "Are you guys alright?"

Shaan blinked, trying to push back the tears that were threatening to escape. He smiled weakly, but it was a smile filled with sorrow and helplessness. "We're fine, Meera," he said, his voice thick. "But how are you feeling? You look... you look well."

Meera waved it off with a small, nonchalant laugh. "Oh, you know me. I'm always fine." She glanced at Aditya, then quickly back at Shaan, as though trying to read something in his expression. But Aditya, still in shock from the revelation, said nothing. His heart ached as he watched her stand there, pretending everything was fine, trying so hard to act normal when they both knew the truth.

Aditya wanted to speak, to ask her how she was truly feeling, to comfort her, but his words stuck in his throat. How could he tell her that he now knew what she had been through? How could he confront her with his guilt, knowing that she had kept her love for him locked away in silence, while he had never seen it?

Meera looked at him now, noticing the strain in his eyes. "Aditya, you okay?" she asked, her voice soft, genuine concern lacing her words. "You're looking a little pale. Have you been getting enough sleep?"

Aditya blinked, his thoughts momentarily clouded. "Yeah," he managed to say, shaking his head slightly as if to clear it. "I'm fine. Just... been a lot on my mind, that's all." His voice sounded distant, even to him.

Meera tilted her head, studying him for a moment, but she didn't press further. She simply smiled again, though there was a slight tremor in the corner of her lips. "Good. You should rest, Aditya. You've been through so much recently... with everything going on. But you're still standing, and that's what matters, right?"

Aditya nodded, but inside, his mind was in turmoil. How could she stand there, so composed, when her time was running out? How could she pretend like everything was okay when he knew it wasn't?

Shaan cleared his throat, trying to regain some semblance of control over his emotions. He glanced at Aditya briefly, exchanging a silent look between them. Then he turned back to Meera, his voice shaking slightly. "You know, Meera, sometimes pretending everything's fine only makes things harder."

Meera's smile faltered, but she quickly recovered, brushing off the remark with a forced laugh. "Well, I don't know about you, but I've always found that keeping a smile on my face makes things a bit easier. No point in dwelling on things you can't change, right?"

There it was again—the strength in her voice, the way she pushed aside her own pain to make others feel better. Aditya felt his heart tighten. She was facing the end of her life, and all she cared about was making sure no one else suffered.

Shaan, sensing the tension in the air, let out a small sigh. "I know you, Meera. You're always the strong one. But sometimes, you don't have to be. You can lean on us too." His voice broke with the weight of his words.

Meera's gaze softened as she stepped closer to him, her hand resting gently on his arm. "I know you're always there for me, Shaan. And Aditya too. But I... I just don't want to burden anyone with my pain. Not now. Not when there's still time for us to make memories together." She paused, and for the briefest moment, her eyes met Aditya's.

Aditya felt a pang in his chest as he held her gaze. Her eyes, filled with so much love and unspoken words, made his heart ache. But he could only stand there, paralyzed by the weight of everything he knew now—everything that had been left unsaid for so long.

Shaan cleared his throat again, trying to change the subject, but the weight of the silence was too much. "We're all here for you, Meera. Just... let us be here for you." He hesitated before continuing. "Don't push us away when you need us the most."

Meera's smile softened, but it was bittersweet. "I'm not pushing anyone away, Shaan. I just... I don't know how to deal with this. It's hard to let go, you know?"

Aditya felt his chest tighten as he looked at her, realizing the depth of her pain. He wanted to reach out, to hold her, to tell her how sorry he was for never seeing her—really seeing her—until it was too late. But he remained silent, his heart heavy with the weight of their shared history and the cruel timing of everything.

"I understand, Meera," Aditya said quietly, his voice barely above a whisper. "I understand."

Meera nodded, her expression softening. "I know you do, Aditya. I always knew you would."

The three of them stood there in the silence, the unspoken truths between them too heavy to be voiced, yet too real to be ignored. Each of them was dealing with their own grief, their own broken hearts, and yet, somehow, they were still together. In that moment, nothing felt certain except the rawness of the love they had for each other, and the painful knowledge that time was slipping away faster than they could hold onto it.

And still, they pretended everything was fine.

The stillness between them hung thick in the air, each one of them carrying a burden too heavy to bear. Meera stood in the center of it all, trying so hard to keep her composure, but Aditya could see the cracks in her carefully maintained mask. Her smile was forced, her eyes betraying the pain she was trying to hide. Shaan, on the other hand, looked like he had given up on pretending. His eyes were red-rimmed, his lips trembling, as though he was holding back all the emotions he had been suppressing for so long.

Aditya felt like an outsider in this moment, like he had stumbled into a space where he didn't belong. He was standing here, pretending to be strong, pretending he didn't know the truth about Meera's condition, pretending that everything would somehow be okay. But it wasn't. None of it was okay.

"Aditya, you're too quiet today," Meera said softly, her voice gentle, as if she were trying to ease the tension between them. "What's on your mind?"

He didn't answer immediately. He couldn't. How could he explain the storm raging inside him? How could he tell her that he now knew the truth, that he knew she was fighting for her life and that it wasn't fair for her to hide her feelings any longer? How could he tell her that he had always cared for her—more than he had ever realized—and now, it felt like it was too late?

Instead, he forced a smile, though it didn't quite reach his eyes. "Nothing. Just... tired, I guess."

Meera studied him for a moment, her gaze lingering with a softness that made his heart ache. She knew he wasn't telling the truth, but she didn't push him. She never did. She had always known when to back off, when to let him have his space. She was always the one who gave, never the one who asked for anything in return.

Shaan cleared his throat, breaking the silence. "We should probably talk about this, Meera. About what's happening. We can't keep pretending everything is okay."

Meera's smile faltered, and for a second, Aditya could see the vulnerability in her eyes. "I don't want to talk about it right now, Shaan. I just want... I want to enjoy whatever time I have left. I want to make good memories, not dwell on the bad ones."

Her words hit Aditya like a physical blow. She was trying so hard to make the best of a situation she had no control over, but in doing so, she was pushing him away. And he hated it. He hated that she felt like she had to shield him from the truth, as if carrying that burden alone was something she could handle.

"I don't want to lose you, Meera," Aditya finally whispered, the words slipping out before he could stop them. "I don't want to pretend anymore. Not when you're... when you're sick. Not when I know you're struggling."

Meera turned to him then, her eyes softening. "You won't lose me, Aditya," she said, her voice breaking slightly. "I'll always be with you. In your heart. In your memories. That's the only way I can be with you... and the only way I can live on. You and Shaan, both of you, are the most important people in my life. And I want you to know that... no matter what happens."

Tears welled in Aditya's eyes, but he blinked them away quickly. He couldn't let her see him like this. Not when she was already carrying so much of her own pain. "I just... I don't understand, Meera. Why didn't you tell me?" he asked, his voice barely audible.

Meera's eyes glistened, but she shook her head, trying to maintain her composure. "Because it's not about you, Aditya. It was never about you. It was about me. I couldn't burden you with this. I couldn't take away your chance at happiness. You deserve more than... than this." She gestured to herself, as though to show that she wasn't enough, that she wasn't worthy of him.

Aditya's heart shattered at her words. "Meera, don't say that. You are more than enough. You always have been."

Shaan, who had been standing quietly in the background, spoke up then, his voice filled with an emotion he couldn't hold back any longer. "She's always put others first, Aditya. She's never cared about herself. She always thought about everyone else—about the NGO kids, about us, about the people around her. She never even lived for herself. And now... now she's not sure if she has the right to live for herself, for her own happiness."

Meera looked at Shaan, a mixture of surprise and sadness in her eyes. "Shaan..." she whispered, her voice trembling.

Aditya turned to Shaan, his confusion written all over his face. "What are you talking about? What does that mean?"

Shaan swallowed hard, the weight of the truth threatening to choke him. He looked at Meera, then back at Aditya, his gaze desperate, but his voice steady. "She always loved you, Aditya. More than friends. More than anything." He paused, the final words coming out in a rush. "She wanted a life with you. A happy life. She always dreamed of being with you, of marrying you... But she never told you, because she didn't think she deserved that kind of happiness."

Aditya's breath caught in his throat as the world seemed to stop. The words didn't fully register at first. He could only stare at Shaan, his heart pounding, his mind racing.

Meera was in love with him.

All this time, all these years, and he had never known. He had never realized how much she had cared for him, how deeply she had loved him, always holding it inside, buried beneath layers of friendship, concern, and selflessness.

His gaze shifted to Meera, her face now pale, her eyes wide in horror at what Shaan had just revealed. She opened her mouth as if to protest, but no words came out. Instead, her lips quivered, and the tears she had been holding back finally began to fall.

"Meera..." Aditya whispered, his voice hoarse, his heart breaking at the sight of her pain. "Why didn't you tell me?"

"I couldn't," she whispered back, her voice barely audible. "I couldn't risk it. I couldn't risk losing you. Not when you had your whole life ahead of you... not when you had so many dreams to chase. I didn't want to be the reason you gave up everything for me."

Aditya stepped toward her slowly, his hands trembling as he reached for her. "But you never had to be the reason I gave up anything, Meera," he said, his voice breaking. "I... I would have chosen you, always. I just never knew. I never knew how you felt."

Tears flowed freely down Meera's face now, and she collapsed into his arms, her sobs muffled against his chest. "I'm sorry, Aditya. I'm so sorry."

Aditya held her tightly, unable to speak, unable to process everything he was feeling. He had always cared for her, but now, hearing these words, feeling the weight of her unspoken love for him, he knew that his heart had always belonged to her too.

But now, it was too late.

....

Aditya sat alone in his room, feeling lost and overwhelmed. His thoughts kept going back to Tara and everything that had happened between them. The past few days felt like a whirlwind—confusion, hurt, and so many unanswered questions. Tara had been pulling away from him, and no matter how hard he tried, he couldn't reach her. She seemed distant, and Aditya had no idea why. But now, it was clear that something was terribly wrong.

Tara had disappeared.

Aditya didn't hear it from her. He overheard a conversation outside his window. He heard one of the men say, "She left... with Manav." His heart stopped as the words sank in. Tara had left without a word, and she was with Manav. The shock hit Aditya like a punch to the chest. He couldn't believe it. How could Tara leave like this? Why hadn't she said goodbye?

Aditya tried to make sense of it all. She couldn't just leave. They had so many plans together. What could possibly make her walk away from everything they had shared? His mind raced with questions, but there were no answers. He couldn't just sit here. He had to find her.

Without thinking, Aditya stood up and walked out into the night. The cool air hit his face, but it didn't help calm his racing thoughts. His heart felt heavy as he walked aimlessly through the quiet streets. Where had she gone? Why had she left? He couldn't understand.

As Aditya walked, his mind kept going back to Tara. He thought about how she had been acting—so distant, so cold. Had he missed something? Had she been trying to tell him something? Had he failed to notice?

His heart ached with the thought of losing her. He needed to know why she left, and he wasn't going to stop until he found her.

After what seemed like hours, Aditya found himself on the outskirts of town. That's when he saw Manav standing alone. A rush of anger and confusion hit him, but he held it back. He needed answers, not a fight.

Manav looked up when he saw Aditya, and for a moment, they just stood there, staring at each other in silence. Then, Aditya took a step forward, his voice filled with fear.

"Manav," Aditya said, "Where is Tara? Where did she go?"

Manav didn't answer right away. His face was unreadable, and he seemed lost in his own thoughts. Aditya's patience was running out.

"Tell me!" Aditya shouted. "Where is she?"

Manav sighed, looking down at the ground. When he finally spoke, his voice was quiet. "She left, Aditya.

Aditya felt like the ground had just shifted beneath him. "What do you mean, 'left'? Why would she leave?"

Manav hesitated, as if trying to find the right words. "She... she needed to leave. She couldn't stay with you anymore."

Aditya's confusion deepened. "But why? We were fine. Everything was fine."

Manav looked up, his eyes full of sadness. "She's been going through a lot, Aditya. She didn't want to drag you into her problems. She needed time to heal. She couldn't stay, not like this."

Aditya's chest tightened. "What do you mean, 'not like this'? What's going on?"

Manav took a deep breath. "Tara... she's been struggling for a long time. She didn't want to burden you with her pain. She thought it was better for both of you if she left."

Aditya shook his head, still in shock. "But why didn't she tell me? Why didn't she talk to me?"

Manav stepped closer, placing a hand on Aditya's shoulder. "She didn't want to hurt you, Aditya. She loved you too much for that. But she thought you deserved better. She thought you needed a chance at happiness—without her."

Aditya stood still, trying to process what Manav was saying. Tara had loved him all this time, but she had left. She had run away to protect him from the pain she thought she was causing him. It didn't make sense. Why would she do that? Why wouldn't she just talk to him?

Manav lowered his gaze, unable to look Aditya in the eyes. "I know this is hard to understand, but she needed to find herself again. She needed space. And I was the only one she could turn to."

Aditya felt a lump form in his throat. The pain in his chest was unbearable. "So, she left ? Just like that?"

Manav nodded slowly. "She thought it was the only way. She thought it was better this way."

Aditya turned away from Manav, his heart heavy with grief. Tara was gone. She had left without even saying goodbye. The woman he loved, the woman who had been everything to him, was no longer in his life. And all he was left with were the memories and the ache of her absence.

He closed his eyes, trying to hold back the tears. It felt like the world was falling apart around him. The love he had for Tara was still there, but now it felt like it was being ripped away, piece by piece.

Manav stood silently behind him, giving Aditya the space he needed to process everything. After a moment, Aditya spoke again, his voice soft but filled with emotion. "Why didn't she just tell me? Why didn't she trust me enough to let me in?"

Manav didn't have an answer. He could only stand there, knowing that Tara's decision wasn't something he could explain. It wasn't something that could be fixed with words.

Aditya's heart was breaking. He had no idea where Tara had gone or what she was thinking. But he knew one thing for sure—she was gone, and he couldn't stop her.

With a heavy sigh, Aditya turned and began walking away, leaving Manav standing in the darkness. He didn't know where he was going or what he was looking for. All he knew was that the woman he loved had walked out of his life, and he didn't know how to fix it.

As Aditya walked through the quiet streets, his thoughts were consumed by Tara. He couldn't believe she had left. How had everything gone so wrong? Why hadn't she fought for them?

His heart felt broken, but he knew that the questions would remain unanswered. Tara was gone, and no matter how much he searched for her, the truth was that she had already made her choice.

Aditya couldn't help but wonder if he had ever truly understood her. Had he ever really seen her pain? Had he missed the signs all along? He didn't know. All he knew now was that Tara was gone, and he was left with nothing but the emptiness she had left behind.

The night seemed colder, and the silence more deafening as he walked, searching for answers that he might never find.

Aditya walked through the quiet streets, lost and broken. Tara's sudden departure felt like a sharp knife in his heart. He couldn't understand why she had left without a word, without saying goodbye. Every step he took felt heavy, as if the weight of the world was pressing down on him.

His mind was spinning with questions. Why had Tara done this? How could she leave without telling him? He loved her more than anything, and he thought she loved him too. But now, all that remained was emptiness.

As he wandered aimlessly, he found himself in a small park. The faint light from a nearby lamp barely lit the path. Aditya didn't care about the cold wind or the silence around him. His pain was louder than anything else.

Finally, his legs gave out, and he dropped to his knees on the ground. Tears started rolling down his face, slow at first, then faster, until they wouldn't stop. His chest heaved as the sobs took over, and he whispered her name, "Tara... why did you leave me?"

He gripped the earth beneath him, as if holding onto something could ease the ache inside. The memories of Tara flooded his mind—her laughter, her smile, the way she always looked at him with so much love. How could she leave after everything they had shared?

"Tara... I thought we had something special," he cried, his voice breaking. "I thought we would always be together."

His tears became heavier, his cries louder. His pain was too much to bear, and he didn't care who heard him or saw him. All he could feel was the emptiness she had left behind.

Aditya's heart felt like it was shattering into a million pieces. He had never felt this helpless, this broken. The love they had was everything to him, and now, it was gone. She was gone.

He kept whispering her name, over and over, as if saying it would bring her back. But deep down, he knew she was gone. She had made her choice, and now he was left all alone.

The hours passed, but Aditya didn't move. He stayed there, sitting on the cold ground, his tears soaking the earth. His body was trembling, his heart aching, but he couldn't stop the pain.

He thought about how much he had loved Tara, how much he still loved her. But now, it felt like love wasn't enough. She had left, and he didn't know if he would ever be able to fill the emptiness she had left in his life.

When the tears finally slowed, Aditya sat there in silence. His eyes were red and swollen, his body exhausted. But the pain inside him still burned, deep and raw.

He didn't know how to move forward, how to live without her. All he knew was that this heartbreak felt like it would never end. For now, all he could do was sit there, lost in the agony of losing the one person who meant everything to him.

....

The hospital room was quiet except for the soft beeping of the machines monitoring Meera's condition. Sunlight filtered through the pale curtains, casting a faint glow over the room. Meera lay on the bed, looking frail yet peaceful. Shaan and Aditya sat nearby, their faces reflecting the weight of the past few months.

Shaan cleared his throat, breaking the silence. He pulled an envelope out of his jacket and held it in his hand for a moment before speaking.

"Aditya," Shaan began, his voice steady but laced with urgency, "this came for you."

Aditya looked up from where he sat, his mind still clouded with thoughts of Tara. He glanced at the envelope but didn't move to take it.

"They love your photographs," Shaan continued, trying to inject a spark of enthusiasm into his words. "They saw your work and decided to give you another chance. This isn't just some small gig. It's a big deal. A once-in-a-lifetime kind of deal."

Aditya didn't respond, his eyes drifting back to Meera. She was resting, her breaths shallow but steady. Her illness had taken a toll on her body, but she still managed to smile when she was awake, hiding her pain for everyone else's sake.

Shaan leaned forward, his tone growing firmer. "Aditya, listen to me. This... this is your chance to start over. To focus on what you're meant to do. To live."

Aditya stared at the envelope, his fingers twitching as if they wanted to reach out but couldn't. His heart was torn between the memories of Tara, the guilt of not being able to hold onto her, and the reality of Meera lying on the bed.

"I don't know if I can, Shaan," Aditya said softly, his voice breaking. "What's the point? I've lost everything."

Shaan shook his head, frustration flickering across his face. "You haven't lost everything, Aditya. Look at Meera." His voice softened as he pointed toward the bed. "She's still here. She's fighting every single day just to stay alive. And for what? For us. For you."

Aditya turned to look at Meera. Her pale face, her fragile body—it broke him to see her like this. But in her quiet strength, he saw something he hadn't felt in months: hope.

"She's given up so much, Aditya," Shaan continued, his voice thick with emotion. "Her dreams, her health, her life—she's spent it all caring for others. And you know what she wants? She wants you to live. To find happiness. To do what you love. Are you really going to let her down?"

Aditya swallowed hard, his throat dry. He looked back at the envelope, his hands trembling as he reached for it. He opened it slowly, pulling out a letter printed on crisp paper. The words blurred in his vision, but the weight of them was clear. It was an opportunity to showcase his photography, to travel, to rebuild the life he had once dreamed of.

He looked at Meera again, her chest rising and falling gently as she slept. In that moment, something shifted inside him. He realized that living for Meera wasn't about guilt or obligation. It was about honoring her strength, her sacrifices, and her unwavering belief in him.

Aditya folded the letter and placed it back in the envelope. He looked at Shaan, his jaw set with determination.

"I'll do it," he said, his voice steady. "I'll take the chance."

Shaan let out a small sigh of relief, his lips curving into a smile. "Good. That's the Aditya I know."

Aditya turned back to Meera, brushing a strand of hair from her face. "For her," he whispered, more to himself than anyone else. "I'll live for her."

The room fell into a calm silence again, but this time, it wasn't heavy. It was filled with a sense of quiet resolve. Aditya knew that moving forward wouldn't erase the pain of losing Tara or seeing Meera suffer. But for the first time in months, he felt like he had a purpose again—a reason to keep going.

And for now, that was enough.

As the room settled into a reflective silence, the door creaked open, and a nurse stepped inside with a clipboard in hand. Her warm but professional demeanor filled the space as she addressed the two men seated by Meera's bedside.

"Mr. Sivaaditya? Mr. Shaan?" she called softly, glancing between the two.

Aditya flinched slightly at the name, still unaccustomed to hearing it used in such a formal setting. Shaan nudged him lightly, giving him a reassuring look.

The nurse continued, "The patient is ready to be discharged. You can take her home now, but please ensure she gets proper care. She's still very weak, and it's important she rests and follows her treatment plan closely."

Aditya nodded, his expression serious. "We'll make sure of it. Thank you."

Shaan stood, folding the letter back into his pocket as if sealing away his earlier words for another time. "Come on, Aditya," he said, his tone lighter but still carrying the weight of the moment. "Let's get her home."

Aditya rose to his feet, his gaze lingering on Meera for a moment longer. She was awake now, her eyes fluttering open to meet his. Despite her pale complexion and fragile state, she managed a small, tired smile.

"We're taking you home, Meera," he said gently, his voice carrying a promise.

Meera's lips curved slightly, though the exhaustion in her eyes was evident. "Home sounds nice," she whispered, her voice faint but steady.

The nurse handed Shaan a set of instructions for Meera's care and reminded them about her medication schedule. "She'll need a lot of rest and support, but with the right care, she'll get through this."

Aditya turned to Shaan, the weight of responsibility now shared between them. "We'll take care of her," he said firmly, as much to himself as to the nurse.

As they helped Meera into the wheelchair, Aditya felt a strange mix of emotions—determination, sadness, and a glimmer of hope. Life had taken so much from all of them, but it hadn't broken them completely.

As they made their way toward the hospital exit, the nurse's parting words echoed in Aditya's mind: *Take good care of her.*

He clenched his jaw and pushed the wheelchair gently but firmly, silently vowing that from this moment on, he would.

The sunlight outside bathed them in warmth as they stepped into the world again, ready to face whatever came next, together.

17

Pages of Now

The small, cozy room was filled with the fragrance of freshly brewed tea. Tara sat by the window, her silver hair glinting in the sunlight that filtered through the curtains. Her hands, weathered by time, held a steaming cup. She turned to Sameer, her face a mixture of curiosity and calm.

"So, what brings you here?" Tara asked, her voice soft yet firm, the weight of years evident in her tone.

Sameer hesitated, his fingers nervously fumbling through the satchel he carried. Finally, he pulled out a neat bundle of aged letters, tied together with a faded ribbon. The sight of them made Tara freeze. Her eyes widened as recognition and shock washed over her.

"These...?" Tara's voice trembled as she stared at the letters, her heartbeat quickening.

Sameer nodded, placing the bundle gently on the table between them. "I found them. I didn't know who you were or why these letters were so important to him, but they led me here."

Tara couldn't take her eyes off the letters, her hands trembling as they hovered over them. She didn't pick them up. Not yet.

Sameer continued, his voice filled with a quiet urgency. "I know it's none of my business, but... I had to find out. I don't know why, but these letters... they've been haunting me. I can't sleep, I can't eat. It's like something—or someone—is pulling me here."

Tara's lips pressed into a thin line, her chest tightening. The past she had buried deep within herself was now staring her in the face, demanding acknowledgment.

"I need to know," Sameer said, leaning forward slightly. "What happened between you and Aditya? These letters... they're full of so much love, so much longing. But they're unfinished. There are no answers, only questions. And I feel like I'm part of this story somehow."

Tara exhaled shakily, her gaze dropping to the floor. Memories she had fought to forget resurfaced, each one piercing her heart like a dagger.

"I... don't know where to begin," she murmured, her voice barely audible.

"Start anywhere," Sameer urged gently. "I'll listen."

Tara looked up at him, her eyes brimming with unshed tears. Sameer's face was sincere, his youthful energy a stark contrast to her own weary demeanor. In him, she saw a spark of Aditya—his determination, his intensity, his heart.

With a heavy sigh, Tara reached for the letters. Her fingers brushed against the ribbon, and it felt like touching a piece of her soul that had been locked away for decades.

"This... this is a story of love, loss, and choices we regret but can't take back," she said, her voice steadying as she spoke. "But if you've come all this way, you deserve to know the truth."

Sameer leaned back, his expression a mix of anticipation and trepidation. Tara held the letters close, her heart racing. For the first time in years, she prepared to unravel the threads of her life that had been left untied for too long.

The garden felt like a sanctuary, bathed in the soft golden light of the afternoon. The gentle rustle of leaves in the breeze, the sweet scent of flowers, and the distant hum of life beyond the walls seemed to hold time still. Sameer sat there, his mind a storm of emotions as he gazed at the woman in front of him. This was Tara, the woman whose letters had haunted his thoughts for weeks, the woman who had once held his father's heart.

There was something almost ethereal about Tara. The lines on her face told the story of a life lived with both joy and sorrow, but her eyes—the same eyes that had gazed at Aditya with love so many years ago—held a deep, quiet strength. She had aged, yes, but there was a timeless beauty to her, as though the years had only added to her grace.

"Do you know who Aditya really is?" Tara asked softly, her voice warm but curious.

Sameer blinked, momentarily thrown by the question. He had spent so much time chasing Aditya's shadow, piecing together fragments of their love story from the letters, yet he still felt as though he didn't truly know the man. He shook his head slowly.

"No... I don't," Sameer admitted. "I've read your letters, but I still don't know who Aditya really is."

Tara smiled gently, as though she had expected that answer. With a small sigh, she stood up, her movements slow and deliberate, as if each step carried the weight of years. "Come with me," she said, beckoning him to follow.

Sameer followed her into the house, a small but cozy space filled with warmth and memories. The walls were lined with shelves holding books and trinkets, and there were photographs—so many photographs. His heart quickened as he looked around, knowing that some of these photos were taken by Aditya, the man who had captured so much beauty through his lens.

In the corner of the room stood an old wooden cabinet. Tara opened it carefully, her fingers trembling slightly, and pulled out a large, weathered photo album. She handed it to Sameer without a word, and he took it, feeling the weight of it in his hands.

When he opened the album, the first image made him freeze. It was a black-and-white photograph of a man in his late twenties, standing by a river, his camera hanging loosely around his neck. His expression was thoughtful, as if he was lost in the moment, completely absorbed in the world he saw through his lens.

Sameer's breath caught in his throat. There was something so familiar about the man's face—the strong jawline, the intensity in his eyes. His fingers brushed lightly over the image, as if touching the photograph would somehow bring him closer to understanding.

"This... is Aditya?" Sameer whispered, his voice barely audible.

Tara nodded, her lips curving into a bittersweet smile. "Yes, that's Aditya. Or, as he is fully known... Shiva Aditya."

The name fell from her lips like a stone dropped into a still pond, sending ripples through Sameer's entire being. Shiva Aditya. His father's name. The man in the photograph was not just Aditya—the mysterious lover from the letters—but his father, the man he had known all his life but never truly understood.

Sameer's mind raced, his thoughts crashing into each other in a whirlwind of confusion, disbelief, and shock. His father—Shiva Aditya—had loved this woman, had shared a life with her before Sameer was even born. The man he had idolized, who had raised him, had lived an entire other life that Sameer had never known about.

His throat tightened, and for a moment, he couldn't breathe. The room seemed to spin around him, and he closed his eyes, trying to steady himself.

"I know it's a lot to take in," Tara said softly, her voice cutting through the fog of his thoughts.

Tara paused for a moment, gazing at the photograph in Sameer's hands. She could see the confusion and curiosity in his eyes, and she understood it well. It was the same look that had crossed her own face many times when she thought of Aditya—of their love, the years they had spent together, and all that had gone unsaid.

With a soft sigh, she gently took the photo album from Sameer and flipped through a few pages, stopping at one particular image. She turned it around and placed it in front of him.

It was a group photograph, a moment frozen in time. Aditya stood in the center, his arms around Meera and Gaurav, with Shaan beside him. The four of them had been so close, so inseparable. Tara could see the vibrant smiles, the happiness radiating from the group. But there was something about the image that made her heart ache. She wasn't in it. Neither was the man who had raised

Sameer.

"Do you see this?" Tara's voice was soft, but the weight of the words was heavy. Sameer nodded, looking at the faces, recognizing them one by one.

"This was our little family," Tara continued, her finger tracing the outline of the photograph. "Meera, Shaan, Aditya, Gaurav, and Mita. They were all a part of my life—of the life I thought would never change. But everything changed the day Aditya and I... well, everything changed."

Sameer looked up from the photograph, his brow furrowed in confusion. "What happened? How did it change?"

Tara's eyes seemed to lose focus, as if she were remembering something that had been buried deep within her heart. She folded her hands tightly together, trying to steady herself before continuing.

"Aditya was my world. He always had been," Tara said, her voice barely above a whisper. "We were in love, Sameer. He was everything I had ever dreamed of. But I couldn't have him. Not in the way I wanted to. There were too many reasons why. And Meera—she was always there for him, a friend, a confidante. I knew she loved him too, and though I tried not to, I saw it. It was in the way they looked at each other."

Tara paused again, a tear slipping down her cheek. She quickly wiped it away, as if embarrassed by her own emotions. Sameer didn't know what to say. There was so much he was hearing for the first time, so much he couldn't have imagined.

"I never had the courage to send him those letters," Tara continued, her voice trembling now. "The letters I wrote, the ones you found. They were all my feelings, my thoughts... the love I had for him, all those years. I wanted to tell him, to let him know how much I cared, but I couldn't. I was afraid. Afraid of rejection, afraid of everything falling apart. And so, I kept them hidden."

Sameer's heart pounded in his chest as he listened to her. He had known Tara as the old woman who lived alone, and until now, he had never realized the depth of the emotions she had carried with her. Tara had loved Aditya. And she had loved him deeply.

"I see now that it was fear that kept me away from him. Fear that I would lose him forever," Tara whispered, a sad smile forming on her lips. "But when I look at you, Sameer, when I see how you've been carrying on his legacy, I can't help but feel a little... a little grateful. Because, in some strange way, you carry his heart."

Sameer was speechless. His mind was spinning. He had spent so many years chasing after the story of Aditya and Tara, trying to put together the pieces of their love from the letters. But now, hearing it all from Tara herself, he understood the depth of the tragedy, the complexity of the love they had shared, and the reasons why things had never worked out.

"I'm sorry," Tara said softly, her voice barely audible now. "I never meant to hurt you, Sameer. But I needed to tell you. I needed you to know how much I loved him. And maybe... maybe it's time you finally know the truth."

Sameer couldn't find his words. His heart was too full, overwhelmed with a mix of sadness, anger, and confusion. Tara had loved Aditya, but so had Meera. And where did that leave Sameer? With the man he had thought of as his father, a man who had always been there for him, a man who had loved and lost. Was Sameer just another shadow of a love story that had never found its happy ending?

"I never told him," Tara continued, her eyes filled with a quiet sorrow. "I never had the courage to say it. But I loved him, Sameer. I loved him more than anyone ever could."

Tara looked up at Sameer, her eyes full of regret and longing. There was no more hiding behind the silence. The years of suppressed emotions and unspoken words had come flooding out, and Sameer could see that Tara had carried this burden for far too long.

Sameer looked up at her, his heart pounding in his chest. "Why... why didn't he ever tell me?" he asked, his voice raw with emotion. "Why did you leave him? If you loved him, why did you leave? And if you didn't... why did he marry my mother?"

Tara's face softened with understanding. She reached out, gently closing the photo album and setting it aside. "There are some questions, Sameer, that only Aditya—your father—can answer. But I can tell you why I left."

She took a deep breath, her gaze turning distant, as if she was looking back through the years, searching for the right place to begin.

"When I left Aditya," Tara said quietly, "it wasn't because I stopped loving him. In fact, it was the opposite. I left because I loved him too much... and I was terrified of what that love could do to us."

Sameer frowned, confused. "Terrified? Of what?"

Tara's eyes clouded with pain. "Terrified of what love could turn into. You see, for me, the only model of love I had was my parents' relationship. They were my world, my ideal of what love was supposed to be. But when their marriage fell apart... it broke something inside me. Their divorce shattered my belief in love, in marriage. If two people who had been together for so long could end up hurting each other like that, what hope did Aditya and I have?"

Sameer's heart ached at the vulnerability in her voice. He watched as her fingers trembled slightly, her eyes filled with the weight of old wounds. "I couldn't bear the thought of staying with him, only to end up like my parents—resentful, broken. I didn't want to be the one who destroyed him."

"But you didn't destroy him," Sameer said softly, his voice full of empathy. "You loved him. And he loved you."

Tara gave a small, sad smile. "Yes, but sometimes love isn't enough. I didn't want Aditya to stay with me out of obligation. I didn't want him to give up his dreams, his future, just for me. So, I left. I thought I was sparing us both from a future full of pain."

Sameer felt a lump in his throat as her words sank in. "But... you got married. You have a daughter..."

Tara laughed softly, shaking her head. "Meera isn't my biological daughter. She's adopted. Aditya and I always dreamed of having a daughter, and we agreed we would name her Meera. But after I left, I raised Meera on my own. She's my heart, but she's not a part of that life I shared with Aditya."

The name Meera struck a chord deep within Sameer. His mother's name. He hadn't realized how much the memory of her still clung to him, like an old song playing softly in the background of his life. Tears pricked the corners of his eyes as he processed the weight of it all.

Sameers expression a mix of confusion and hurt. His voice trembled as he asked, "If you loved him so much, Tara, why did you leave these letters behind?"

Tara's eyes softened as she let out a heavy sigh. She looked away, her gaze settling on the flickering flame of the lamp on the table, its gentle dance mirroring the turmoil in her heart.

"When Meera came into my life," she began, her voice steady but tinged with sorrow, "everything changed. She became my world, my only priority. I couldn't afford to think about myself anymore."

She paused, her words hanging in the air like a fragile thread. "I decided then that I had to leave all my emotions behind. My love for Aditya... it felt like something I couldn't carry anymore. Meera needed me, and I needed to be whole for her."

Sameer's grip on the letters tightened, and he whispered, "But why keep them at all? Why not tear them up or burn them?"

Tara's lips trembled as she gave him a faint, sorrowful smile. "I wasn't strong enough to destroy them," she admitted, her voice quivering. "Those letters... they held all the feelings I couldn't express, the words I couldn't say out loud. Destroying them felt like erasing a part of myself. So, I left them behind, hoping they'd stay hidden, forgotten—like I tried to forget him. But I never really did."

Her voice broke on the last words, and she turned to meet his gaze, her eyes glistening with unshed tears. "Even then, Aditya were always there, in my heart."

Sameer stared at her, his silence heavier than any words.

Without thinking, Sameer leaned forward and wrapped his arms around Tara, pulling her into a tight embrace. She gasped softly in surprise, but then she relaxed into the hug, her hands gently resting on his back. The warmth of her touch, the soft scent of jasmine in her hair, it was everything Sameer had needed without realizing it. He held on to her like a son clinging to his mother, feeling the raw surge of emotions that had been locked away for so long.

"Oh, Sameer," Tara whispered, her voice trembling. "It's been so long since I've felt this. I'm so happy to see you, such a handsome grown-up man."

Sameer didn't say anything for a moment. He was overwhelmed by the flood of emotions—grief, love, longing. For the first time in years, he felt the kind of warmth and comfort that only a mother could provide. Tara's embrace reminded him so much of his late mother, and it broke something inside him, something he didn't even know had been hurting.

After what felt like a lifetime, Sameer pulled away, wiping the tears from his face with a sheepish laugh. "I don't even know why I'm crying."

Tara smiled, her eyes soft with understanding. "It's okay. You've been carrying so much for so long. You needed this."

Sameer nodded, his heart full, but there were still questions gnawing at him. "But how did I find you? Why did I even come here?"

Tara tilted her head, a knowing smile playing on her lips. "Your friends' father gave you my address, didn't he?"

Sameer blinked. "Yes... Shaan off course."

Tara chuckled, shaking her head fondly. "Shaan. Of course. I should have known. He's been there for me through everything. But I never thought he would tell anyone, not even you."

Sameer smiled weakly. "He didn't tell my father. He gave me the address."

Tara's eyes twinkled with amusement. "Shaan... that boy never could resist helping people." She paused, her expression softening. "I'm glad he gave you the address, though. Seeing you here... it's like a weight has been lifted off my heart. For the first time in years, I feel at peace."

Sameer stared at her, his heart aching with everything she had said. "But I still don't understand. If you and Aditya loved each other so much, why did my father

marry my mother?"

Tara's smile faded slightly, and she looked away, her eyes distant. "That's a question you'll have to ask Aditya yourself."

Sameer felt a deep, unshakable confusion settle in. "But why didn't he ever talk about you? About any of this?"

Tara sighed softly, her gaze drifting to the garden outside. "Some stories... are not mine to tell. But I can promise you this—you will find the answers you need. You just have to be patient."

As the sun began to dip below the horizon, casting a soft, golden glow over the garden, Sameer sat there, lost in thought. He had come so far, pieced together so much, but there were still so many unanswered questions. And yet, there was also a strange sense of calm that settled over him, as if the hardest part of the journey was behind him.

Tara smiled at him, her eyes filled with love and wisdom. "Go to him, Sameer. Ask your father. You'll find the answers you're looking for."

Sameer nodded, his mind swirling with everything he had learned. But for now, he stayed with Tara a little longer, savoring the peace of the moment, knowing that soon, he would have to confront the man he had known all his life—and the secrets that had shaped their family's history.

As the golden light of the setting sun bathed the garden in warmth, Sameer looked at Tara, his heart heavy with everything he had learned. He hesitated for a moment, unsure of how to phrase the question that had been on his mind since he walked through her door. Finally, he took a deep breath and asked, his voice soft yet filled with quiet resolve.

"Tara... will you come with me? To see him?"

Tara's eyes flickered with emotion—surprise, sadness, something unspoken that Sameer couldn't quite place. She looked down at her hands, her fingers tracing the rim of her tea cup, the silence between them thick with uncertainty. Then, slowly, she raised her eyes to meet his, a small, bittersweet smile playing at the corners of her lips.

"I..." she began, her voice soft and full of meaning, but before she could finish, the wind stirred the leaves in the garden, and the moment lingered, the answer hanging in the air, unfinished.

18

The Last Page

The long journey back home felt surreal. Sameer sat in the train, staring out of the window as the landscape blurred past him. The world outside seemed distant, detached, like a silent film playing on repeat. His mind was still wrapped around Tara's words, her unspoken answer to his question lingering in the air.

Would she come with him?

He had left without an answer, but her eyes—the quiet, bittersweet expression she wore as she looked at him—had said so much more than words ever could. Sameer had sensed the weight of something unspoken, something unfinished. But as the train rattled on, he knew he couldn't wait any longer to face the man who had been both his father and, in some ways, a stranger.

Shiva Aditya.

The name echoed in his mind like a riddle he was still trying to solve. His father, the man who had raised him, had lived a life Sameer had never known about. A love that had shaped him long before he became the man Sameer knew today. How could someone hold on to such a story in silence for so long?

The landscape began to change as the train neared the familiar edges of Sameer's hometown. The bustling streets, the small cafes, the towering trees that had shaded his childhood—they all greeted him with a sense of homecoming, but there was an unsettling tension in his chest.

He wasn't sure how this meeting with his father would go. Would it break something between them? Or, perhaps, for the first time, bring them closer?

By the time Sameer reached his house, the sun was setting, casting a soft, golden hue over the quiet neighborhood. His father's car was parked outside, and the garden was as meticulously kept as always. The sight of it brought a pang of familiarity, of the countless evenings he'd spent playing there as a boy, his mother's laughter echoing in his ears, his father's calm presence just beyond the doorway.

But today, everything felt different. He was different.

Sameer stood in the doorway, his heart racing as he faced his father, Shiva Aditya. The room was still, the quiet tension palpable. Sameer could feel the weight of the moment pressing down on him, knowing that what he was about to do would change everything. His father had been carrying a secret for years—a secret that Sameer had only just uncovered. And now, standing here in front of him, Sameer knew it was time for that secret to come to light.

"Baba," Sameer said softly, taking a step forward. His voice was steady, but his heart was pounding in his chest. "I... I brought something for you."

Shiva looked up, his brow furrowing in confusion. There was a slight hesitation in his eyes, as if he sensed something monumental was about to happen. "What are you talking about, Sameer?"

Sameer swallowed, his throat suddenly dry. He could see the curiosity and caution in his father's expression. "Actually... it's not something." He paused, feeling the gravity of his next words. "It's someone."

Shiva Aditya's face grew still. His eyes narrowed slightly as he tried to understand what Sameer was saying, but before he could ask anything further, Sameer stepped aside, his heart pounding in his ears.

From behind the door, Tara emerged.

For a moment, time seemed to stop. Shiva Aditya's eyes locked onto hers, and everything around them faded into the background. His face froze in an expression of disbelief, and for a heartbeat, it was as if he couldn't comprehend what he was seeing. His body stiffened, as if bracing for an emotional impact he wasn't prepared for. His hand, which had been resting casually on the armrest of his chair, slowly clenched into a fist as if trying to ground himself in the reality of the moment.

Tara took a step forward, her eyes fixed on him, her gaze full of love, sorrow, and the weight of years gone by. There was no anger, no bitterness—just a quiet acceptance of everything they had lost, and everything they had once shared.

"Aditya," she whispered, her voice trembling as it carried the years of separation, the countless nights spent wondering, regretting, hoping.

For Shiva Aditya, it was as if a dam had broken inside him. His breath hitched, and a myriad of emotions washed over his face—shock, joy, confusion, anger, and an overwhelming sadness that seemed to weigh down on his very soul. He blinked rapidly, his eyes growing moist as he stared at her, as if afraid that she might disappear if he blinked too long.

"Tara..." he whispered, his voice breaking as he said her name for the first time in what felt like a lifetime.

The room filled with a thick, emotional silence as they both stood there, staring at one another. It was a moment suspended in time—two people who had once been everything to each other, now standing on the edge of something so profound, so overwhelming, that neither could speak.

Sameer, realizing the depth of what he had just set into motion, took a step back. He could feel the electricity in the air, the unspoken words between his father and Tara. There was nothing more he could say. This was their moment, and he knew they needed to face it alone.

"I'll... give you both some space," Sameer said softly, his voice barely above a whisper. He glanced at his father, who hadn't taken his eyes off Tara, and then back at Tara, who gave him a small, grateful nod. Without another word, Sameer turned and quietly left the room, closing the door behind him.

Inside the room, the silence stretched on as Shiva (Aditya) and Tara continued to stand across from one another, each moment bringing back a flood of memories. His heart ached as he looked at her—this woman he had once loved with every fiber of his being, the woman who had disappeared from his life so abruptly, leaving a void he had never been able to fill.

Tara took another step forward, her hands trembling slightly as she moved closer to him. "It's been a long time," she said softly, her voice carrying both the weight of their shared past and the tentative hope of reconciliation.

Shiva Aditya shook his head slowly, as if still trying to make sense of it all. "I thought... I thought I'd never see you again," he said, his voice thick with emotion. He took a deep breath, trying to steady himself. "I tried to move on, Tara. I tried to forget."

Tara's eyes filled with tears, and she nodded, understanding his pain. "I know, Aditya. I know you did. And I'm sorry. I'm so sorry for everything."

He looked at her, his brow furrowed in a mixture of sadness and anger. "Why did you leave? Why didn't you tell me? I would've... I would've done anything for you."

Tara closed her eyes for a moment, gathering her thoughts. When she opened them again, they were filled with a deep sadness. "I was scared. After my parents' divorce... after everything fell apart, I stopped believing in love, in marriage, in forever. I didn't want to be the reason your life fell apart too. I thought... I thought leaving was the only way to protect you."

Shiva Aditya let out a shaky breath, his fists clenching at his sides. "You didn't need to protect me, Tara. I needed you. I loved you. I still do."

Tears welled up in Tara's eyes as she heard the raw emotion in his voice. "I know. And I loved you too. I still love you, Aditya."

They stood there, the weight of their shared past filling the space between them. Slowly, almost hesitantly, Shiva Aditya took a step toward her. His hand reached out, trembling, as he touched her face gently, as if confirming that she was real, that she was standing in front of him after all these years.

"I thought I'd lost you forever," he whispered, his voice breaking.

Tara leaned into his touch, closing her eyes as the tears finally spilled down her cheeks. "I thought... I thought it was the only way. But now, seeing you... I realize how wrong I was. I never stopped loving you, Aditya. Never."

Shiva Aditya pulled her closer, and in that moment, it was as if the years of pain, regret, and longing melted away. They stood there, wrapped in each other's arms, holding on as though letting go might break them all over again.

For what felt like an eternity, they stayed like that—two souls reunited after so long, clinging to the love they had thought was lost.

Outside the room, Sameer paced the hallway, his heart heavy with emotion. He could feel the intensity of what was happening behind the closed door, and part of him wished he could see it, to understand the depth of what his father and Tara had once shared.

But he knew this was something they needed to experience alone.

As the minutes ticked by, he leaned against the wall, closing his eyes and letting the gravity of the situation sink in. His life had been changed in ways he never could have imagined. The story of his father, of Tara, and of the love that had shaped their lives was more complex than he could have ever anticipated.

But as emotional as it was, there was a strange sense of peace. Sameer had brought them back together. He had helped them find closure.

And now, he had to face his own questions.

The door creaked open, and Tara stepped out, her eyes red from crying, but there was a softness to her expression, a quiet relief that hadn't been there before. She gave Sameer a small smile, her gratitude evident in the way she looked at him.

"Thank you," she whispered, her voice thick with emotion. "You've given us something... something we never thought we'd have again."

Sameer smiled back, nodding. "You deserved it. Both of you."

Tara wiped at her eyes, her hand trembling slightly. "He's waiting for you," she said, gesturing toward the room. "Go talk to him."

Sameer hesitated for a moment, feeling the weight of what was to come. But with a deep breath, he stepped forward, ready to face his father—and the answers that still lay ahead.

As he walked into the room, he saw his father standing by the window, his back to the door. The air was thick with emotion, and Sameer knew that the conversation they were about to have would change everything.

But for now, as father and son stood in the same room, there was an unspoken understanding that whatever came next, they would face it together.

Sameer stood in the doorway, his heart still heavy from the whirlwind of emotions he had experienced. The room felt thick with the weight of everything that had just transpired between his father and Tara. He hadn't even had the chance to process fully what it meant for him, his family, or his life. His eyes, still moist, moved to where his father stood by the window, his back straight, though there was a sadness hanging over him, as if the years of silence had finally caught up with him.

Shiva Aditya turned around slowly, his eyes meeting Sameer's with a deep, quiet understanding. He motioned to the chair beside him, inviting Sameer to sit. Sameer hesitated but finally lowered himself into the chair, his mind buzzing with unanswered questions, doubts, and confusion.

Shiva let out a slow, deep breath. "I know," he began, his voice soft, almost apologetic. "I know you have a lot of questions in your mind right now, Sameer. I can see it in your eyes."

Sameer didn't say anything. He simply looked at his father, waiting, knowing that whatever was about to come would change the way he understood everything.

Shiva stepped closer, sitting across from his son. "But before you ask anything... let me tell you one thing clearly: I never cheated on your mother."

Sameer's heart clenched. He had wanted to believe that, but the whirlwind of revelations had left his mind in turmoil. Now, hearing it from his father, the weight of those words seemed to lift something inside him.

Shiva's eyes softened, and there was a gentle but tired look in them as if reliving these memories was pulling him through the deepest parts of his soul. "Your mother knew everything, Sameer. From the beginning to the end. She knew about Tara—about the love we shared. She knew that I wasn't capable of loving her the way I loved Tara."

Sameer's breath caught in his throat. His father's confession was raw, vulnerable, and full of emotion. He had always seen his father as a strong, distant figure, never someone who could admit such deep feelings of guilt and pain.

Shiva's voice dropped to a whisper. "But she also knew that Meera... your mother... was always close to me since childhood. Meera was with me in every single moment, Sameer. Every step of the way, every time I thought I'd lost everything, she was there."

Sameer blinked, his tears threatening to spill over as he listened to his father's words, the depth of emotion in them making his chest tighten.

"When Tara left, I was lost," Shiva continued, his voice wavering slightly. "But Meera and Shaan, they were there for me. Meera—she was more than just a friend, Sameer. She... she loved me."

Sameer's eyes widened as he heard this. He had always known there was a deep connection between his parents, but this? He had never expected to hear such a confession from his father.

Shiva's gaze became distant as he continued, his voice trembling slightly. "When Meera found out she didn't have much time left, it was Shaan who told me... how much she had always loved me. Part of me always knew, Sameer. Somewhere deep inside, I always knew that Meera had feelings for me, but I... I never allowed myself to see it."

Sameer's heart ached at the thought of his mother, of the love she had silently carried for so long.

Shiva rubbed a hand over his face, his eyes glassy with the memories. "When Tara left, Meera and Shaan were my family. They held me together when I felt like everything was falling apart. And when I found out Meera didn't have much time... it broke me, Sameer. It broke me in ways I didn't know I could break."

Sameer felt tears streaming down his face, the sadness of his father's words sinking into him like a weight he hadn't anticipated.

"I couldn't lose her," Shiva whispered. "Not after everything. So... we got married. Not because of some great romantic love, but because we were both there for each other. We both needed each other. Meera knew from the very beginning that I couldn't love her the way I loved Tara. She accepted that, and she never asked for more."

Shiva's voice cracked then, and Sameer could see the tears welling in his father's eyes. "But you know what she did ask me for?"

Sameer shook his head, his throat too tight to speak.

"She asked for a child," Shiva said, his voice barely audible. "That was the one thing she asked me for—the first thing and the last thing. She wanted to have you, Sameer. And I gave her that. I gave her all the love I could muster. And in return, she gave me more love than I ever deserved."

Sameer was openly crying now, the full weight of his father's words pressing down on him. He had always known his mother loved him deeply, but hearing this—hearing how much she had sacrificed, how much love she had poured into their family despite everything—left him shaken.

"And when she died," Shiva continued, his voice breaking, "the last thing she said to me, Sameer... she said two things. The first was that she had given me enough love so that I would never feel the loss of my mother. She told me to take care of you, no matter what. She didn't want you to ever feel the pain of losing both your parents."

Sameer closed his eyes, feeling his chest tighten. His mother had always been selfless, always putting him first, even in her final moments.

"And the second thing she said," Shiva continued, tears now streaming down his face, "was that in our next life, I should marry Tara. That was her only wish, Sameer."

Sameer's breath hitched as he tried to process his father's words. The depth of Meera's love, her sacrifice, her acceptance of his father's past... it was almost too much to bear.

"I feel so sorry, Sameer," Shiva whispered, his voice filled with guilt. "I never saw your mother as more than a friend. Even after all these years, I carry that guilt with me. But when Tara left, and I was broken, Meera and Shaan were there for me. And when I learned Meera didn't have much time, I knew I had to be there for her. It was my time to give her the love she deserved."

Sameer wiped at his eyes, trying to hold himself together as he listened to his father pour out years of suppressed emotions.

"But she knew," Shiva said, his voice softening. "She always knew that after she was gone, I'd be alone again. That's why she asked for you. You were the one thing that kept me going, Sameer. You were her gift to me, the one thing she left behind to make sure I was never truly alone."

Sameer's heart broke at those words, at the realization of just how much his mother had loved both him and his father.

"And now," Shiva said, his voice shaking with emotion, "I look at you, and I see everything she wanted for me. I see her love in you. And I'm so sorry... so sorry that I never gave your mother the love she deserved. But I tried, Sameer. I tried to be the best father I could be."

Sameer reached out, grabbing his father's hand, the tears streaming down his face. "You were, Baba. You were the best father. And Mom... she was the best mother. I know she loved you, and she loved me. She never needed anything more."

Shiva closed his eyes, nodding slowly as the tears continued to fall. "I just... I hope she knows how much I loved her in my own way."

Sameer hugged his father tightly, feeling the years of unspoken love and guilt between them finally breaking free. They held onto each other, letting the tears flow, the silence between them now filled with an understanding that had been missing for so long.

And in that moment, Sameer realized that love—whether it was romantic, familial, or something in between—wasn't always simple. It wasn't always perfect. But it was there, in the quiet sacrifices, in the unspoken promises, in the things people do for each other without ever saying a word.

As they pulled away, Sameer wiped at his eyes, looking at his father with a newfound sense of understanding.

"I think Mom knew, Baba," he said quietly. "I think she knew everything."

Shiva nodded, his voice thick with emotion. "I hope so, Sameer. I really do."

For a moment, they sat in silence, letting the weight of their conversation settle. Then, Sameer smiled through his tears, his heart full of love for both his parents.

"I love you, Baba," Sameer said softly.

Shiva smiled back, his eyes full of warmth. "I love you too, beta."

And in that moment, father and son were closer than they had ever been.

....

Sameer sat quietly in front of his father, holding the bundle of letters in his hands. The old ribbon tied around them looked fragile, much like the stories they carried—stories of love, hope, and pain. He looked at his father, Shiva Aditya, whose face showed curiosity but also calmness.

Taking a deep breath, Sameer held out the letters. "I think these are yours," he said softly.

Aditya took the bundle, his hands brushing against the worn paper. At first, his face showed confusion, but as he looked closer, recognition dawned. His expression changed—his eyes reflecting memories, emotions, and something too deep for words.

Sameer watched his father carefully, feeling as though he was handing over not just letters, but pieces of a story that had been waiting for this moment to come alive again.

....

The warm afternoon sun bathed the garden in a golden glow as Sameer and his father, stepped through the back gate of the house. The moment they arrived, they could hear the lively chatter of their closest friends—voices filled with laughter, teasing, and warmth.

As they walked further into the garden, they saw the familiar faces gathered together. Shaan was there, standing by the table, gesturing animatedly as he spoke to Rhea and Rohan, who were both laughing at something he had said. The air was filled with the smell of freshly brewed tea and the sound of rustling leaves, a perfect scene of friendship and love.

But it was Tara's presence that caught Sameer's attention. She was sitting at the far side of the garden, smiling as she looked at the group, her hands gently resting in her lap. She looked peaceful, almost serene, as if a weight she had carried for years had finally been lifted. But as Sameer approached, he could see the tears glistening in her eyes.

Tara's gaze moved to Rhea, who was standing beside her father, Shaan. For a long moment, Tara looked at her, as if searching for something in the younger woman's face. Then, with a bittersweet smile, she spoke.

"Shaan, your daughter... she's beautiful," Tara said softly, her voice full of emotion. A single tear slipped down her cheek, but she quickly wiped it away. "No wonder you're old now, Shaan. You've raised her well."

Shaan, ever the joker, immediately grinned and replied, "Old? Me? I still have the energy to take you on, Tara! Just say the word!"

Rohan, never one to miss a chance to tease, jumped in. "Old? Oh, come on! Shaan is a fossil at this point!"

The group erupted in laughter, and for a moment, everything felt light and carefree again. Sameer watched as his father joined the group, standing beside Shaan and exchanging jokes like they had done for years. The weight of the past seemed to ease off his father's shoulders as the group bonded over their shared history.

But then, as the laughter quieted, Rohan, always curious, turned to Sameer with a serious expression. "Sam, there's something I've been thinking about. What kind of coincidence is it that you, of all people, ended up in that exact apartment? The one where you found the letters. What are the odds? It's like the dots were somehow... connected."

Sameer furrowed his brow, the same thought having crossed his mind more than once. He turned toward Tara, whose expression had shifted. She wasn't laughing anymore. Instead, she was looking at Shaan with a knowing, almost guilty look, as if there was more to the story than anyone had realized.

Shaan, sensing the tension, let out a deep sigh. His usual lighthearted demeanor shifted, and he exchanged a glance with Tara before turning back to the group. "Well," he began, rubbing the back of his neck awkwardly, "I suppose it's time to come clean."

Sameer's heart skipped a beat. He stepped closer, his eyes narrowing as he asked, "What do you mean, Uncle Shaan ? What's going on?"

Shaan took a deep breath, then looked at each of them in turn before finally resting his gaze on Sameer. "It wasn't really a coincidence, Sameer," he confessed. "It was me. I connected those dots."

The group went silent. Even Rhea, who had been smiling a moment ago, suddenly grew serious. She looked at her father, confusion clear in her eyes. "Wait, Baba... what are you saying?"

Shaan nodded, taking a step toward her. "Remember, Rhea, when you told me Sameer was looking for an apartment, and I suggested that specific one?" He glanced at Sameer before continuing. "I didn't choose it at random. That apartment... it used to be Tara's. She lived there for five years after she and your father, ended their relationship."

Sameer's jaw dropped. His mind raced, trying to process what Shaan was saying. "What? You knew Tara lived there?"

Shaan nodded again, his expression serious. "Yes. After Tara found out that Shiva and Meera had moved back to the city, she left the apartment. But it belonged to Manav, her younger brother, after she left. When Manav decided to rent the place out, I knew... I knew there was a chance that, if you stayed there, you might find something that would make you understand your father's story."

Sameer blinked, stunned. "So, you set this whole thing up? You knew I'd find the letters?"

Shaan admitted. " All I knew was that it was the right place for you to learn about your father, to connect with the past. I thought... maybe you could learn something important from his story. Something that could help you in your own life."

Sameer felt a wave of emotions crash over him—shock, confusion, gratitude. He turned to his father, who had been listening quietly the entire time, his expression unreadable. "Baba... did you know about this?"

Shiva shook his head slowly. "No, Sameer. I had no idea Shaan had done this." His voice was quiet, thoughtful. "But I'm not surprised. Shaan's always been good at putting people in the right place at the right time."

Rhea, who had been watching the exchange with wide eyes, suddenly let out a small laugh. "I can't believe it. My own father, the puppet master."

Shaan smiled sheepishly. "I just wanted to give you all a little nudge in the right direction. Sometimes, life needs a little help connecting the dots."

The group fell into a comfortable silence, the weight of Shaan's confession sinking in. Sameer looked around at the people who had been there for him—his father, Tara, Rhea, Rohan, and Shaan. This was his family, bound together not just by blood, but by love, friendship, and shared history.

As they stood there in the garden, surrounded by laughter and love, Sameer realized that he had finally found the answers he had been searching for. The pieces of his father's story, Tara's story, and even his own, had come together. And though there were still some mysteries left unsolved, he knew that he could live with that. Life, after all, wasn't meant to be perfectly understood.

Tara reached into her pocket, pulling out a small, worn photograph, and with a tender smile, she held it up for Sameer and Shiva to see. "Look at her," she whispered softly, her eyes glistening with emotion. "This is Meera, my daughter."

The picture showed a young girl, full of life, her eyes sparkling with the innocence and joy of childhood. Shiva's breath hitched the moment he saw it, his hand instinctively reaching out as his gaze locked onto the image. His emotions, once carefully guarded, unraveled in an instant. His eyes welled up, a flood of tears threatening to fall as he took in the sight of Meera, the daughter Tara had adopted in memory of their lost friend.

Sameer, standing beside his father, couldn't help but smile fondly. "Oho, I met her!" he said with warmth in his voice, trying to lighten the emotional atmosphere. "She's really cute. And finally, I have a little sister."

Tara blinked in surprise, her heart skipping a beat. For a moment, she hadn't expected such an immediate embrace of her daughter, and she looked at Sameer, almost stunned by the ease with which he had accepted her and Meera into his life.

"You... you think of her as your sister?" Tara asked, her voice soft and full of wonder.

Sameer nodded without hesitation. "Of course. You, Meera—both of you—you're family now."

Tara's eyes filled with tears, and she clutched the photograph tightly, her emotions swirling between joy, relief, and disbelief. Shiva, still gazing at the picture, smiled through his tears, feeling the deep connections that were now forming between them all, like threads of love and healing that were finally weaving their fractured lives together.

Sameer had said it with such certainty, such love—it wasn't just words. It was a promise. A promise that, after all these years of pain, loss, and separation, they had found a way back to each other.

"Family," Tara repeated softly, her voice trembling, as if the word itself held the key to everything she had ever wanted.

Aditya sat in the dimly lit room, his hands trembling as he turned the delicate pages of Tara's letters. Each word brought back memories, some sweet, some painful, but all so vividly alive. Tears streamed down his face, falling silently onto the faded ink. The room was quiet, save for the occasional sound of him catching his breath, overwhelmed by the emotions spilling over.

Lost in the letters, he didn't notice Tara enter the room. She stood in the doorway, watching him with a mix of tenderness and longing. Slowly, she walked closer and leaned against the doorframe, her voice soft and playful.

"Told you," she said, a small smile curving her lips. "When you'd finally read my words, they'd make you cry."

Aditya looked up, startled at first, but her presence immediately softened his expression. He wiped his face hastily, attempting to regain his composure, but the raw emotion in his eyes couldn't be hidden.

"You always knew how to put your heart into words," he replied, his voice cracking slightly. "I just... I never realized how much of it was for me."

Tara stepped closer, sitting beside him on the floor. Without a word, she leaned her head gently against his shoulder, her warmth filling the space between them. For a moment, neither of them spoke. The silence wasn't awkward—it was filled with the weight of all they had shared, and all they had lost.

After what felt like an eternity, Tara whispered, her voice barely audible, "I missed you."

Aditya's breath hitched, his chest tightening at the sound of those words.

"I love you," she added, her confession floating softly in the still air.

Aditya closed his eyes, letting her words sink in. He didn't say anything in return, but his hand reached out, gently resting over hers. It was a simple gesture, yet it spoke volumes—of love, of forgiveness, of all the feelings they had held onto for so long.

For that moment, it felt as if time had stopped, and the years that had separated them melted away. It was just Tara and Aditya, together again, hearts quietly beating in sync.

The Day of the Exhibition

The day of the photography exhibition had finally arrived. The gallery buzzed with excitement, filled with the quiet hum of voices, the soft click of shoes on polished wooden floors, and the occasional murmur of admiration as people moved from one photograph to the next. Large, elegant prints adorned the walls—each one a story captured in a single frame, the culmination of months of work, emotion, and discovery.

But for Sameer, this exhibition wasn't just about his photography—it was about telling a story that had transcended time, love, and heartache. It was about Aditya and Tara.

He had worked relentlessly to bring their story to life, and now, as he stood at the entrance of the gallery, watching people admire the photos, he felt a mixture of anticipation and vulnerability. These weren't just images to him; they were fragments of a love story that had shaped his own understanding of life, and he was about to share it with the world.

Sameer took a deep breath and stepped inside, moving past clusters of guests and fellow photographers. His eyes scanned the room, taking in the sight of his work displayed for all to see. The walls were filled with a mix of old and new photographs—some taken by Aditya himself, others captured by Sameer during his journey to find Tara. The images worked together to create a powerful narrative, each photograph holding a piece of the past, intertwined with the present.

One wall in particular drew the most attention. It was the centerpiece of the exhibition, showcasing a series of photos that told the story of Aditya and Tara's love.

The First Photograph: "The Meeting"

The first image was a candid shot of Tara sitting by the riverbank, lost in her own world. The light of the setting sun bathed her in a soft, golden glow, and her profile was serene, her gaze distant. Her lips were slightly parted as if she were caught in the middle of a thought, and in her eyes, there was something quietly hopeful, like someone waiting for a dream to unfold.

Beneath the photograph was a small plaque that read: "The Meeting: The beginning of a story told through silence, where two souls saw each other for the first time."

The Second Photograph: "The Lovers"

Next to it —an intimate portrait of him and Tara together. In this image, Aditya had captured the two of them sitting under a tree in a garden. Tara's head was resting on his shoulder, her eyes closed, and Aditya was looking down at her with an expression of pure love. The photograph was raw and tender, capturing a moment of complete vulnerability between two people who were bound by something deeper than words. Their connection seemed almost sacred, as if time itself had stopped just for them.

The plaque beneath it read: "The Lovers: In moments of silence, their hearts spoke to each other in ways that words never could."

The Third Photograph: "The Wait"

But it was the third photograph that held the most power. It was one of Sameer's own, taken during his time with Tara. In this image, Tara stood in the garden outside her house, looking off into the distance. She was older now, her hair streaked with silver, but her beauty remained. Her eyes, though, were what drew everyone in—eyes filled with longing, with a quiet, aching wait that had lasted for decades. There was pain there, yes, but also acceptance. Her lips were pressed together in a faint, wistful smile, as if she had made peace with the waiting, even though the years had passed without the reunion she had once dreamed of.

Sameer had captured her in a moment of stillness, her hands resting on the edge of an old wooden chair, her posture regal yet weary. Behind her, the trees swayed in the wind, a symbolic reminder of the passage of time, of things that change while others stay the same.

The plaque read: "The Wait: Time passes, but the heart never forgets. In her eyes, the story of a love that waited, even when the world moved on."

The Final Photograph: "The Unfinished Story"
The last photograph was one of Sameer's most personal. It was a collage, combining two images—one of Aditya's, taken of Tara in their youth, and one of Sameer's, taken of Tara in her later years. The two photographs were placed side by side, showing Tara at different stages of her life. In both, she was smiling, but the smiles were different. In the first, her eyes were bright with youthful excitement, full of dreams and possibilities. In the second, her smile was soft, almost bittersweet, as though she had lived a lifetime of love and loss, but had come to terms with it all.

The title of the photograph read: "The Unfinished Story: Some love stories never truly end—they simply change, grow, and find new ways to exist."

The crowd moved through the gallery, absorbed in the beauty and emotion of the photographs. Sameer stood back, watching as people reacted to the images, his heart swelling with a mix of pride and nervousness. He could see some wiping away tears, others standing in quiet contemplation. This wasn't just about photography—it was about connection, about seeing parts of themselves in the love story he had uncovered.

As the evening wore on, friends and family gathered around Sameer, congratulating him on his work. Rhea and Rohan were there, beaming with pride as they hugged him. Shaan stood nearby, laughing and joking with some of the guests, but he threw a knowing look at Sameer, silently acknowledging the journey they had all been on together.

Even Shiva Aditya, Sameer's father, stood proudly by his son's side, his eyes misty with emotion as he took in the story of his past displayed for all to see. He hadn't said much since reuniting with Tara, but Sameer could tell that the experience had moved him deeply.

It was then that Sameer noticed someone standing in the corner of the room, lingering near the photographs. At first, he couldn't see her face clearly, but something about her posture, the way she stood so still yet so poised, drew his attention.

His heart skipped a beat as she turned around.

There, standing in the soft glow of the gallery lights, was Siya.

For a moment, Sameer couldn't believe his eyes. He had been so caught up in everything that he hadn't expected her to be here. She had been his anchor throughout this journey, always supporting him from afar, but seeing her here, in person, was something else entirely.

He couldn't control the surge of happiness that flooded through him. A wide grin broke across his face as he moved toward her, his steps quickening with excitement.

"Siya!" he called out, his voice filled with disbelief and joy.

She smiled at him, her eyes lighting up as she took a step forward. "I wouldn't miss this for the world," she said softly, her voice like music to his ears.

Sameer reached her in a few long strides, and before he knew it, he pulled her into a tight hug. He had spent so much time thinking about her, talking to her through a screen, but now, having her here, in his arms, felt like everything was finally falling into place.

"You're really here," he whispered, his voice thick with emotion.

Siya pulled back slightly, her eyes glistening as she looked at him. "I told you I'd always be here for you, Sameer. I meant it."

The two of them stood there for a moment, lost in the warmth of the reunion, surrounded by the beautiful photographs that had brought them all together. It was a night of stories, of love both old and new, and as Sameer looked into Siya's eyes, he knew that this was just the beginning of a new chapter in his life.

A chapter filled with love, hope, and the promise of a future that he had once thought would never come.